IRON COWGIRL

Michal "Mike" Dunn is Wyoming born and bred and the most respected and sought after farrier in the Big Horn Basin. At forty-two, she has no intention of leaving Ten Sleep or marrying a second time. Nature has taught her that a family with a house full of children wasn't in the cards for her. Her job, friends, horses, and the Bighorn Mountains are all she needs. That is, until a big Marine with bigger dreams comes to Wyoming for a visit and has her wishing on lucky horseshoes that he'll be always faithful.

1st Sgt Nick "Mule" Walsh was passed around from foster home to foster home until he found a family in the United States Marine Corps. Watching his brothers settle down brings back the suppressed longing for a family of his own. When visiting his fellow Marine Reservist in Ten Sleep, Wyoming, Nick he meets Michal and aims straight for the heart. But the farrier has an iron will. She's given him the summer, and he plans on using every ounce of stubborn Marine determination he's got to show her their age difference doesn't matter, and just the two of them together is all the family he needs.

With enough heat, even iron bends...

IRON COWGIRL

TEN SLEEP DREAMING SERIES, TWO

KIRSTEN LYNN

www.kirstenlynnwildwest.com

Sign up for Kirsten's Newsletter
(www.kirstenlynnwildwest.com/contact_kirstin.php)

Printed in the United States of America
First Printing 2016

Print ISBN-13: 978-1537053806
ISBN-10: 1537053809

Editor: Ekatarina Sayanova, Red Quill Editing, LLC
Cover Design: Scott Carpenter
Formatting: BB eBooks

DEDICATION

To the amazing people of Ten Sleep, Wyoming who have supported my writing, assisted as resources, and served as inspiration for this series. From my heart, I thank you.

CHAPTER ONE

NICK LIFTED HIS sunglasses and let them drop back on his nose. He wasn't imagining things. Giving a low whistle, he took in the place First Sergeant Worrell called his hometown. From what he'd seen as they made the long drive through Wyoming, the people of the state weren't too particular how they tossed the label *town* about. A bar and post office pretty much established a town, post office optional.

"This is home sweet home, huh?" Nick scanned the buildings of Ten Sleep quickly before he blinked and missed the whole thing. Names like Dirty Sally's and Crazy Woman Café caught his attention.

"Don't start your shit, Walsh."

"Roger, but… Damn me, Worrell, there's more men in our company than in your whole damn town."

"Some of us prefer this life to growing up in your charmed existence in Baltimore."

Nick could feel the hostility emanating from his buddy and fellow First Sergeant, Jared Worrell. One of his closest brothers from the Marine Corps used to be just short of the intensity of The Incredible Hulk about the fact he'd never return to Wyoming. Returning home to care for his dying mother and meeting a red-haired wonder had his buddy doing a one-eighty. And Nick couldn't fault him for wanting to stay with Lucy wherever he could. Hell, Nick might give Green Acres a try for a woman like Worrell's.

"Yeah, it was an honor and a privilege growing up in an orphanage in Baltimore." He glanced back in the side mirror. *But at least we had a Mickey D's and movie theaters.* Nick didn't dwell on the shit life he was dealt as a kid. He gave up on having a family when he left the fifth foster home. After graduating high school, he joined the Marines, and they issued him a family with more brothers than a man could want.

"Sorry 'bout that."

"No harm, no foul." As they pulled around a corner and passed a log building, once a house, which now bore a sign heralding Circle Dub Chocolates, Nick nodded to the house and back to Jared. "Nice, Worrell. No shit."

"Thanks."

Jared put the truck in park in the driveway of a small brick house behind the log home-turned-chocolate shop. "You sure Lucy is okay with this?"

"Yep. She likes your sorry ass for some reason."

"Yeah, you're an asshole."

Jared opened his door and stepped out of the truck. "Nice, man, I bring you to my home..."

"Chocolate man!"

Nick stood by on the other side of the truck and watched as Worrell's wife plowed into his friend. Her legs locked around Jared's waist; her arms wrapped around his neck, and she planted a kiss on him that would make a weaker man blush. As it was, Nick tried to push down the overwhelming envy he felt for a moment as he observed the couple. Their love was almost suffocating as it surrounded the area.

After what seemed like a decade, they unlocked lips, and Lucy nuzzled Jared's ear and whispered something. Jared whispered something back. She brushed a kiss on his neck and looked up, smiling at Nick. "Hey, Nick, sorry about the shameless display, but three weeks is an eternity."

Even as she apologized, Lucy showed no sign of releasing Jared, and the first sergeant held her close. "Not a problem. I'd expect nothing less from you two. Shameless seems to be the name of the game."

"What have you been telling him?" She laughed and dropped another kiss on Jared's lips.

"Just the truth about my wild, red-haired wonder. Where's my son?"

"He was napping, but I might have ruined that."

Jared still didn't release Lucy, but started toward the house. "Come on, Walsh, you won't recognize the weed that's my son."

Nick grabbed his seabag. "My bedroom isn't close to yours, is it?"

Lucy's laughter rolled over them in pure joy. Jared gave him the one-finger salute.

"I thought you might be more comfortable in the shop."

Nick lifted an eyebrow. Lucy slid down Jared's body and sighed. "Jared walled off an area as a guest room. It's nice with its own bathroom. But if you'd rather stay with us, you're more than welcome."

Nick smiled at Lucy; you couldn't look at her without smiling. "Negative. I like the idea of a little privacy."

"You'll eat with us and everything, though. No arguments."

"No, ma'am."

"Momma." The cry of a child filtered through the screen door.

"Jared, show Nick his room. I'll get supper going."

Jared kissed Lucy hard and hungry once more before he nodded to Nick. "This way."

Nick's shoulders relaxed at the thought of being in a separate building from Jared and Lucy. Hearing them through the walls laughing and possibly screwing was more than he could stand at the moment. He didn't begrudge Jared his good fortune in finding Lucy, and he didn't even want Lucy per se, he just wanted what Jared had with Lucy and their other Marine buddy Tim had with his wife, Hailey. Someone to jump in his arms after three weeks with Fox Company 2nd Battalion 23rd Marines at Twenty-Nine Palms active-duty training, like he'd been gone on a year-long deployment. Hell, he bet Lucy attacked Worrell after their weekend drills in Salt Lake City with the rifle company.

Stepping in line with Jared, Nick shook off his crap mood and turned his attention to his surroundings. They went in the front door, and Nick smiled at the picture of Claudia Worrell, Jared's mom, hanging on the wall behind the counter. Around her picture were photographs Nick suspected Lucy had taken of mountains, valleys, and what Nick surmised was the Circle W Ranch. But the picture holding his attention was Claudia smiling brightly.

"Nice touch." He nodded to the photograph.

"Without her, none of this would be here, and I sure as hell wouldn't."

"She was a wonder. I'm glad I got to meet her."

Jared's forehead wrinkled in a deep scowl. "What the hell is goin' on, Walsh?"

"Not a damn thing. I compliment your mom and you blow up?"

"No bullshit, man, you know what I mean. You grilled Tim and me about our families for two weeks. You look at Lucy like she's the sun and almost earn a fist to the face, and now you're looking at Mom's picture the same way. What the hell is goin' on?"

"Thinking about family."

"And?"

"And fuck off, Worrell. When did you become a headshrinker?"

"Whatever, brother. Your room's back here."

Nick followed Jared through the living room-turned-storefront and into the revamped galley. Tim had come out and helped Jared gut the log home and install a state of the art galley. Jared opened a door and nodded.

"You sure you're okay staying over here?"

Nick stepped into the room and smiled at all the touches that spoke to Lucy's hand in decorating. A cream-colored comforter with huge orange poppies covered a queen size rack with a wrought iron headboard but no footboard. On the wall were framed pictures of mountains, many featuring slopes covered in wildflowers. Something about the room and the photographs gave Nick a peace he lacked.

"Affirmative. This works."

"The head's through that door." Jared pointed to the far wall with his chin. He leaned a hip against the doorframe, and Nick braced against the frown his friend shot him. Out of the three, Worrell had the most fierce Devil Dog frown. More than one private had almost cried with one look.

"What are you looking for here, Walsh?"

"I honestly don't know yet."

Jared nodded. "Fair enough. Get settled in and come on over for chow."

"Aye, aye."

Jared pushed off the doorframe and headed out the back door. Nick tossed his seabag in a corner and released a deep breath. For all the crap he'd given Worrell about the town and lack of people per square mile, he'd had almost the same feeling as he did when he joined the Marines—he was just a step away from finding out what he was made of, but he was going to have to fight for it. And he was right where he should be.

CHAPTER TWO

"SO THIS IS the ranch you grew up on?" Nick tapped the top of the truck's window rim as he rested his elbow on the bottom rim.

"Yep."

Nick scanned the area from what appeared to be unending pastureland to the red dirt hills and rims around the vibrant green fields. "Lucy's dad still hung up on you wanting the place?"

Jared laughed. "Not since Eli came along. He's ready to hand it over to his grandson."

Nick joined in the laughter. "What do you have to say about that?"

"Eli will choose his own path. I won't have anyone telling him what he's going to be."

"And he'll want to be…"

"A Marine of course."

"Oo-Rah!"

As they pulled into the ranch yard, Nick turned back to his inspection. The main house was not what he expected. Before him stood a modern two story house with beige siding and a redwood deck wrapped around the entire structure. He'd been caught up in old Westerns, and pictured a rustic structure with the door swinging from a rusty hinge. Of course, what he knew about ranching could fit in a thimble. Just what Jared shared, which boiled down to fields with cows and horses.

Stepping out of the truck, Nick inhaled the fresh summer air. He'd been a million places, but the air had never been as sweet as he'd found during these couple of days in Wyoming.

"Lucy's probably in the barn with Mike. You comin'?"

"Right beside you."

He fell in line next to Jared, and they headed toward the barn. The sound of Lucy's laughter seemed to make his friend's feet move faster. Nick almost halted at the throaty laugh joining Lucy's. Pulled toward the sound like someone was tugging him by a rope, he continued on and stepped into the barn.

Out of the corner of his eye, he watched Jared kiss his wife and take his son from her arms, lifting the boy in the air overhead until small giggles filled the musty old building.

"Hey Nick."

"Hey," he mumbled and tried to keep his gaze on Lucy and not on the woman tossing iron tools into a steel box. She was decked out in a western shirt, jeans, boots, and chaps. Sweat glistened on her top lip and forehead, and she wiped her cheek, leaving a black smudge from her leather gloves.

The barn sizzled from the ninety degree late June temperatures, and when the woman bent over, Nick caught sight of the curve of her muscular thighs. The muscles in her arms flexed when she lifted the steel anvil. A thick, caramel-blonde rope braid swung from her back over her shoulder. Nick swallowed hard and felt a drop of sweat roll down the side of his face. He almost choked on the spit he barely got down when she lifted her face to his. Her eyes were the prettiest green and sparked when she smiled.

"This is Mike Dunn. Mike this is Nick Walsh; he serves with Jared."

He canted his head. "*This* is *Mike*?"

"Nice to meet you. It's Michal, but people call me Mike." She tugged off a glove and held out a hand. Nick took it. Her strength was evident in her handshake. He gave her hand a small squeeze before releasing it and held onto a smile at the sparks of awareness shooting through her eyes before her forehead creased.

"Nice to meet you, too, Michal." He wasn't sure how a woman who looked like she did got saddled with a guy's name, but for reasons he wasn't going to examine, he refused to be lumped in with the general populace that called her Mike.

When she released his hand, he let her go for the moment. He stepped back, giving her space, and caught the looks Jared and Lucy were shooting from Michal and back to him.

"Well, I better get on my way to the Cross V."

Lucy grabbed her camera from the top of a hay bale. "Thanks for letting me get some photographs while you work. They're going to be awesome. And thanks for putting up with the stops as Eli needed attention."

Michal chuckled. "I'm sure with your talent you've managed to turn even a subject like me into something to look at. Eli's welcome anytime. He sure is a cute one."

For a fleeting moment, Nick caught while Michal's smile at Eli was genuine, she never reached for the toddler and didn't look at the family standing like a portrait for more than a second.

"What do you do, Michal?" Nick scanned her box of tools hoping for any clues, but none of the tools looked the least bit familiar.

"I'm a farrier."

"Pardon, ma'am?"

He ignored the chuckles from his so-called friends and focused on Michal's tempting smile. "A farrier. Horseshoeing, the various kinds, trim and balance hooves, make sure the horse's legs are in good condition, all that, you know?"

"No, I didn't. What are the kinds of horseshoeing?"

Jared's eyebrow lifted, and Nick willed him to keep his damn mouth shut about how uninterested Nick had been about horses until right that second.

Michal's gaze narrowed as if she was also judging his sincerity. "Hot shoeing, cold shoeing, therapeutic, corrective and lameness shoeing. I shoe reining and ranch horses and horses for barrel racers, ropers, draft horses, mules, donkeys, and so on. I can also treat some diseases if needed."

"Hot shoeing versus cold shoeing? Which is better?"

Her mouth turned in a slow smile. "Do you really care?"

"I don't even know what the hell I'm talking about, but tell me anyway."

Her laughter made him grip the side of the truck so he didn't haul her to him and kiss her like she deserved to be kissed.

"Really, if the horse is healthy, both are fine. I shoed the horses here with cold shoes. Meaning I bought the shoes at the ranch supply store in Riverton and used the hammer and anvil to shape them as needed. Hot shoeing requires forge work and me building the shoe with bar stock. I usually only do hot shoeing for therapeutic, corrective, training, or other specialized shoeing." She leaned a hip against her truck, facing off with him. "You have any other questions, Nick Walsh? You lookin' for a farrier?"

He smiled and leaned forward an inch, bringing her closer. "I am now."

Her smile vanished, and she pushed off the truck. "Well, like I said, I better hit the road. Good meeting you, Nick. Take care, Worrells. See ya around."

With a final wave, she had her tool box in the back of her truck before he could offer to help. Nick admired the woman's hustle. He watched the red truck disappear.

"Give her five more seconds and she could've put a bit in his mouth and led him around."

Nick narrowed his gaze at Worrell. "Shut the—"

"The baby." Lucy cut him off for the thousandth time since his arrival.

He nodded. "Sorry, Lucy. Michal involved with anyone?"

"Not that I'm aware of."

"You just met, man. Although your interrogation style is as effective as always."

Nick lifted an eyebrow and cut a look between Jared and Lucy then held Jared's gaze.

"Roger."

Lucy laughed. "Anyway, I've never seen Michal with anyone."

"Outstanding. You're going to see her with me."

MICHAL FOUGHT WITH catching a final look at the big blond Marine in her rearview mirror. He'd startled her when he squeezed her hand, and she felt the heat emanating from him hotter than any fire in her forge. It was as if he'd transferred all that heat through his hand, warming her from head to toe. She'd felt surrounded by him even though he'd kept his distance. Lord, he must be six foot six with muscles stretching his t-shirt taut. She enjoyed the looks he'd given her, and she wouldn't lie to herself, she'd stayed bent a few seconds longer than necessary when she sensed him watching her ass.

Her mouth tugged into a smile at him standing there nodding during her description of hot and cold shoeing like he really gave a crap, but damn, she believed he really did. He didn't care because of any love for horses but because he wanted to know about what was important to her.

The last thing she needed was to be some young Marine's summer fling. Losing her battle, she glanced in the mirror, and her gaze shot back to the road when she caught him looking down the road. Like he could see her from where he was. She brushed off the feeling he could, in fact, see her.

That he called her Michal and not Mike had thrown her off balance as much as the light squeeze he'd given her hand. No one called her Michal but her mother who was still fighting the good fight to have a refined daughter instead of a tomboy. Hadn't she told him people called her Mike? And what really irked? She'd melted a little inside hearing it.

She shook her head and focused on the road. There were plenty of younger women around closer to his age, and since Lucy snapped up Jared before anyone had a chance, they'd be circling the handsome Marine like a turkey buzzard on roadkill. At forty-two, she'd be content to stand by and watch the entertainment. She lifted her gaze to the review mirror not expecting to see anything from this distance, and she didn't. The fact disappointment hammered her hard at not seeing Nick Walsh made her press harder on the accelerator to flee from the temptation her daddy always preached about.

CHAPTER THREE

NICK TRIED HIS damndest not to plow over Lucy to get to the spot on the bleachers next to Michal. He glanced at Lucy as he sat down. Her smile said he'd failed at acting cool and collected. Turning his attention back to why he'd run over his friend and his friend's wife, he smiled at Michal's wide eyes. "Hey, Michal."

She nodded. "Hi, Nick." She looked around him. "Jared. Lucy. Glad to see you made it to the rodeo."

"Wouldn't miss it." Lucy lifted her camera with a lens that reached to Montana. "I'm in charge of photographs."

"As it should be. I was in charge of shoeing most of the horses."

Lucy chuckled. "As it should be."

When her green gaze landed back on him, Nick had to fold his hand into a fist to keep from running his fingers over her cheek.

"This your first rodeo?"

"Actual rodeo, affirmative this is a first."

She chuckled at the meaning; he'd witnessed and been involved in many rough rides, just not on a bull or horse.

"You want to join me for some chow after?"

Her forehead folded in a frown. "I'm sorry, I've got an early day tomorrow."

He snorted a laugh at her lame excuse. "Okay."

The rodeo would start at one thirty—in about ten minutes. He couldn't imagine it'd run too late, but if she didn't want to, she didn't want to. He stared at the dirt arena and chutes across from the covered stands where they sat. Not a complete rodeo novice, he knew most of the main events like saddle bronc riding, team roping, and bull riding. He glanced at the program, mutton busting…that was a new one.

He caught the sight of little fingers on his legs and moved the program to meet Eli's big hazel eyes. "Up." The toddler stretched his arms for Nick, and with smile, he lifted the tyke and settled him on his lap.

Lucy kept a steady click on her camera as she cleared her throat. "What do you say, Eli Worrell?"

"Than' ew."

"You're welcome anytime, buddy."

Nick felt a gaze on him and shifted his to meet Michal's. Her gaze cut from Eli to him and back to Eli before settling on him. "I am sorry about later."

He shrugged. "Don't give it a second thought. Your privilege to say no." He tipped his head to Lucy. "You want to sit by Luce, so you can talk?"

"No."

He laughed. "See, that word seems to slip awful easy from your mouth."

"Nick, I'm really not trying to brush you off. It's just there are a lot of things…" Before she could finish, the announcer asked everyone to stand for a prayer and the National Anthem. He could live to be a thousand and that song, played in a place like this, on the Fourth of July, among people who really gave a damn, would settle a lump in his throat and a surge of pride through his blood. His smile grew when Eli, standing in front of him, stood ramrod straight, rivaling him and Jared for Marine posture. The song ended, and everyone clapped except Eli who clapped and did a little dance before demanding his position on Nick's lap.

Lucy's parents, Patty and Gerald Thomas, joined them, sitting on the other side of Jared, who quickly changed places with Lucy. His friend liked his parents-in-law just fine, but only a man who didn't value his sanity would sit between Patty and Lucy who were already talking like they hadn't just seen each other a couple days ago. Jared slid next to Nick and rolled his eyes with a nod to his wife.

"Daddy!" Eli reached for Jared, and he took his son.

"We're not playing back-and-forth all afternoon, son."

" 'K."

Nick angled his attention back to Michal. She was visiting with a few people in front of them. The bareback bronc riding had already seen three contestants go, and he'd missed each. At the parade that morning and in the stands, he felt a real sense of community. This was more of a family reunion than a town Fourth of July celebration.

"Nick, this is Ned and Kaylee Mitchell. They work on the Cross Bar T."

Nick came out of his thoughts and shook hands with the couple, Michal had introduced him, too. "Nice to meet you both."

"You're here with Michal?"

"He's visiting Jared and Lucy. He serves with Jared."

Jared tipped his hat to the couple. Nick stayed with the conversation, but was confused at Michal's sweet move to include him, and at the same time, keep her distance. He took advantage of the fact she was even speaking to him.

"So, what's mutton busting?"

Her smile warmed to a natural feature instead of the stilted formal action she usually sent him. "The little ones"—she nodded at Eli—"ride sheep."

"Ride sheep?"

"Yep. It's really sweet." She looked around him to Jared. "Is Eli riding later?"

"Yes, ma'am. Don't let the clicks from Lucy's camera fool you. She's just acting like she cares about the other contestants. That thing is going to go wild when this cowboy saddles up."

Nick chuckled. "You let your son ride a sheep?"

"I'm good."

Nick stopped with the jokes and assumed a serious look. "I bet you're the best, Bud."

Jared nodded in appreciation, and Nick turned back to watching what the program called steer wrestling. Now that looked like something he could get into. Riding hell bent and launching off your horse to take a steer by the horns and wrestle it to the ground. It took balls.

"How many people are here?"

"They said yesterday's rodeo brought in about a thousand." Michal adjusted her cowboy hat.

He watched her more than the rodeo. Damn, she was the finest woman he'd ever known. "Almost five times the size of Ten Sleep on any given day. Impressive."

"It is. And it's not even a PRCA-sanctioned event. Just a good old Western rodeo as it should be."

"Amen to that, Michal." An older man behind them rested his hand on her shoulder.

"Nick Walsh, this is Marv Townsend."

Nick accepted the man's hand. "Nice to meet you, sir."

"Same here, young man."

"Damn, Mike, good thing you're here, I'm falling down on introduction duty."

"Language, Jared." Lucy said from behind her camera.

"Thanks for introducing me to some folks."

The red on her cheeks had nothing to do with the July heat and crammed stands. "It's good Wyoming manners."

"Well you've got those in spades." He let his gaze wander over her and let her see it wander. "You've got a lot in spades."

"Nick. You don't understand."

"Go out with me tonight and enlighten me."

Pain shot through her eyes, and Nick stopped the shit. "I really can't."

He saw the truth in her gaze and the fact it had nothing to do with getting up at the butt crack of dawn. "Let's compromise. You sit by me at the fireworks, so I'm not the third wheel on the Worrell wagon and I won't push...tonight."

"I sit by you, nothing more?"

"Well, you could say 'hi' maybe ohh and ahh at the show."

"But no street dance or anything?"

"There's a street dance?" He shot a glare to Jared who'd failed to keep him informed.

Jared shrugged. "I didn't know you'd need a place to meet Mike."

He sent another glare to his brother and turned back to Michal. "No street dance, if that's what you want?"

She offered her hand. "Fireworks. I'll even bring dessert."

He took her hand, letting his swallow her soft flesh, and held tighter than he needed to. Her gaze dropped to their joined hands, and he watched her throat work. "Deal."

"Deal." She tried to take her hand back, but Nick laced their fingers together and held tight. He almost let out a whoop when she didn't try to yank her hand away. But any joy was dashed when he saw her quickly swipe at a tear.

"Michal?" He went to let go of her hand, but she held on.

"I'm fine. Just don't move," she whispered.

He froze not willing to lose the connection for all the awards and medals the Marines could offer. Giving her some space, he turned his attention back to the rodeo and watched youngsters ride around poles showing an extreme amount of talent. Every once in a while, Michal squeezed his hand and the tenderness shot straight to his heart. This was the woman for him. In all the world, he never thought he'd find his soul in Ten Sleep, Wyoming. It was going to be a fight, but she was worth every wound and every battle.

Michal fought the pull to Nick Walsh, but she couldn't deny it when he took her hand in his. They'd be declared a couple by tonight, but she didn't mind her name connected to his for a few hours. That's all it could be. She wasn't going to waste his time and hers on a dream she could never turn to reality. Later, at the fireworks, she might hold his hand again and wish it would end with their bodies as entwined as their fingers.

One after another, the events started and ended, and Michal couldn't tell anyone who had the better time in the timed events or who stayed on for eight seconds in the rough stock. She came out of her daze when Nick untangled their hands.

"Sorry, sweetheart, but I've gotta cheer on my boy."

She nodded, and he stood. "Come with us."

"Yeah, come on, Mike."

Michal shook her head at Jared and Nick. "I'll cheer from here.

Don't worry, I'll be really loud."

"You sure?"

"Yeah."

"Okay. Save my seat."

She patted the still warm spot next to her. "It'll be here."

He stopped short of following Lucy and Jared. "Will you?"

Michal smiled at how well he knew her. "I will."

The words were out before she could train her voice to keep the intensity from the promise. He looked like he was about ready to bend down and kiss her, so she pointed to the Worrells. "You better hurry."

"Nice deflection, Michal."

Before she could answer, he made his way through the others in their row and followed the Worrells and Thomases behind the chutes where the little ones where being decked out in helmets and chaps to take their place among the rough stock contestants.

Michal kept her word and cheered the loudest for Eli Worrell, who ended up holding on for dear life to his sheep the longest—a whole three seconds. She stood and whooped for him as his little hand was lifted in victory. Her smile spread when Nick gave him a high five and slapped his back, almost sending him ass over teakettle. Nick was a natural with children. One of those men who should have six or seven. She sank back onto her seat, her stomach turning sour. She had to stop this train before she couldn't and it crashed leaving them both shattered.

MICHAL REMINDED HERSELF to breathe as she made her way to the Thomas' deck. Lucy had caught her after the rodeo with an invitation to her parents' ranch for a Fourth of July picnic and a small fireworks show. When Michal opened her mouth to decline, Lucy reminded her she'd promised Nick she'd watch the fireworks with him, and this would be where he'd be watching them.

The street dance had kicked-off at dusk, and as she made her way to the people on the deck, she almost wished she'd suggested she and Nick go to the dance. There'd be lots more people there and a chance to break away and visit with others when she needed a break from his touch. Like a sane woman would need break from him.

"Mike, you made it."

Michal lifted the cake pan she brought filled with chocolate chip cookies. "I brought some cookies. Thanks for having me, Patty."

"You're welcome anytime." Patty Thomas took the pan.

"Mike, good to see you. You know that Roan…"

"No way, Dad, Mike gets today off."

Michal turned her attention to Gerald to avoid Nick's hot gaze. "If you want…"

Gerald stood, but Patty and Lucy gave him a look that made him sit back down. "It can wait."

"Okay."

"You hungry? There's plenty of chow left." Jared nodded to a table set up buffet style with fried chicken, potato salad, rolls, and chips.

"Thanks."

She went to the table and started filling a plate. A large shadow fell over her, and her heart kicked against her chest harder than any mule.

"Our deal was you'd say *hi*."

"Hi, Nick."

"And sit with me."

"I will, as soon as I get my plate fixed."

He leaned a hip against the side of the house. "Heard you say you brought cookies?"

"Chocolate chip."

"My favorite."

She narrowed her eyes at him. "Why do I get the feeling you'd say the same thing no matter which flavor I brought."

"Because I would. Why are you so late getting here?'

"Because I was trying to avoid you."

"Direct hit, Michal. Not interested?"

"Very interested. I'm not going to lie. You are hot, and not only on fire with the looks, but you're kind and a little goofy, and I like that. But you and me? It's not going to happen, Nick. So give it up."

"Sorry, Michal, but it's not in this Marine's blood to quit. You should have said you weren't interested."

Her shoulders sank a bit. "Would you have given up then?"

"Hell no."

Nick pushed from the side of the house. He tossed a wink as he walked by her. Michal fought the urge to trip him.

NICK KNEW HE'D been pushing his luck all evening, but he wasn't about to let up on the assault to bring down the walls Michal was building fast. They'd all moved the party up a hill so they could see the city's fireworks without the hassle of parking. Spreading out a few blankets on the grass, they sat. Michal was true to her word and sank down next to him on their own private blanket.

She lifted a Tupperware bowl. "Cookie? They're going fast."

Nick nodded and reached for one of her chocolate chip cookies. He took a bite without thought and groaned as the explosion of rich chocolate and the perfect dough hit his tongue.

"Marry me, Michal?"

Her laughter tied him to her like it had the first day. But he caught her gaze and her laugh died on a strangled, "Glad you like them."

Satisfied she'd caught how little he was kidding with his proposal, he patted the quilted material between his legs. "Why don't you move over here?"

Her gaze shot to the spot between his legs and to the other couples. Lucy was relaxed between Jared's thighs, her hands on his shins. Patty was equally relaxed with Gerald.

She turned her gaze back to Nick. "You're bound and determined to make something out of this impossible situation."

Even as she scolded, she climbed over one leg and nestled back against him. "Until you tell me why it's impossible, yes, I'm determined to make something of us."

Unable to resist any longer, he brushed a kiss to the exposed skin on the back of her neck, pleased at the soft gasp-turned-moan. "Don't."

"Roger. But you did promise to hold my hand."

Michal took his hand and laced their fingers together. In the distance, the sky lit up with red, white, and blue flashes as the town celebrated America's independence. He stared at his hand linked with

Michal's again and noticed, as much as she tried to keep her distance, she pressed closer throughout the night and glanced at their hands.

"Give me a chance, Michal."

"There isn't a chance for us, Nick."

"I won't believe that."

"Then you'll make both of our summers miserable."

"You miserable now?"

"No, I'm way too content."

"Me, too."

"Nick…"

"Just enjoy tonight. We can fight about how much you're going to give in to me later."

With a heavy sigh, she fell silent, and Nick did the same. As the others watched the fireworks, Nick used his mental whiteboard to plan out the next maneuver.

CHAPTER FOUR

Michal sat at a corner table and released a deep breath after swallowing a drink of Outlaw Amber. She had a beer maybe twice a month, and the week she'd put in called for one of those times to be that night. The Friday night local band playing at the Ten Sleep Brewing Co was playing some of the older country tunes, and the music from outside where the band played on the unique stage of the flatbed of the 1950s era truck floated over her as she chose a seat inside. She allowed herself the slightest smile at the twang of a Mark Chestnut classic, "Ol' Country". Only in her mind, instead of a country boy and city girl meeting up for a weekend tryst, it was a Wyoming gal and a very well put together city Marine getting together to set the sheets on fire.

"Hey, Michal. You savin' this chair for me?"

The well put together Marine she'd been dreaming about slid into the chair opposite her wooden booth bench and winked before she could say yes or no. Michal rolled her eyes and sighed. She shouldn't have let her fantasies run loose; somehow they'd conjured the subject of most of them since she'd spent the Fourth of July between his strong legs, his arms wrapped around her. He'd declared his intention to marry her when he bit into one of the chocolate chip cookies she'd brought. Instinct told her he was only half teasing.

"Guess so." Why she said that and not 'go to hell' she could only blame on the lack of desire to fight and the memory of his hand caressing her arm. She just wanted to relax, but at the moment, there wasn't a relaxed muscle in her body.

He leaned forward, and long blond eyelashes shielded the dark blue of his narrowed gaze. "You look beautiful tonight."

Her gaze dropped to the plain blue v-neck t-shirt top and her jeans. Plain brown boots finished the outfit.

"Not your clothes, woman, you."

Michal kept her gaze lowered, hoping to hide how much his words hit right to her heart. "Kind of forward, City, for just one night watching fireworks."

"But not too early for nicknames. Okay, Lucky Charms."

She frowned and met his gaze so he could clearly see her displeasure. "What the hell does that mean?"

He tipped his beer mug toward her chest where her horseshoe necklace rested. "Horseshoes, Irish heritage, makes sense. That's how we do it in the Corps." He leaned in closer, and his mouth curved in a wicked smile. "And I bet you are magically delicious."

Michal took a drink of the amber brew to hide her pleasure in the name. "Aren't you supposed to be with Jared and Lucy?"

"They're out on a date, and her parents are watching Eli. I saw the big "BEER" sign like a beacon welcoming me home."

She laughed despite the silent vow she'd made that Nick wouldn't get to her.

"You wanna dance?"

"Ummm?"

"Come on, Lucky Charms, I'm not on one knee; I'm just asking for a dance."

He stood and held out a hand. Michal placed her hand in his and smiled as his large, calloused hand swallowed hers. He gave a tug, bringing her up. He didn't let her hand go as he led her outside to an area cleared for dancing. He tugged her close, and she almost groaned as the band covered Doug Stone's, "A Different Light". It was a favorite of hers—the part of her wishing a man would see beyond the tough farrier to the woman who needed to be held just as Nick was holding her at that moment.

She roped his neck with her arms and pressed close as he rested his hands on her hips, and they moved to music. She would enjoy this dance and this man holding her for the almost four minutes of the song. After the song, she'd point out a few of the women Lucy's age, or Jared's age. Nick must be about thirty-five like Jared since they were the same rank.

He pulled her closer, and she felt all those iron muscles brushing against her. And when she inhaled deeply, his spicy scent acted like a drug, drawing her closer and leaving her aching for more. The night air was heavy, and the music swallowed them. They were in a darkened area, leaving Michal feeling like they were in their own world. He brushed a kiss on her forehead; Michal lifted her gaze to meet his, and her lips parted, inviting him to taste her.

The last note played, and Michal broke from his arms. "I've gotta go. Thanks for the dance."

She weaved through the other couples taking their time to part from each other's arms instead of running like a scared deer, but she continued the flight. Michal had just made it to her truck when a large hand landed on her shoulder.

"What the hell, Michal?"

She pivoted on her boot heels and shrugged his hand off her. "Look, Nick, I'm not the woman who's gonna warm your bed while you're in Wyoming. There are plenty of younger women here who will be more than willing to spread their legs for you and show you a nice time while you're visiting. But it's not gonna be me."

He stumbled back like she'd kneed him in the groin. He smoothed a hand over the wheat-colored hair he had left after the Marines took their share. She had the irrational thought of how much she'd like to see him with a full head of hair. She bet it was thick and gorgeous. Just another way the man toyed with her emotions.

Before Michal could gather her thoughts, he cuffed her upper arms and hauled her so close her curves melted against him. He opened his mouth and she prepared for a few choice words to be tossed her way. Instead, his mouth crashed onto hers, and all those sappy books and movies that talked about fire and fireworks didn't come close compared to the inferno Nick's kiss sent through her. He pressed her against the truck and released her arms, and she wrapped her arms around his neck again. When he gripped her thighs, she gave a little hop and secured her legs around his waist.

Nick responded by pressing closer so she could feel his erection pressed between her thighs. He broke the kiss for a second to join her in a deep moan before his mouth was on hers again, and he deepened the kiss, gently tangling his tongue with hers as if he savored every taste and the feel of being connected to her.

Michal heard the small cry coming from her when he broke the kiss. He brushed kisses over her face as he continued to move against her.

"This wasn't supposed to happen."

He chuckled, and she squeezed him close as it rumbled through him. "This is exactly what was supposed to happen, Michal."

"Why won't you call me Mike?"

He shrugged. "Everyone else does."

Michal lowered her head and rested her forehead on his chest. "Let me go, Nick."

"Negative."

"I'm forty-two."

"I'm thirty-five. Do you want to do height and weight next?"

She laughed again, despite wanting to be mad at him. She bet he'd make her laugh a lot. Somehow the thought made her sad, because she wasn't going to find out. Unhooking her legs, she smiled when he lowered her legs slowly and rested his hands on her hips to keep her steady. She couldn't quite bring herself to lower her arms even after asking him to let her go.

"Nick…"

"No, you listen, Michal. I don't give a fuck how old you are. I want more of you. And before you let that scowl completely form, I don't mean just screwing, I want to hang with you, get to know you. And yeah, I'd like to fuck you silly a few times a day."

"That's quite a proposal."

NICK COULDN'T KEEP his own scowl from forming. "So now you're gonna lie and say you didn't feel anything. Damn, Michal, you're practically choking me."

Her arms fell from his neck, and Nick cursed his mouth for spouting off. She leaned against the truck. "You know that kiss was nuclear, and I'm not denying anything. I just think you'd be happier with one of the younger gals."

He brushed a kiss over her cheek. "Let me decide who'll make me happy."

Her green gaze held his. "If I go home with you tonight, will you let it go after that?"

He felt the tug of a frown crease his forehead. "Hell no."

"Hey, Mike!"

Nick pushed away from the truck where his hands caged Michal's head when she startled at the greeting.

"Hey, Charlene!"

Nick locked his jaw for a second when the pretty brunette made her way over to the truck. Couldn't she see he and Michal were kind of in the middle of something?

"You headed in?"

She asked her question like she was talking to Michal, but she was looking at him.

"No, I'm headed home. This is Nick Walsh, Jared's friend. Nick this is Charlene Granger; she and Jared dated in high school."

And he could see why Jared fell hard and fast for Lucy. He shouldn't be a jerk even in his thoughts, but anyone could see Charlene wasn't the woman for Jared, and she wasn't the woman for him.

"Nice to meet you, Nick."

He took her hand in quick handshake. "Same here."

"Hey, I'm headed out, but Nick shouldn't have to end his night early. Why don't you take him back for a drink or over by the band for some dancing, Charlene?"

Nick never wanted to strangle a woman more than his hands ached to wrap around Michal's neck. Then he caught the quick flash of jealousy as he released Charlene's hand.

"Yeah, I think Michal and I are done with our conversation."

Charlene shrugged. "Okay. Have a good night." She waved back to Michal and Nick fell in step beside her. "Night, Mike." He tossed back over his shoulder.

He felt like a number one asshole at her crestfallen look, but it was her own damn fault. If she wasn't as stubborn as a Marine bulldog. He wasn't a man who had ever used a woman to make another jealous, and he wouldn't if he'd seen any real interest in Charlene's gaze or touch, but he got the feeling she wasn't any more interested in him for the long term than he was in her. If it was the kick in the ass Michal needed, he'd give it a try. Still it didn't feel right.

"Hey Charlene, I want to set the record straight before we get there…"

"Michal's being a pain in the ass about her age, and you want to make her a little jealous." She shrugged. "I'm game."

"How'd you know?" He followed her inside past the brewery equipment and into the tap room.

"Because there was enough heat between the two of you to cause a wildfire, and then she's pushing you off on me after announcing we're the same age. I wasn't a math wiz, but I can add two and two."

"Thanks."

"My pleasure. Mike's a good woman, and after her asshole of an ex-husband did what he did to her years ago, she deserves a real man." Her eyes took him in from top deck to lower. "You definitely fit that bill."

"Thanks, again. Let's have a beer and dance."

"Sounds good."

Nick wanted to ask about the asshole ex, but he wasn't into small town gossip, and if Michal wanted him to know, she'd tell him.

CHAPTER FIVE

*N*IGHT, *MIKE*.

Michal swallowed around the pain in her throat. He'd tossed it back as if she was just another one of the guys. Like he was with everyone else. She choked back the vicious tears threatening to fall. He hadn't wanted to be in the same category as everyone else, but she'd forced him there all the same. Her big dumb ass thought to force him to go back with Charlene. Well, it worked.

She watched as the new couple walked side-by-side toward the Brewing Co. At least he didn't hold Charlene's hand. He was city, but he fit in the country real nice in the purple cowboy shirt, Wrangler jeans, and black boots. Her gaze followed the long legs back up to his hands. He'd be holding Charlene with those hands, maybe more.

The couple stopped just short of the wood fence and disappeared as they continued to the tap room, chatting like old friends. Charlene's laughter rolled over the parking lot. Michal turned and got into her truck, resenting the younger woman's laughter that should have been hers.

Driving to her small farmhouse, Michal retraced the whole evening. There had been a number of younger women at the Brewing Co when Nick arrived, but he'd sought her out, told her she was beautiful, and gave her a silly nickname. When they'd danced he held her so tight she felt his heartbeat, and his breathing was as harsh as hers. He'd followed her to her truck and kissed her senseless. None of this sounded like a man who found her too old for him. Hell, he'd told her he didn't give a fuck about her age.

She pulled into the farmyard and scanned the small green house. All the windows were dark except for a soft glow from the kitchen window, the only light she left on so she wouldn't have to walk into a completely dark house. There was nothing worse than a dark house.

Stepping out of the truck, Michal went to her barn where she was sure to be welcomed. Her feet crossed the threshold and Max, her barn cat, circled her legs until she bent and petted him for a few minutes before moving on to show love to Bailey, the Paint gelding. As she stroked Bailey's neck, she smiled. This was it—her stock—a cat and a horse. When she'd moved to Ten Sleep after her divorce, she wanted her own land, a place to escape. It wasn't much, her little piece of land tucked against the Bighorns, but she could sit on her porch and listen to Ten Sleep Creek bubble over the stones. How much nicer to have someone sitting on the porch with her?

"Damn him, he has me thinking all kinds of sappy thoughts."

Bailey pushed her shoulder with his nose and Michal sighed. "Fine. I'll go back, but you know he's probably halfway to Charlene's by now."

She mumbled all the way back to the truck and back through town and out to the old Smith barn, now the Ten Sleep Brewing Co, at the base of Signal Cliff. When she parked the truck, she scanned the parking lot, and her heart picked up the pace when she spotted Lucy's truck. He must have borrowed it. She continued her search until she found Charlene's car. Her stomach twisted, half relieved they were still there and not in Charlene's bed and half sick she'd now have to look like a fool.

She made her way inside and, after a quick scan of the tap room, headed back outside. With a deep breath, she let her gaze wander over the dancing couples. She waved to a few folks and mumbled a greeting to others as she made her way to the dance area and the couple in the center. Of course, they looked amazing together, Charlene's dark contrasting with Nick's blond, and both were too beautiful for their own good.

As she took the final steps, she prepared for anything, from them laughing in her face to Nick telling her to go to hell. Charlene saw her first and took a step from Nick's arms pointing to Michal with her chin.

He turned around and Michal cleared her throat. "Sorry to interrupt, but can I talk to you, Nick?"

"Sure." He turned to Charlene. "You'll be okay?"

"Absolutely."

He was such a gentleman. Why couldn't he be a jerk?

His full focus came back to Michal. "You want to talk here?"

All eyes and ears were tuned in to them. She shook her head. "Away from everyone, if you don't mind."

"Lead the way."

She turned on her boot heels and shoved her hands in her pockets, leading Nick through the cars and trucks past the Indian Taco truck. He rested a hand on the small of her back, and she lifted her gaze and smiled. Her smile fell when he didn't return the gesture.

She kept walking until they got to her truck, then she turned to face him.

His gaze moved over the area. "This seems familiar."

"I don't want you with Charlene," Michal rushed before she lost her nerve.

His eyebrow hitched. "You don't?"

"No."

"And who are you, Mike, to make that decision?"

She stepped closer and tipped her head back so she could meet his gaze. "To you, I'm Michal."

A fire sparked in his eyes, but he didn't reach for her or smile. "So who do you want me with, if I'm not with Charlene?"

"Do you have to be with someone?"

"Yes."

She held onto her smile. "Me. If you still—"

She was backed against the truck with his hands braced on the truck on either side of her head, his strong arms acting like iron bars keeping her where he wanted her. "No more shit about age?"

"No. But no acting like this is a forever thing, either."

He stared for what seemed like years, and she held her breath, hoping she hadn't blown it again. He pushed off the truck and gave a sharp nod. "For now."

His stance and eyes said it was the best she was going to get. "Okay."

He leaned forward, and Michal didn't hesitate, meeting him halfway and wrapping her arms around his neck, bringing him closer when his mouth met hers. His kiss was hard and possessive, as if his words were lies, and he meant to own her forever. Nevertheless, Michal met his need with her own. As quick as the kiss started, it was over, but she held on, making her own words lies that she wanted things to ever end.

"Glad you came back, Lucky Charms."

She squeezed him harder for using her nickname. "Me too, City. Do you want to follow me home?"

An unexplained sadness entered his eyes, but disappeared so quick she wondered if she'd seen it there. His mouth tugged up in a wicked smile. "How easy do you think I am, ma'am? We haven't even had a first date, and you're trying to get me into bed."

"But I thought you wanted…"

"Oh, I want that a lot. But I think we both need to step back tonight."

Michal dropped her arms and nodded, unable to voice consent to his logic. At least he wouldn't be going to anyone else's bed.

"You want to go back?"

"No. I think I've caused enough commotion for a night. Are you?"

His smile said he knew what she was thinking. Charlene was still inside. "No. I think I'll head back to the shop."

"Would you like to come along with me tomorrow? Learn what I do?"

"Love to."

Michal lowered her gaze, suddenly feeling a bit shy and uncertain in the shadow of the big Marine. "I'll pick you up at seven."

"I'll be waiting."

She shifted and turned to open her truck door. "See you tomorrow then."

"See you tomorrow."

She wished she could wipe the smug smile off his face, but it was so darn cute, she couldn't stay mad long. Getting in her truck, she gave a wave and pulled out of the parking lot. Again, she had to take one last look in the rearview mirror. Her smile grew when she saw him rooted where she'd left him. He lifted his hand and waved, and her triumph turned to a something much hotter.

CHAPTER SIX

NICK WHISTLED AS he got in the truck he'd borrowed from Lucy. He turned off at their street even as he watched the taillights from Michal's truck continue down 2nd Street. The temptation to flip a U and follow her was strong, but she'd used the magic word. Home. The one word that could cut him. And she'd used it right after making it clear that, to her, this was just a summertime affair.

He'd agreed to her terms, because he saw in her something he hadn't seen in any other woman he'd dated. He saw how perfect she was for him. He'd been a summertime affair before; hell, he'd been an affair for all seasons, but no woman ever chose him. They wanted the uniform, the title, not the man. Michal could be the one to choose him. Shit, she'd come back to the Brewing Co, and everyone had to have known what was going on, but she still did it.

What the hell was he doing? He could be balls deep in the woman instead of dreaming about it again that night like he had every night since he met her. He shot a text to Jared, hoping he wouldn't be interrupting anything.

The answering text came back. Nick shot off a second text and Jared responded in the affirmative. Armed with the information he needed, Nick shoved some gear in his seabag and got back into the truck. He checked his phone to confirm the directions Jared sent and headed through town toward the Bighorn Mountains.

He took the turnoff and slowed the truck as he closed in on Michal's place. He couldn't see much with night fully descended, but there was a light in one window. He turned off the truck and looked up to see Michal on the porch. He swallowed hard. She'd changed into a pair of yellow yoga pants and a tank top; clearly, she'd taken off her bra.

Grabbing his seabag, he headed toward the porch where she stayed rooted. Her face was so sweet, but the muscles in her arms showed the years of hard work. She wasn't ripped, but he'd felt her strength when she held him, and with the tank top, the definition of her muscles was pronounced. When his gaze dropped to her bare feet, he smiled. Curves, muscles, sweet, tender, and sassy. She was everything a man needed. He lifted his gaze to hers. And wanted.

She crossed her arms over her chest. "I thought you weren't coming?"

He stayed at the bottom of the steps so they were eye to eye since her five foot six wasn't near his six foot six. Opposites in every way.

"You mind?"

"No."

They stood there staring for a bit. It was still warm as the summer heat held on, but a cool breeze drifted over them. The creek running over the rocks, crickets, and the sounds of the country rang louder than any big city noise as he waited. He filled his lungs with a deep breath of the fresh air filled with pine, soil and the smells that made up a farm.

She stood aside. "Come on in."

Nick passed her and entered the small house. A galley to his right looked like it hadn't been refurbished since the fifties. To his left was a living room just big enough for a couch, chair, a couple of end tables, and a TV.

"You want some coffee?"

He tossed his seabag by the archway cutout leading to the passageway. "Didn't come here for something to drink, Michal."

"No, I guess not."

"Take down your hair, sweetheart."

"Pardon?"

He smiled at her wide eyes. "Your hair, I want to see it down."

Bringing her braid forward, she slipped off the band and started unraveling the thick braid. Nick felt his heartbeat kick up like he was about to bust through an insurgent's door. She kept her gaze lowered as she released the thick, honey-colored locks.

"Look at me, Michal."

Her gaze shot to his, and she combed her hair with her fingers as she kept her emerald gaze locked on him.

"Do you like it?"

"Hell, yes."

He took the step necessary to close the distance and ran his fingers through the spun silk cascading to the middle of her back in soft waves. He fisted a hunk and tugged, bringing her face to his, and her mouth dropped open in shock.

"You are so damn beautiful, Lucky Charms, you know that?"

"Not until you said so."

He loosened his grip on her hair, massaging her scalp with the tips of his fingers. "How do you want it?"

Her face couldn't have gotten more red, and he was sure she would have dropped her gaze if he wasn't holding her steady. "Me under you," she whispered. "I want to feel you on me."

"That sounds real nice."

"Yes, I want it nice." She angled her head and kissed his forearm.

Nick bent and captured her mouth. Keeping his fingers in her hair, he guided her head to deepen the kiss and then ran kisses along the column of her neck. Bringing her closer, he slid his other hand under the elastic of her pants to find she wasn't wearing any panties. He groaned and ran two fingers along her slick sex. Michal grabbed both of his wrists and gasped into his mouth, her eyes shooting wide open.

He removed his hand from her pants and broke the kiss. "You okay?"

"Yeah, it just surprised me."

Nick held her gaze and had the feeling he was Michal's first since her husband, but he didn't want to bring another man into this, so he kept his thoughts to himself. "Want to head into the bedroom?"

"Yes."

He stopped by his seabag and snagged his head kit where he kept his condoms. Michal took the kit and tossed it back on the bag.

"I've got birth control covered. Unless…"

Nick lifted her and carried her to the bedroom. He tossed her on the bed and covered her. He didn't let her say anything, but crushed his mouth to hers, planning to kiss her until their lungs popped for want of air. She wasn't idle under him. She was tugging his shirt out of his jeans and smoothing her palms over his chest. Nick returned the favor, running his palms over her soft belly and over her breasts, molding the mounds as Michal squirmed under him.

She had his fly unzipped and his cock in her hand, and Nick broke his promise and tore his mouth from hers, moaning as she stroked his dick from root to head. Damn, she was good, knew just how much pressure to use and caressed the thick ridge and the sweet spot under the head.

Nick let her have her way for a few more amazing seconds before grabbing her wrist. "No more, or I'm not going to last."

Michal released his cock and brushed her lips over his. "Same here with my breasts. Please stop; they're so sensitive."

He nodded and smoothed his hands back down over her breasts, ribs and belly. "Lift up."

Stripping her of her yoga pants, Nick moved back up her legs and pressed them wide with his palms. He ran his tongue from her vagina to her clit. "Nick, please, I'm ready."

He smiled. She didn't have to tell him, he could taste and feel just how ready she was. He shifted and made quick work of ripping off his clothes. When he turned to find her stripping off her tank top, he almost swallowed his tongue. She reached for the lamp by the bed.

"Leave it on."

Her eyebrows nearly reached her hairline. "You want the lights on?" Even as she asked, she was giving him the once over. When she finished, she traced her lips with her tongue.

He let his gaze trail over every inch of her. Lord, he was going to have a hell of a good time mapping those curves.

"Yeah, I want the lights on. Lie back."

MICHAL RESISTED THE urge to flip off the light no matter what he said. He'd just flip them on, and she didn't want to argue about lighting. She followed his directions and laid back and tried to will herself not to blush.

The positive was, while leaving the lights on meant he could see her, it also meant she could see him, and the view was worth a lifetime of embarrassment. He was golden from head to foot; only his backside was white. His chest was broad and covered in a smattering of golden curls. His stomach was what exercise machine commercials promised, and a happy trail led to a thatch of gold and his impressive cock, thick and heavy, stretching toward her.

She opened her legs, and he took his place there. He kissed her tenderly and brushed a kiss by her ear. "Why wouldn't I want to see every outstanding inch of you?"

She shrugged. "I think you're exaggerating."

Nick cuffed her wrists together over her head, and Michal gave a sharp cry as he pushed his full length deep inside her.

"Damn, you are tight."

Michal bit her lip and arched to take him deeper. "You feel so good, Nick. God, it's so good."

He started to rock in and out at an agonizingly slow pace. "You have no idea." He took her mouth in a hard kiss, his hand tightening around her wrists. His thrusts turned harder and deeper.

"Don't let me hurt you."

Michal brushed her lips over his neck and licked the salty skin. She lifted her face and held his gaze. "Same here."

His jaw turned hard as he locked it, understanding she was talking about his heart not his body. Michal struggled against his iron grip and wrapped her legs around his waist. "Please," she whispered.

Nick released her hands, and Michal held him tightly, digging her fingers into his biceps as he pounded into her, kissing her hard, and consuming every sense. She slammed one hand against his chest and held tighter to his arm with the other when he pinched a nipple as he angled to hit her clit. He did it again, and Michal felt her body clamp down around his thick length, making her tighter as she trembled under him. She came again when he continued to move until he rammed deep and emptied himself into her. The bellow of her name was so loud, it almost broke her eardrum.

Michal gasped repeatedly, unable to come down from the intense orgasm. Nick's chest rubbed against her sensitive breasts, sending her over the edge again and again with each breath. She gave a little shove, and he understood and lifted from her just enough.

His kiss was tender and soothing as he brought them both down to earth, and his smug smile floated above her until Michal's vision finally cleared and she could focus on his amazing face.

"Your breasts really are sensitive?"

She nodded and swallowed hard around an emotion she didn't want to express. Glad for his teasing comment, she clung to that. "Yes. Extremely."

"Hmmm, let's see how sensitive."

He started to move. Michal gripped both of his arms. "Don't, Nick. I need a minute. This was…You were…"

His mouth curved into a tender smile, and he brushed a kiss on her forehead. He rolled a lock of her hair between his forefinger and thumbs. "Yeah, it was, and you were, too."

CHAPTER SEVEN

"**W**HERE ARE YOU from?"

His chuckle rumbled through her before he shifted off her and onto his side. Michal shifted to her side, too, so she could meet his gaze and so she wasn't so exposed. His frown told her he didn't like it.

"Why? Because the sex was out of this world?"

He was trying to tease, but Michal didn't laugh and pushed a hunk of hair off her face and over her shoulder. "The sex was out of this world, but I'm asking because I just let you into my home and body without blinking, and I barely know you. It's a bit backward, but I'd like to know something about you."

"Fair enough." He hooked his arm around her and pulled her closer. "You want to know where I'm from now, or where I grew up?"

"Both. And no just rank and serial number. I want real information."

He laughed, and Michal enjoyed the deep, rich sound. "Aye, aye, ma'am. I currently live in San Diego, and work with a buddy of Jared's and mine, Tim Hayes. He and his wife have an IT business, and he recruited me, but his wife, Hailey, is the boss."

"But I thought Lucy said the Hayeses lived in New Mexico."

"They do. Nice thing about IT, all I need is a computer. I can work from anywhere. Even here."

She frowned at the slight derision in his voice when he said here. She wasn't stupid. Ten Sleep wasn't a place most people settled down in, but it still stung. Boy, were they night and day. He was high tech, and there was only one occupation in history older than hers.

She smiled when she caught him watching her. "What are you thinking, Michal?"

"Just how different we are."

"True."

"No deflecting. Where were you born and raised?"

"My birth certificate says I was born in Norfolk, Virginia. My parents gave me to the state of Maryland when I was seven, and I spent most of my time in foster homes."

Michal pressed closer and smoothed her palm over his face, resting it on his cheek. "That's horrible. Who would want to give you up?"

He choked out a laugh. "Seems a lot of people. You're talking about doing it after the summer."

"Nick. No...it's not like that..."

He kissed her hard. "Pity over. It's a part of my life that's done. The Marines gave me a family, and now I'm looking for my own like Jared and Tim found."

Michal felt sick. He wanted a family. She should stop this right now and send him on his way to find the woman who could give him what he wanted. What he deserved. But she couldn't let go. Not after this night. Not yet.

"You from here?"

She jolted out of her thoughts. "Wyoming? Yes, I grew up in another bustling metropolis called Dubois."

"Your parents?"

"Are still there. Along with my two brothers and their families." She tipped her head back and held his gaze. "I left when I got married. He was from Kaycee." She laughed when he didn't even blink. "I should have known someone told you. How much do you know?"

"Just that he's an *ex*-husband."

"Very ex. He was one of my instructors when I was getting my degree in Farrier Science." She winked. "Obviously, he mentored me in more than horseshoeing. I was twenty and he was thirty-six when we married. It went downhill pretty fast, but I hung on until he let go."

"Why stay with him if things went downhill?"

"I blamed myself for why things were the way they were. He blamed me, too, which made it easier for me to take the blame. My parents begged me to leave him, but I'd said for better or worse. I sure was relieved when he took off with another woman."

"Sounds like an A-1 asshole."

Michal shifted to her back not caring Nick could see her not-so-perky breasts and imperfect body. She wanted to defend Trevor by telling Nick he only wanted the same thing Nick did, but she couldn't defend him and knew Nick would never treat his wife the way Trevor had treated her no matter what issues they faced.

"Well, like you said, it's a time of my life that's done. It's been done for ten years. So, you're involving yourself with an old divorcee."

"What'd we agree to about that age shit?"

She ran two fingers over his forehead smoothing the wrinkles of his frown. "I was kidding…kind of."

He took her hand and kissed her wrist. "I'm not kidding…at all."

"Thank you for coming over tonight."

She laughed when he pulled her on top of him.

"Best damn decision of my life next to the Corps."

Michal didn't take the compliment he'd given her lightly. She snuggled into him, content beyond her dreams to be pressed against his hard muscles. She pressed her lips to his and ran her tongue over his lips. Her hair fell forward, and she sighed against his lips, prepared to flip it out of the way, but he dug his fingers through her hair and took over the kiss.

NICK GATHERED HER hair with one hand and gave a small tug, exposing her neck. He trailed kisses down her neck while smoothing his other hand down her back and squeezing her butt cheek.

"Shit you are so hot, Michal. Your turn to be on top."

Her smile wavered. "I'm a little out of practice."

"What do you Wyomingites say? It's time to get back on the horse."

Michal's laugh flowed through Nick like the peace he'd been searching a lifetime for. She moved down his body, kissing his neck, down to his chest and his belly. Nick was praising God she was going to pleasure him with her hot mouth, but she moved back up. His disappointment didn't last long when she took his cock deep inside her sex and started riding him.

Nick watched her, entranced by the woman over him. Her long, caramel-colored hair flowed down her back and over her shoulders. She tried to hide imperfections only she could see, but Michal had the finest body he'd ever seen. He arched up, and her forehead wrinkled as her eyes glazed over in lust. She moaned and fell forward, bracing her hands on his chest as she continued to alternate between riding his cock and grinding. Nick grabbed her hair and pulled her mouth to his, feasting on her sweet lips and tasting her deep with his tongue.

For a woman out of practice, she was giving his body more pleasure than he'd ever known. With his other hand, he brushed the side of her breast, and Michal came apart in his arms, bucking wildly, her already tight sex clamped hard around him. Nick drove his cock hard and deep and ravaged her mouth as he released his cum into her channel.

Nick cupped her face and continued to kiss her as they rode out their orgasms. When he broke the kiss, she remained over him, and they shared each other's breath.

"I think I underestimated you."

He kissed her again. "How?"

"You're getting to me, Nick. I didn't want that."

"I did."

The faint sound of a country song floated from the living room. Michal's head popped up.

"Shit. It's my business ring."

She was gone before he could ask anything. He followed behind her.

"I'll be there as soon as I can."

She hit *end* and met Nick's gaze. "I'm so sorry, but I have to go. There's an emergency."

He cut his gaze from the phone back to her. "You're on call?"

"Yes. Sorry."

She shut the door to the head. When she came out and started dressing, Nick stepped in line. "I'll go with."

"Really?"

"Absolutely."

Michal pulled her hair into a ponytail, and Nick almost ordered it down until he gave himself a mental shake; she'd want it out of her way. He was getting to her? Fuck that, she had burned past getting to him into almost an obsession.

"I'll go get my chaps and tools and meet you at the truck."

He tugged on his second boot. "I can help with the tools."

"Okay."

They headed out and loaded her gear without talking. He could see where her muscles came from, hauling all her tools around.

He got in the passenger side, and she gave him a small smile. "You mind me driving?"

"Not as long as you keep it on the road."

Her smile grew, and she put the truck in gear and headed out. They didn't talk as Michal drove through town and turned off onto a dirt road. It wasn't uncomfortable, and Nick wondered if she was trying to process this thing between them like he was.

She turned into a ranch yard, and they met an older man outside the stables.

"Came out and found her limping around."

Michal nodded and Nick grabbed her tools before she could and followed her inside the stables. He set the tools next to the stall she entered.

"Thanks." She gave him a quick smile.

"Consider me your assistant. Just tell me what you need."

MICHAL TURNED HER full attention to the mare in front of her. The task was made more difficult with Nick so close and his handprints still on her body. She wouldn't think of his touch on her heart. Smoothing her hand down the mare's neck, she spoke in soft tones. She continued her caress but brought it down to the horse's haunch and down her leg.

She didn't feel anything wrong with her leg, so she straddled it, holding the hoof between her knees. "Dammit."

Michal frowned. "Who shod Mable last, Marv? This isn't my work."

"Sorry, Mike, I asked this other guy out. He was a bit cheaper."

"I can see why. Her hoof is severely heel cracked. Whoever's responsible for this mess didn't even put the nails in right. That takes real skill since nails are marked. Hell, Marv, he even left the front shoes hanging over, and Mable's still your best roper. You want her accidently stepping on a front shoe and tossing it?" She didn't let him answer. "Looks like she could have a contracted heel on the other front hoof. I'll get these off first and we'll go through what has to happen next. You'll need to call Dr. Paulson for one, but tell him he won't need to come out until tomorrow. I don't have any anti-inflammatory drugs so tell him to bring those. I do have sedatives, thank god."

"Yes, ma'am. And thanks, Mike."

She nodded and walked the few steps outside to her truck, digging in the glove box for sedatives. Michal stepped back inside. "This will help us both 'cause the gal's not going to like me messing with her sore hooves. Next time, remember, cheap isn't always better. She'll have to be boxed for a time; the doc will tell you how long."

"All right. Anything you need."

"What do you need from me, Michal?"

She startled at Nick's voice. In her anger about poor Mable's condition, she'd actually forgotten he was there. She filled the syringe and tapped the barrel to clear any air bubbles. Marv was a few feet away, calling the veterinarian.

"If you want to hand me the tools, nurse, maybe sponge my brow." She tried to smile.

Nick lifted the eighty-five pound anvil like it was nothing, but she shook her head. "I won't need that tonight. I'll leave her barefoot until tomorrow when I can forge some corrective shoes." She narrowed her gaze as her anger flared again.

Michal kept to the side of the mare and patted her hind haunch. "Okay, honey, this will take you to a happy place while I fix that dipshit's mistakes."

A sharp slap of tail to her face was her answer. Nick frowned, but Michal ignored it and him. If she was only slapped in the face once by the tail and managed to avoid Mable deciding to relieve herself during the process, it would be a stellar operation.

"Doesn't that hurt?" Nick lifted an eyebrow when she felt the lash of the tail across her cheek again after inserting the needle and injecting the sedative.

"Doesn't feel good, City."

She smoothed her hand over Mable's back. "But neither does a needle to the butt, so we're even."

"You need this?" Nick held up the stand she'd made her first day of class. It was a simple pipe welded to a flat piece of iron, but she'd been so proud when it was complete.

"It's my stand, and no, I won't need it. I use it for finishing."

He shrugged and opened her toolbox. "What's first?"

"Rasp. The better looking one."

Michal kept talking to Mable and facing away from Nick. She cradled the hoof between her legs with Mable's leg almost underneath the horse's chin to keep the patient comfortable. When she felt Nick nudge her arm with the rasp, she took the tool and started rasping the nail head down to undo the clinches.

"What are you doing?"

"I've got to get these nail heads down and nice and rectangular so, hopefully, the nail will come out easier. I usually like to have the nail head bent over. Who knows what this asshole was doing."

She pivoted to the other side. "Come closer and look if you want." Michal used the rasp to file down the four nails on the other side. "See, and I only use three nails on each side, but this isn't necessarily wrong, about the only thing that isn't."

She felt Nick's gaze on her hands as she worked, and her heart chipped off another piece and offered itself to him. He genuinely cared what she was doing. She had to keep adjusting Mable's hoof on her lap. It might have been better to use the stand, but she'd always done it this way. Also, even with the sedative, Mable couldn't help pulling away as someone tampered with her sore hooves.

Michal set down the hoof and handed the rasp back to him and even offered a small smile to Marv. Money was tight all over; she couldn't necessarily fault a man for trying to save, but there were some things a person shouldn't pinch pennies on.

She swiped the sweat from her brow. "I'll need the nail pullers, shoe pullers, and nippers."

"It's that bad you'll need the nail pullers? Can't just use the shoe pullers?"

She shook her head and turned to Marv. "Don't want to take the chance with that crack, Marv. It's that bad."

The poor old rancher looked like he wanted to cry. "He shoed a couple others, Mike, you mind?"

"Nope. Would rather take care of it tonight."

"Sorry to interrupt, but I don't have a damn clue, are any of these right?"

She adjusted Mable's leg between her knees at the ankle so she could see the hoof. She pointed to the tool with the smallest head. "Nail pullers, perfect."

"Sorry."

She shrugged and went to work on the nails, rockering them out. "Not a problem. I should have been more specific. If you started hollering out IT terms I'd..." She chuckled. "Well, my head would explode since I barely passed Googling 101."

He laughed, but didn't comment. Again, Nick kept his gaze riveted to her hands and Mable's hoof as she worked the nails out one by one. Mable pulled away, and Michal sighed, shifting with the horse. "Come on baby just a couple more."

She handed Nick the nails. "Shoe pullers, Nick, they're the ones with the more rounded clamp." She hoped that was a fair description. When the steel tool hit her hand she smiled. "Thanks."

"Why do I get the feeling this would be easier without me?"

"It might be." She started rockering off the shoe. "But the gesture is very much appreciated." She lifted her gaze and caught his for a second. "Thank you."

"Glad to help. You can't just yank it off?"

She pulled up on the toe and pushed with her other hand rocking the shoe puller. "I don't. Especially when the hoof is damaged or sore. Also, this way it's leverage not strength needed."

"You seem tough enough."

She laughed and blew her bangs out of her eyes. "I appreciate the compliment, but I have three more shoes on this horse and eight more after this. No use flexing the muscle."

Mable pulled away again, and Michal gave a huffed laugh as she was tugged along. She gripped the hoof. "Come on Mable. Cut me some slack."

Michal finished pulling off the shoe and inspected the hoof more thoroughly. "This crack is heartbreaking, Marv. I'll need to fill it with a polymer, and we'll have to get a poultice on it."

Putting the hoof down, giving them both a rest, Michal dug in her box for the polymer. With a smile at Nick, she grabbed the hoof knife, nippers, and rasp. Laying them on the ground she tucked Mable's hoof back between her knees.

She started cleaning up the hoof and frog with the knife and then gave the knife a small toss and grabbed the nippers, trimming the hoof down.

"You're really quite the woman, Michal Dunn."

She bit her lip and started smoothing and flattening the area with the rasp. "You're good for a woman's soul, Nick."

"Only one woman I care about."

She swiped the sweat off her forehead with the back of her arm again and gave him a quick smile. Not trusting herself to say more, she stuck with business. "Hand me the polymer, please."

He handed her the plastic tube and winked. "Here you go, doctor."

She let her shoulders relax when he went back to the playful mood instead of saying sweet things. A man who lived in California, really all over the world with the Marines, who would have thought he'd saunter into Ten Sleep, Wyoming, and turn her universe upside down?

Nick continued to *help* and study every move as she continued to work on Mable and moved on to the other two horses. "Flash has a contracted heel, Marv. You'll need to soak it once I get it trimmed up to let the tissues expand. We'll see about putting on a corrective shoe, or letting this guy go barefoot for a bit. You using him much?"

"Not much."

"Then we'll let him barefoot it."

Michal finished up with the gelding and stood with one hand on her lower back she groaned and stretched. "I'm getting too old for this."

"Michal."

The warning was clear in Nick's tone. She frowned. "Don't get all wound up. I meant for horseshoeing." She sidled close to him. "Especially after pre-horseshoe activities."

He smoothed the back of his fingers along the curve of her face, and she cringed at how sweaty she was. "You're so beautiful."

"Wow. I…"

The sound of a voice clearing cut off her response, and she wanted to thank Marv for interrupting, because she really had no response.

"Thanks again, Mike. Nick. I'll get to soaking Flash's foot, anything else before you come back tomorrow?"

She patted the old rancher's arm. "Nope, just keep an eye on them all."

With a nod, she turned to get her tools loaded, but Nick already had everything loaded up.

She could get used to having him as an assistant. She took off her chaps, tossed them in the truckbed, and glanced at her watch. "Can I treat you to breakfast at the Crazy Woman?"

"Sounds good. Keys." He held out his hand and Michal gratefully handed him her truck keys.

As they headed toward town, Michal rested her head back and closed her eyes.

"After breakfast you should catch some z's."

"Can't. I have to be out at the Bar 4. They have some new horses needing to be shod. Then I have to meet Dr. Paulson at the Rocking L where we're working together on a case and will also have this new one to discuss."

"Damn, woman."

She tried to laugh but it came out as a yawn. "When are you getting some sleep?"

"When you do."

"You're sweet."

"I am not sweet."

He parked the truck in front of the café. She started to get out when she noticed he was coming around to get her door. He was sweet. Sweet, and caring, and a white-hot lover. Michal almost cried, wishing she could keep him, but a man wanting a family had destroyed one marriage. She didn't want to destroy Nick.

CHAPTER EIGHT

"**O**H, I CAN'T work with that in the room." Nick nodded to the poster sized framed picture of Jared leaning against a pickup truck all decked up cowboy style. He leaned closer to the poster. "Shit."

Lucy laughed and shoved his arm. "I'm very motivated by that picture. It's one of my best."

"I'm not saying anything against the skill. It's the subject I question."

"Well, I love it."

"Yeah, you love him. And from the look in his eyes in the photograph I'd say my brother is gone over his wife."

"Thanks, Nick."

"Nick!" Eli stumbled into the room on chubby toddler legs, his red hair matted on one side and reached for Nick. Nick obliged and picked up the boy he saw as a nephew.

"Hey, little Sergeant. Naptime over?"

Lucy tugged on the little guy's shorts. "Naptime doesn't last near as long as it used to. Especially when he hears your voice. Children from around the state are probably heading toward the Pied Piper Nick."

He shrugged off her bullshit. "Marines don't need sleep. Right, Devil Pup!" Nick assumed his First Shirt tone and almost smiled when it didn't faze Eli. Instead, the boy raised his hand.

"Oo-ah!"

"Oo-Rah! Close enough."

Lucy shook her head. "Between you and Jared, this poor kid doesn't stand a chance."

"Wrong, he stands the greatest chance of all. He'll be a Marine."

"Okay, I give. But speaking of sleep, from what Jared said, you could use a little after last night."

Nick felt heat crawl up his neck. "You're makin' me blush, ma'am."

Lucy slapped his arm. "Not that, jerk. Working all morning with Mike."

"Oh, oh. Roger. Nah, too much going through the cranial matter. I decided to get some work done. But the woman doesn't even have a computer, so…"

"So here you are."

He jostled Eli. "So here I am."

"You gonna be here for supper?"

"You invitin' me?"

"Yes. You are so irritating. Why don't you invite Mike, too?"

"Aye, aye."

"Aye," a little voice echoed.

Lucy took Eli from his arms. "I'm taking my son before you have him doing pushups, and we're going to Dirty Sally's for raspberries and ice cream. If you're good, I'll bring some for you. Invite Mike to dinner."

Nick stood at attention and saluted. "Yes, ma'am, inviting Michal to dinner, ma'am."

Eli saluted back and Nick smiled when Lucy rolled her eyes. "Be glad I love you guys so much."

"We are, Lucy. Believe me, we don't take it for granted."

She nodded and her hazel eyes softened. "Make yourself at home. I have coffee on. If you need something just bark."

"Bark?"

"Isn't that what Devil Dogs do?"

Nick laughed and waved to Eli who was peeking over Lucy's shoulder as she walked away. He shot a text to Michal who was probably still dead to the world in bed where he'd left her after they got back from her second appointment. He'd made sure she went to sleep extra tired.

MICHAL TUGGED HER phone out of her back pocket when she heard the ding telling her she got a text.

Nick: *Lucy's and Jared's for supper.*

6:30

Michal glared at the text wishing it was the man.

Michal: *Are you inviting me?*

Or ordering me?

Nick: *Both.*

WTF are you doing up?

Why was she smiling? He'd just ordered her to supper and swore at her, albeit in abbreviated form. She pivoted on her heel so Dr. Paulson and Marv couldn't see her grinning like a lovestruck fool.

Michal: *Needed to get Mable her new shoes.*

You know how we women like our shoes.

An angry face emoticon showed on her screen and her smile grew.

Nick: *6:30?*

Michal: *I'll be there. Gotta go.*

Nick: *Better.*

Her fingers itched to type the closing that would change everything, and she resisted. One night…and an afternoon of good sex. She shook her head. The best sex wasn't a reason to give her heart away. But him carrying her gear and helping her at every stop, opening doors for her, making her laugh over breakfast when she was so tired she didn't think she could, and stealing kisses throughout the day might be. And it didn't feel like just sex that afternoon when he'd stripped her like she was something precious. It felt like making love as he rocked in and out of her body, whispering how beautiful she was, how amazing she made him feel.

"Hey, Mike, you need any help?"

She shook her head. "Nope. Just about finished."

Michal: *I will be.*

She hit *send* and put the hoof she'd been shoeing back between her knees, trying to put Nick from her mind. It didn't work, and she thought again about telling Nick she was falling for him. She picked up the clinch block and secured it under the rounded nail, giving it a quick pound with the hammer and doing the same with the other nails. She finished each hoof by using the rasp to make sure the hoof and shoe were the right length followed by the clinchers bending the nails better.

Nope, she wouldn't say it. If she did, Nick would never leave. He was that kind of man. And out there was a woman who could give him a houseful of children and the family he'd missed growing up, and she'd fit in with his city lifestyle. Hell, she'd have a computer.

"All right, this guy's ready to go dancing."

Marv's chuckle was low and a bit uneasy. "Thanks for shoeing the other horses, Mike, I know you just stopped by to see to Mable."

"Not a problem. She's already looking better." She tilted her head back to meet Dr. Paulson's gaze. "Good thing you got those anti-inflammatory meds out here first thing."

"Bullshit, Mike. It's all on your quick timing and thinking. You should go ahead and finish up vet school. You already do it all. I just follow behind with meds and foaling. Hell, you even did that a couple times."

She shrugged. "I'm happy doing what I do. I'm not real content in a classroom."

"Well, I'm glad you're here. You have plans for supper? I don't know what Lindy has cooking, but…"

"I've been invited to Jared and Lucy Worrell's. Thanks though."

"Sure thing. Tell Jared those chocolates I gave Lindy last week got me out of the doghouse and then some for missing our anniversary."

Michal laughed. "I will. If you've got things here, Dan, I better get home, take care of Bailey, and get cleaned up."

"Yep. Mable and I will be just fine."

"Thanks, and enjoy your evening with the Worrells and their friend

Nick."

Michal stopped short. "Nick?"

"Mike, did you actually think you could go into the Crazy Woman for a very early breakfast then travel throughout the countryside with a man and it not get around?"

"I hoped."

"Well, consider that hope dashed. Just do what we've all done."

"What's that?"

"Not give a damn and do whatever the hell you please."

"Think I'll do just that."

"Good evening."

"You, too. If you need…"

"Go, Mike."

She chuckled and headed for her truck. After a day of Nick lugging her gear she had to turn back. With a sheepish smile she grabbed her gear and finally headed down the road.

CHAPTER NINE

ICHAL STEPPED OUT of the truck a bit more carefully than she normally would. She pretended she didn't know what possessed her to change into a summer dress and leave her hair down, but she knew what or who possessed her.

"Hey, Mike."

She gave a small wave. "Hey, Jared. How's everything with you?"

He stopped short of walking up the steps to his house and waited for her. "Nothing I can think of to complain about. You?"

"Things seem to be under control for the moment."

His dark eyebrow hitched. "Really?"

"Well, until I step through your front door."

"Gotta give you props for being honest."

"Dan Paulson thanks you for your magic chocolates. It seems they redeemed him in Lindy's eyes."

His smile said he knew exactly what she was doing, and she hadn't made the transition smoothly. "Always happy to help a man smooth it over with his wife."

He turned and Michal put her hand on his arm. "You okay with this?"

"Mike, it's not me who has to be okay with it."

"I know, but I feel like I have to explain. I don't want you to think I'm one of those women who sleeps with the uniform. I care, I really do, it's just complicated."

"First, I'd never think that about you. Second, that it's complicated for you gives me hope."

"Don't. Don't hope."

"What the hell is the problem, Mike?"

"I'll tell him why, Jared, I swear I will, but not yet."

"Jared." Lucy stepped outside. "Oh hi, Mike, glad you came." Lucy cut a glance from her husband to Michal.

"What's going on?"

Michal's gaze snapped to Nick as he pushed the screen door open. Eli sat snug in the crook of his arms and Michal felt the blood rush from her head as she swayed. It was all the images of him holding Eli, cheering the boy on at the rodeo, the high-five, and now at home walking around carrying a toddler. The scene became fuzzy and her ears rang.

"Mike!" Jared's voice boomed and she felt a large hand circle her arm.

Jared was replaced by Nick holding both of her arms. "Michal, sweetheart." He gave her a little shake and she started swimming up from the fog.

"Sorry, just tired I guess."

"Yeah, well, if I were you, I'd run on fuckin' empty all day."

"It's my job." She shrugged his hands from her arms. "I'm forty-two years old; I don't need you telling me what to do."

"No fuckin' way."

Michal turned her attention to Jared. "What?"

"You're forty-two? Damn, you don't look any older than Lucy."

"Don't be ridiculous."

Nick's mouth was on hers, and he was kissing her like he hadn't seen her in years. His hands ran over her body. She vaguely heard Jared and Lucy go back inside, but she didn't care if they were making a scene. She wrapped her arms around his neck and held on tight.

"You look so fuckin' hot, Michal."

She nuzzled his neck. "Thank you."

"You know you broke the age rule."

"No I didn't. I just meant I was old enough to make my own decisions."

"Yeah, but you brushed off Jared."

"Because it's ridiculous…" His mouth crashed down on hers again, and he kissed her until they had a hard time catching their breath when it ended.

"I'll do better."

"Good." He squeezed her close. "You leave your hair down for me?"

"Yes."

"Thank you, Lucky Charms. You feelin' better?"

She stayed on the balls of her feet, her arms around his neck and tried not to think of the perfect image of him holding a little one. "Yes. Eli likes you." She almost bit her tongue.

"Yeah, he's my little buddy. But I'm ground round when Jared's around."

He stepped from her and took her hand. "Come on let's get inside and get you some chow."

NICK KEPT AN eye on Michal throughout the evening, and caught her gaze landing on Eli more than once. During dessert she caught him staring and smiled over her coffee mug.

"Did you get your work done?"

"Almost."

"So you'll be staying here?"

"For a bit."

She turned her attention to Lucy. "Are you staying close to home this summer?"

"Between Wyoming and Montana. We were heading to Glacier this weekend and thought Nick might want to come along."

"I think Mule has his own wonder right here, Flash." Jared scooped up a sleeping Eli and started down the hall.

Lucy looked between them. "Hmmm, I think you might be right."

Nick gave a fake laugh. "You guys fail subtlety 101, but you're right. I'd rather stay here."

"Glacier Park is beautiful though, Nick."

"Would you go?"

"I can't this weekend. Sorry."

"Then I'll stay here." He stopped the beer bottle he was raising to his mouth and looked to Lucy. "If that's okay? I don't want to seem ungrateful."

"Not at all. It's your trip."

"How did you get the nickname, Mule?"

"Cause he's a stubborn ass." Jared returned to the table.

Michal laughed. "Well, I knew that."

"Yeah, like either of you should be talking." Jared clinked his beer bottle to Michal's coffee cup in a salute.

Lucy stood and started cleaning off the table, and the rest fell in line picking up their plates and clearing.

"How long have you known each other?" Nick looked between all three.

"I've known Lucy for about..."—Michal looked to the ceiling as if the answer was there—"...about five years?" Lucy nodded. "When her family bought the ranch from Jared's mother. I've only known Jared personally for the three years he's been back. But I knew Claudia from going to the ranch and caring for her horses."

He pointed between Michal and Jared. "She try to set you guys up?"

The three laughed. "No way, she wanted Lucy for Jared. She wanted only the best for him."

Nick scowled and noticed Jared and Lucy frowned, as well.

"I think it was more she knew Lucy and I were right for each other."

Michal nodded. "Of course. Can I help with the dishes?"

"No, I'll just toss 'em in the dishwasher."

"I hate to eat and run, but it has been a long day. Would you mind..." She pointed toward the door.

Jared leaned a hip against the counter. "Not at all. From what I heard, you've had a run of fixing another farrier's mistakes."

"It's been interesting. I'm thinking of visiting this guy and having a chat."

"Not alone you're not."

"Listen, City..."—she shoved a finger in his chest—"I'm getting tired of you telling me what I can and cannot do. I've survived just fine without anyone backing me up."

Nick ignored they had an audience and stepped forward towering over her. "Now you've got someone on your six. You won't visit this asshole alone."

He held onto his smile as Michal straightened her spine in a feeble attempt to meet his height. "Nothing in our deal said you could boss me around."

"I just said it."

"You are so damn stubborn."

"That's why we call him Mule."

Michal's gaze shot to Jared at the same time Nick's did. Nick leaned back in a belly laugh.

"Thanks for supper. Goodnight."

Michal plowed through them all, and Nick let her go. Something a lot deeper than him being an obstinate ass fed her outburst, and it had been riding her hard all day.

"You need to go after her, Nick."

"Not yet, Lucy. She's fighting something, and it's a battle I can't help her with because she won't open up."

"She said she'd tell you everything." Jared's words sent a cold dread through Nick.

"Why'd she tell you?"

"She didn't tell me shit, except she promised she'd tell you everything. Just not yet."

"Great, because being patient is something I excel at."

"Not that it's my business man, but what's the endgame? Mike calls you City and she's right; you've never shown a desire to live small time. You think Mike wants to head to San Diego?"

"Right now, according to Michal, the endgame is we're lovers through the summer, and I head home, she stays here."

"I didn't ask for her endgame, brother."

"Growing fond of a little farmhouse in Wyoming and more fond of the farrier who owns it."

"Are you serious, Nick?"

He laughed at Lucy's wide-eyed, shocked expression. "Can't think of a time I've been more serious."

"That says it all in my book. We're here if you need anything."

"Time is all I need. Enough time to break through the walls."

"If that's the case, you better get on out to that little farmhouse and see if you've still got a room. This hotel's closed."

"No, it's not, Jared."

Nick shook his head. "I really do have to finish a couple of things for Hailey. I'll head out after I'm finished. My first change at the farmhouse will be internet service and wifi."

CHAPTER TEN

MICHAL GROANED WHEN she heard the diesel truck coming down the drive. She'd made such an ass out of herself from the minute she arrived to tucking tail and running. Wrapping her arms around her legs, she rested her chin on her knees and stared at the creek. A light breeze washed over her and cut through the heat of the night. She'd wanted someone to sit by the creek with her on a summer night. Here he came.

Nick folded and plopped next to her, his long legs stretched out, and Michal noticed he'd taken off his socks and boots. He was sexy even with bare feet. "Hey, Lucky Charms. You still mad?"

"No, just embarrassed. I'm sorry."

He nudged her arm with his. "Nothing to be sorry about."

He tugged the hairband on her ponytail and freed her hair. "That's better."

She smiled. "Maybe for you. You're not mad I lost my shit in front of your friends?"

"No." He turned and stared at the creek. He rested back on his hands. "Beautiful night."

She frowned. "Yes, I love summer nights when it stays light longer."

"What are you frowning at?"

"You just seem awfully relaxed and okay after I stormed out."

"Michal, I'm not pissed. Jared and Lucy aren't pissed. You think you're the first one of us to lose our shit? It happens. I'm not going to fight with you."

She turned her attention back to the creek, and they both sat there, watching it for a time. The splash of water running over rock relaxed her muscles, and she closed her eyes and inhaled the fresh air, cleansing her mind. The breeze washed over her and ruffled the skirt of her dress, tickling her skin and turning her thoughts to other soft touches. She opened her eyes and angled her face to watch Nick. His gaze was locked on the creek and the rush of the water as if he wanted to follow it to its source.

"What do you do for Hailey and Tim? What's your job?"

He didn't turn his gaze. "I started physically testing their security systems. Meaning I tried to break into buildings. I still do that some for their military contracts. I choose some of the young Marines at Twenty-Nine Palms who volunteer for this. We try to break into the buildings every way possible. Now, I've moved more into trying and sometimes succeeding in hacking Hailey's security programs for company computers, some high ranking individual computers."

"You're a hacker?"

His mouth lifted in a slow smile, and he winked. "Sometimes I hack. Sometimes the programs Hailey's created are like iron walls."

"I'm sorry; I don't really even know what to ask."

"Michal, it'd bore you to tears for me to get into all the coding, decoding, zeros and ones, binary versus quantum. It's not really as tangible as what you do to try and explain. Thanks for giving a shit."

"I do."

He brushed the back of his hand over her arm. "And the Marines?"

"What about them?"

"What do you do there?"

He lifted his head, pointing to her with his chin. "Why don't you unbutton the top of that pretty dress, lie back, and let me have some fun instead of the chit-chat?"

"Nick, we're outside."

"Outstanding. Now that we've narrowed down our location, get the dress off, Lucky Charms."

Her gaze met his, and no amount of breeze was going to cool her down. She knew no one was around for miles, but she still scanned the area before she started unbuttoning her dress. When she got the top unbuttoned, she stripped the top of her dress down and lay back as ordered.

"No bra?"

"It's the kind of dress I don't need one."

He traced one of her breasts with a finger. "I like that kind of dress."

"Why don't you kiss me?"

He smiled and lowered his head. "Don't mind if I do." But he didn't capture her lips; instead, he brushed a kiss over her breast taking her nipple in his mouth and sucking.

"Nick, I told you...oh god." She cupped his head and held him to her. Her hips lifted as he continued to suck, and with his other hand, he molded her other breast. Sweat broke out on her upper lip, and Michal screamed as her orgasm hit.

Nick's face was over hers when she opened her eyes. "You can come like that?"

"Yes! I told you..."

"No, you didn't tell me that. That was amazing, Michal. God, you are outstanding." He reached under her dress and pushed her panties aside. Michal bit her lip and moaned as he slid two fingers inside her and pressed her clit with his thumb. "I want to see it again."

Her breasts were beyond sensitive, and his fingers found her g-spot. Michal jackknifed up at the intensity of her orgasm. Her legs slammed together, and she pushed against his head. With one come-hither move with the two fingers against her g-spot, Michal came apart again.

"Stop, Nick, stop." She flopped back. He took his fingers from her. Nick was over her again, only this time, he was between her legs and the head of his cock was at her opening.

"You okay, Michal?"

"Yes."

He nodded and thrust deep. There was nothing nice about this time. She was as desperate as he was, and she met his thrusts as she dug her fingernails into his back. It was hard and wild, and Nick sat back and tugged her forward so her thighs rested on his. In this position, he hammered into her body.

"Play with your breasts."

Michal shook her head.

"Do it."

She did, and his groan was her reward before her climax slammed into her, and she arched back at the same time Nick plunged deep; she felt almost torn in two.

Michal fought for breath until his mouth covered hers in a hard, demanding kiss. His tongue tangled with hers, and he sucked her tongue back into his mouth. His kiss seemed to last forever until he was moving inside her again. He kept the kiss and his thrusts hard until she stroked the back of his neck, silently begging for him to ease up.

He complied, and his kiss became tender as he pulled his cock from her and sank deep again and again. Michal's inner muscles tightened around him, and they both came on a low groan shared between them.

He broke the kiss and trailed kisses over her face. "Did I hurt you?"

"A little. Nick, you need to…" He eased his cock from her, and she sighed.

"Sorry, Lucky Charms. I'd never hurt you."

She smiled. "I know. My body's not used to this. Used to you."

"Good thing you're on something."

Her emotions were too raw after his intensity, and Michal couldn't stop the tears.

"Michal, what is it? Come on, sweetheart, let me in."

"You want a family."

"Yes."

"I can't give that to you."

"What?"

"If I tell you, will you agree it doesn't change our standing agreement? You won't try to keep me?"

"Hell no."

"Nick, please."

"Michal, I've never planned to let you go. So nothing you tell me or not will change that. I've always planned on keeping you."

She scrubbed her hands down her face. "This is so messed up,

Nick, you promised you wouldn't see this as a forever thing."

"No, I said 'for now' a day ago and that *now* is long gone. So tell me. Is this more about your age?"

"Yes, Nick, you have to think about it. You have to. I know I'm not ancient, but it will make it more difficult to have children. If we could even if I was twenty."

"But that's not it?"

"No. You see, Trevor wanted a family, too, just like you do. And when we married, I couldn't give him one. I don't know if I can for you."

His scowl was so ferocious Michal almost pushed from under him, but he wouldn't hurt her. "You're comparing me to your ex-asshole? I can deal with it if you can't get pregnant."

She cupped his face and ran her thumbs over his cheeks. "I'm not comparing you to Trevor except your desire to have a family. Nick, I can get pregnant, I just can't keep my babies alive. After four miscarriages, I couldn't take it anymore. My body hurt; my mind hurt, and my heart was shattered. So I had the doctor implant a IUD. When Trevor found out, he was furious. He was right; a woman's body shouldn't reject her baby. So, he found a woman whose body wouldn't."

"That fuckin' bastard should have his dick cut off for ever saying that shit to you, Michal. You didn't reject your babies. He rolled from her and stood adjusting his clothes. "If I ever see the fucker, I'll beat the shit out of him."

Michal adjusted her clothes, suddenly wanting a barrier between them because he was breaking every other barricade she had. "Whether he was right or wrong, the fact remains I couldn't carry a baby to term. I couldn't even get to the fifth month."

"And you think I'd leave you? If you can't have my baby, I'd fuckin' leave?"

Michal flinched at the accusation in his voice. "No, I know you'd stay. You'd stay forever and give up all your dreams to keep your word."

He cuffed her arms and lifted her to stand in front of him. "You listen to me, Michal Dunn; you don't know shit about my dreams. I want a family. I never said how big that family had to be. If it's you and me, that's outstanding. You and me, we could be a family."

"I can't believe you."

"You're calling me a liar?"

"No. I've seen you with Eli. I know you want children."

"There are other ways to get children, Michal, if that's something we decide. You need to think about what you want. I know what I want and what my dream is."

He let her go and took a few steps and Michal panicked. She took his arm. "Don't go."

"I have no intention of going anywhere but to the house and a nice soft bed."

She hugged one of his arms and fell into step beside him. They took the steps up to the porch. Michal took a deep breath, deciding to take a chance. "Nick."

"Hmmm?"

"I'm falling in love with you."

"What?"

"I'm falling for you. It started when you said hello, but then you made me laugh; you made me feel beautiful and desirable, but mostly, I'm falling because you made me laugh when I didn't want to. I wasn't going to say anything…"

"I'm falling, too, Michal. I'm falling hard."

"And that doesn't scare you?"

"Scarier than a door-to-door in Ramadi. But I'm willing to risk it." He tucked a strand of hair behind her ear and traced her cheek with his fingers. "What are you willing to risk, Michal?"

"We're so different. I live here; you live in San Diego."

"People can move. And I wouldn't want a woman who was like me. We'd be in a terminal standoff."

Michal leaned back against the side of the house and away from his tempting touch. "Would you be willing to compromise?"

He rested a shoulder on the side of the house, bringing him close again. "Not usually, but for you, yes."

"We'll stop considering this a summer fling." He cleared his throat, and Michal smiled. "*I'll* stop considering this a summer fling and see where it might go. *I'll* try to be open-minded about the possibilities." She frowned. "So, really I'm doing all the compromising."

"Sounds like it."

"But you won't push."

"Nope."

"And you'll seriously think about what I told you and everything. If you decide you want something different you won't feel—" His mouth covered hers, but this time, she didn't fall into the kiss. She pushed him back. His frown was harsh and his eyes a dark indigo in anger.

"Nick, shutting me up won't change things. Let me finish. You won't feel obligated to stay with me."

"You just don't get it, Michal; obligation is not what binds me to you." He pushed off the house and went inside. Michal followed, unable to respond.

Nick flopped on her couch and turned on her TV. She studied the domestic scene.

"Do you want anything?"

"Yes, but you're sore."

Michal felt her face heat. Only Nick could make her blush. "Yes, I am. So, do you want some coffee or anything?"

"No."

"Okay, I'm going to wash off. If you change your mind, help yourself."

She started toward the bathroom but turned and bent, brushing her lips over his. "I know obligation doesn't bind you to me, Nick. And it's my heart binding me to you, too."

"I'll let it all process and won't dismiss your concerns again."

She smiled. "You're going to stubbornly wait me out, aren't you?"

"Even if it takes a hundred years."

"A city mule, that's what I've got on my hands, a citified mule."

"At your service, ma'am."

CHAPTER ELEVEN

MICHAL SET THE horse's hoof off the stand and swiped her forearm across her forehead, removing the sweat. She stretched her back after leaning over for hours shoeing and trimming hooves at a local ranch the Lazy CU.

"At least you didn't fall victim to the man posing as a farrier."

Percy Olsen hooked a foot over the lower board of the stall door. "Heard about every horse he shod has come up lame. I think me and Gerry over at the Circle Dub are about the only ones who didn't try to save a dime."

"Seems so. Dr. Paulson and I have been hoppin', fixin' his mistakes. I can see why others gave it a try though. The prices he gave were well below mine."

"Well, I wouldn't use another farrier, and that's for damn sure."

"Thanks, Percy."

"Rumor is the chocolate man is being a Marine this weekend?"

"Yep."

"Guess his friend is with him?"

Michal turned to shape a shoe on her anvil. "Yep. He's in the same company." She hoped she used the right term. The two weeks they'd spent together, Michal never asked Nick again about his service. He'd mentioned names like Ramadi, Fallujah, and others, and she listened, but she never questioned him. Not because she feared his service, she was actually very proud. She'd just been so wrapped up in them...in him, she hadn't wanted to let anything from the outside in. Only when he and Jared left the day before did she regret not pushing him to share more about what he'd done and what he was doing now.

"You and Lucy must be proud."

Michal smiled at the old rancher and brought the hammer down on the horseshoe. The din of metal-on-metal calmed her nerves and drowned out Percy's commentary.

She thought she'd have a few days without thinking of how much she was falling in love with Nick. Falling nothing, she'd fallen and was drowning in it. But every ranch she visited they all brought up Nick, wanting to be first with the news of when they'd be married, she was sure. Even the café and brewery offered no refuge. She didn't know how much of a town project she was until Nick showed up.

She bent over the hoof of the gelding and fixed the shoe in place. "Hi, Mike."

She lifted her head and yanked the nails out of her mouth setting the hoof down. "Hi, Lucy. What brings you out here?"

"I was taking a few photographs over at the Circle W, and Dad said you were over here. I thought you might like some books on the Marines in Iraq and Afghanistan."

Michal slipped the nails back in her mouth before securing the gelding's hoof between her legs and, one by one, pounding the six nails through the shoe and into the hoof. She used the other end of the hammer to do a quick rounding of the nail on the other end. A fly was determined to torture both horse and woman, and she had to keep nudging the geldings haunch with her shoulder to keep him steady.

She stood when the shoe was secure. "Thank you, Lucy. That's nice of you."

"When Jared and I started out, he recommended them. They're from the History Division so they're not the *I won the war by myself* books, as Jared calls them."

Michal grabbed her clinch block. "I'm almost done here, and this is my last place. Would you mind coming over and talking. I'm afraid I've made a real mess of knowing anything about Nick the Marine."

Lucy's smile stretched. "I'd love to. Eli is with Mom and Dad for couple hours. Talking to Hailey—that's Tim's wife—has been wonderful, but it will be so nice to have another 2/23 wife right here."

Michal shook her head. "I'm not that, Lucy. Don't rush this. I just want to talk."

The younger woman's smile fell. "Sorry. We'll just hang out. But, I thought when we got back from Glacier, Nick said you guys were moving forward?"

"Slowly, we're moving ahead slowly."

"Okay."

Lucy waited while Michal finished up and helped her carry out her tools. Michal refused to look at the redhead who nodded in agreement all while hope sparked in her gaze.

"Is this about what you said the other night about Claudia not wanting you for Jared?"

Michal stopped short. "Absolutely not. I was just stating fact. Claudia knew about me and my past from us talking. Also, I'm a bit older than her son...than all of you. And let's just hit the nail on the head— you two belong together, and she knew it from the start."

"But I don't think your age, or your past would matter to her."

"It doesn't matter, Lucy. I'm sorry I was such an idiot the other night. I'm going to plead lack of sleep and awakened hormones. Nick and I...I'm going slow because I need to."

"All right. I'll keep my nose out of it."

"I don't mean to be an ass, and I know you care for Nick. Still want to come over for a chat?"

"Absolutely, because whether you're a 2/23 wife or not, I'd love to have a good friend here. And I care about you, too, Mike."

NICK SHIFTED IN his chair in the classroom at the University of Utah as a major lectured on the history of the 2nd Battalion 23rd Regiment from World War II to the War on Terror. He'd worked his bolt and got transferred from a reserve unit in California to the rifle company of the infantry battalion a year ago. It worked out with working for Tim since he had to go to New Mexico a few times a year. He usually planned those trips around drills in Utah.

It was good working with Jared and Tim again, and Nick was proud of the Marines he commanded. He was usually fired up for weekend drills, but he was restless this weekend. He wanted to get back to Michal. They'd made some major headway over the last few days; he didn't want to lose the momentum.

If only they'd been doing something physical this weekend, he could forget everything while barking orders and running ten miles. Esprit de Corps wasn't getting it done.

As the lecturer wrapped up, Nick forced himself to stay seated until the end and rise with some dignity. He stood ramrod straight with arms locked at his side. "Oo-Rah!" He shouted with more gusto when they were dismissed.

"You'd think he had a woman waiting for him."

"Fuck you, Hayes."

"Mike doesn't need iron to shackle this one."

"And a pleasant fuck you to you, too, Worrell. I don't see you walkin' slow with Lucy at home."

"Direct hit."

Jared joined Nick in flipping Tim off. "And if I hear one more story about how beautiful Hailey is eight months along, I'll puke."

"Okay, okay. I give. Just gotta give the new guy taken down by a woman shit."

Nick held back his smile as each of their strides seemed to get longer as all thoughts turned to the women waiting for them. They managed to toss salutes to the officers above them and line of ranks below as they pushed ever forward.

"You staying the whole summer in Wyoming?"

"That's my plan, but I'll still come down to your place in early August."

Tim shook his head. "No need, unless you want to. Sounds like you've got the project of a lifetime going on up in Ten Sleep. Hailey thinks the Skype meetings will work."

"It okay if I keep my truck there?"

"Affirmative. We'll sell it if it gets in the way."

"Hardy har har. You're a riot."

Tim looked around him to Jared. "You okay with Mule on your turf that long?"

Jared snorted. "The shithead's threatening forever. But he's Mike's problem."

"You're both dicks. You give each other this much crap?"

"Affirmative. All the damn time."

CHAPTER TWELVE

N ICK'S HEART KICK-STARTED and he couldn't keep the smile from stretching his face when Michal walked through her front door as he pulled into the farmyard. He'd hustled home, forcing Jared to pick up fast food on the way out of town instead of stopping for chow. It wasn't much of a struggle since Jared had wanted to get home to his wife and son. Michal had waited up for him...waited up and came out to meet him. He tried to suppress the rising hope, but he couldn't deny the dream coming true the closer she got.

He stepped out of the truck and pulled Michal into his arms. Not even letting her speak, he captured her lips in a kiss and pressed her against the truck. She was wearing a skirt again, and that really pleased him. He broke the kiss and started reaching under her skirt.

"Nick!" She pushed against him. "Oh god," she whispered as his fingers slid inside her. "Nick stop."

"What I'm gonna do to you, Lucky Charms, will have you blushing for years."

"Nick stop." She pushed at his hand, and Nick frowned taking his hand from her.

"What's up?"

"My parents are here."

Nick pushed away from her like she was fire. "What the hell?' His situational awareness had been tragically compromised by the vision of her meeting him after weekend drills because, until that blinding moment, he hadn't noticed a couple of black F-150s parked a few feet away.

KIRSTEN LYNN

Michal started adjusting her clothing, and Nick reached to help, but she slapped his hand away. "I came out to warn you." She laughed. "I didn't know I was the one who needed a warning."

Nick cut a look toward the house. "Isn't it a bit late for company?"

"No."

"Are they staying here?"

"I missed you, too, City. I missed you a lot."

Nick melted, but there were greater concerns. "When did they come?"

"First, they're staying in town. Two of my brothers are here, too. They called yesterday saying they'd be getting here today and staying the night before going up to Sheridan for the WYO Rodeo."

"Do they know I stay here?"

Her cheeks turned red. "Yes. I told them earlier today."

"Let me grab my ruck, and I'll be right in."

"I'll wait to walk in with you. I'd like us to go in together."

"Roger."

Michal slipped around the other side of the truck and dug through the glove compartment. She tossed a packet at him. "Wet wipe." Her eyes glistened with lust. "For your hand. You have me on you."

Nick tore open the package and used the wipe on his hands. "Thanks. Though I hate wiping you off. That was a prime moment."

"You can do all those things you had planned later."

"I may never get hard again, Lucky Charms."

At the sound of her laughter, he was proved wrong. Tossing his bag over one shoulder, he hooked his other arm over her shoulders and started walking toward the house.

"How big are your brothers?"

She took his hand over her shoulder in hers. "Big. But I'll protect you."

He laughed and kissed the top of her head. As he took a deep breath before taking his arm off her to get the door, he felt the rise and fall of her shoulders in an equally deep breath.

"You nervous?"

"Yes."

He winked. "Me, too."

He opened the door and let her enter in front of him. A woman who looked like an older version of Michal stood from the table in the galley and smiled, extending her hand.

"You must be Nick."

He nodded and took her hand. "Yes, ma'am."

"I'm Esther Dunn." She waved to the older man who'd pushed out of his chair. "And this is Michal's father, John."

"Sir." He shook hands with Michal's father.

"And these are her brothers, Jason and Ben."

Nick shook everyone's hand then turned to Michal. "Dunn's your maiden name."

Her forehead wrinkled like she couldn't understand why he wouldn't know that. "Yes. I didn't want to keep his name."

"Who would? The asshole."

"Ben!" Mrs. Dunn scolded, and Nick saw his mistake in bringing it up.

"Would you like some coffee, Nick?" Michal's gaze begged him to give her something to do.

"Sure. It was a long drive."

"Mike tells us you're a Marine."

"Yes, sir." Nick sank into a folding chair they'd pushed up to the table.

"That's very admirable of you. Can't say I had the guts to join. I admire those who do."

Nick took the coffee mug from Michal. "The Marines have been good to me, aside from the four vacations to Iraq. But at least all expenses were paid."

All gave a nervous chuckle. No one seemed put out about the situation or seemed ready to kick his ass, so he settled in.

"What do you do, if you don't mind me asking?"

"In the Marines, or the rest of the time?"

"Both."

"I work in IT, a bunch of computer junk, testing security systems. In the Marines, my MOS is Infantry Unit Leader, my rate is First

Sergeant with a rifle company. Which means I'm a grunt leading other grunts."

Her father gave a huffed laugh. "I suspect there's more to all of that, but I won't pry any further."

Nick nodded and took a swallow of coffee. "All I can really say about either."

"Would anyone else like something?"

"I'll take some more coffee, Mike."

"Me, too, Mike."

Her brothers lifted their mugs. Nick frowned. "So not to sound like a real ass..." He cleared his throat when he caught Mrs. Dunn's gaze. "...jerk, but who has a beautiful baby girl and gives her a boy's name?"

"Nick?" Michal gasped. Everyone else laughed.

Esther shook her head. "It's actually a biblical name after King David's first wife it's spelled M-I-C-H-A-L. I'll admit we set her up to be called Mike with two older brothers."

"Named after a queen. I can see that."

"Yeah, a queen whose husband finds another woman." Her brother, Jason had to chime in.

Nick felt his frown return. Michal surprised him running her fingers over his forehead smoothing the wrinkles like she'd done before. "Don't look so stern. It's okay."

Mr. Dunn cleared his throat. "Well, it's getting late, and you've just gotten home from a busy weekend, so we'll head to the Carter Inn."

Nick saw the flash of pain in Michal's eyes at the same time his heart raced when her father used the word *home*.

"Thanks for understanding, sir." Nick stood. He wasn't sure what his role in all this was, but for now, he'd pretend he and Michal were as set up domestically as her parents and brothers seemed to think.

"We'd like to meet for breakfast if you can?"

"I'm free. Michal?"

"Yeah, I actually have tomorrow off."

"Good. How about seven-thirty?"

"Okay."

Michal hugged her family and Nick shook their hands again.

"And call us Esther and John, Nick."

"Thank you."

With a final round of goodbyes, her family drove off. Michal turned and led the way back into the house. "Sorry about the ambush."

"They're your family. They have a right to visit."

She smiled at him, but it turned into full-blown laughter. "The look on your face when I told you didn't say they had the right."

"Yeah, well, hearing daddy's here when my fingers are deep in your pussy and my tongue in your mouth is kind of a dick shrinking moment."

Her laughter died. "I'm sure it was a sight."

He stepped toward her all humor gone. "Oh, it was a damn beautiful sight."

She stopped short when her back hit the wall. "I really did miss you, Nick. I missed you too much."

Nick pulled the band from her braid and unraveled her hair. She turned her head and kissed his palm then locked her gaze on his. "Tell me you missed me, City. That you thought of me every minute of every day, like I did you. Not just my body, but me."

He rubbed his cheek against hers. "I missed you like crazy, Lucky Charms, and you were on my mind every second, day and night." He kissed the side of her mouth. "Every part of you, but especially your laugh. But I'll be honest, sweetheart, your body crossed my mind a time or two."

She smoothed her hands under his t-shirt and up his chest. "Well, if we're being honest, your body crossed my mind more than a couple times. The bed was too empty." Nick closed his eyes as her palms mapped his chest and over his abs. Her hands stopped just above the waistline of his jeans and his eyes opened. Her green eyes flashed with passion and need and what he wanted to see most. Love.

"I'll admit City, I slept on the couch because I couldn't sleep in bed without you wrapped around me."

Nick captured her lips and kissed her like she was life, because for him…she was. Michal responded in kind like always. For all her talk about letting go and this being temporary, she held him close whenever she could. He gripped her hips and lifted, spreading her wide.

"Get my fly!" he ordered.

Michal obeyed, opening his fly and releasing his hard dick.

"Take me in."

She nodded, pushed her panties aside, and took his cock inside her hot sex.

Her head fell back, and she arched against him. Nick dug his fingers into her thighs and moaned at the feel of her surrounding him. He'd been turned on for hundreds of miles, and all of it returned in his first thrust. Taking her lips in a hard kiss, he pounded into her. Lord, she was so tight and stretched around him in the sweetest way he'd ever seen. She was spread so wide he could feel every inch of her as her pussy muscles worked him and tried to hold him deep inside.

Michal's arms were wrapped around his neck, and she held him tight even as her hips bucked.

"Mmmmm." She tore her mouth from his, and her head arched back again. Her moans and grunts kept him hard, and he pushed harder with every thud against the wall.

"You okay?" he panted.

"Mmmm hmmm." Her lips were pressed together tight, and she nodded. "Nick, I need…"

He dropped his head and sucked her breast through the cotton of her dress. Her back bowed, and when he lifted his gaze, her mouth was open. Nick pushed through the pain of having her sex clamped down around him and continued to pump until he slammed deep and emptied his essence into her. Her back bowed again, and she pushed against him as he felt her sex contract around his cock once more. Damn, she was so good.

Her head fell forward as they started to come down. "You know my body too well."

"See, I was just thinking I don't know it enough."

She kissed the side of his neck. "You said you had plans for me. I'd love for you to show me those plans."

Nick kept holding her and started walking. Her legs snapped around his waist. "You have tomorrow off?"

"Yes."

"Then I'll give you a preview tonight and tomorrow after we choke down eggs with your parents, we're going to come home, strip down, and you're mine in every way, all day."

"I'm all for that plan. Except I will need to see to Bailey."

"Aye, aye."

He laid her on the bed and followed on top of her. Michal traced his face with her fingertips. "Your face can be so hard, and then so kind, but it's always so strong."

His gaze caught a stack of books on the bedside table, and he recognized the names of battles and people from Iraq. "What are those, Michal?"

She arched her head back to see the stack. "Lucy loaned them to me to read about the war in Iraq."

"Why?"

She laughed. "You want to talk about that now? You're still inside me."

"And I'm staying there. Why?"

"She thought I'd want to understand your life as a Marine a bit more, and I was grateful."

Nick frowned. "Did you read those?"

"Not all. What's wrong?"

"Nothing. I just didn't think you cared about my tours and the war."

"I know, and that's my fault. I didn't want to think beyond us here in this house, this bed." She kissed his neck. "When you were gone, I realized I really knew nothing." She kissed his neck again. "While reading the books, I realized I didn't really need most of the information, although I might finish a couple, but I want you to tell me what you want to when you want to." She kissed his neck a third time and smiled against him. "Do you know what I'm realizing now?"

"What?"

"Tonight I just want you to make love to me and not talk about all this other stuff."

"I like that realization best."

"Me, too, Marine, so get to it."

"At your service, Ms. Dunn. All damn night."

CHAPTER THIRTEEN

N ICK CAME SLOWLY awake and moaned. He shifted only to have a
hand on his belly bring him fully out of the best damn dream of
his life to find it wasn't a dream at all. Michal's full pink lips were
wrapped around his dick, and she was outstanding at giving head. He
gathered her hair back and held the thick ponytail in a fist. She lifted her
green gaze to meet his, and he arched his neck and moaned as she
sucked harder, her fingers fondling his balls.

"Take more, Michal."

Her forehead wrinkled for a second before she swallowed more of
him, then pressed her tongue flat and licked him from balls to head
where she swirled her tongue around his sweet spot.

"Sweet fuck!" His grip on her hair tightened, and she swallowed his
cock again, sucking and pumping him until Nick saw bright lights and
arched, feeding her every inch as he came hard. Her throat continued to
work him, and she took her sweet time releasing him. She brushed her
lips over his belly, and his muscles flexed. He still gripped her hair until
she cuffed his wrist.

"You're hurting me."

He instantly released her hair. "God, Michal. Why haven't you done
that before?"

"Glad you liked it."

"Liked it? Holy shit!"

She knelt beside him and ran her hand over his chest. Nick put his
hand over hers. "What are you thinking?"

"I like pleasing you." She met his gaze, and her smile spread like a cat that had just had a cream and canary feast. "No, I *love* pleasing you. It makes me feel sexy, hearing you groan and swear because of me."

He gave her hand a tug, and she pressed those fabulous breasts against his chest. "It hits the heart square on when you admit things like that. I should think of sweeter things to say in the heat of the moment, but damn, you wiped my brain clean."

Her palm skimmed over him. "I don't mind the swearing at all. You're so cute when you come apart."

"Cute?"

"Okay, so hot I could fry eggs on your rock-hard abs."

"That's better."

She pressed her lips to his chest where his heart beat like he was in downtown Fallujah. "You're easy to talk to, Nick. I've felt comfortable sharing with you from the start."

Her lips touched his chest again, but the kiss went straight to his heart. She snuggled closer even as she sighed. "We better get ready to go."

He flipped her on her back and smiled at her laughter. "I'm a man who likes to give as well as receive. We'll be late."

Pushing her legs wide, Nick kissed her sex and found the same pleasure in her moans as she had in his.

MICHAL GRABBED HUNKS of sheets as Nick continued kissing her sex with the passion he usually kissed her lips. He pushed his tongue deep inside her and pressed it against her g-spot. Her back arched, and his fingers replaced his tongue while he sucked her clit and tongued her labia.

Michal felt an intensity she'd never known before along with the need to release. She squirmed under him, trying to get away, but Nick kept up the pressure on all her sweet spots.

"I don't...Nick..."

Her head fell back, and with a low cry, Michal felt a rush of wetness. Nick took his hand from her and brushed kisses over her belly, imitating her actions to help bring her down. She stroked his head with her hands.

"We really should get going."

"Five more minutes, sweetheart."

He brushed kisses up her body, being his usual considerate self and not kissing her breasts so soon after an orgasm. His mouth covered hers, and Michal fell into the minutes of stroking, kissing, and enjoying each other.

"You make it damn hard for a man to leave you." He nuzzled behind her ear.

"Nick Walsh, you know just how to turn a woman's head and melt her heart."

"Yours is the only head and heart I care about. Now turn that pretty head."

Michal rolled from him, laughing even as she ached at being apart. "No, City, you cannot mark me. It's blazing hot outside and I'm not wearing a turtleneck or scarf."

His forehead wrinkled but the spark in those dark blue eyes told her he wasn't really mad. "Fine. Might as well get into town and get some chow."

He winked and Michal sighed, both loving and hating how much the simplest thing he did got to her. She returned his wink. "It's been dry this year, we should probably do our part to conserve water and shower together."

"I was right; you are perfect, Lucky Charms."

"I'LL GET THE check." Nick took the check from the waitress.

John Dunn frowned. "You don't have to do that."

"Not a problem. Next time, it'll be on you."

"You've got a deal."

Nick hated to feel like he was a big fake, acting like he was even going to be around the next time they came through Ten Sleep. Michal's walls were coming down, but she hadn't said shit about him staying or her going. He didn't understand her wanting to read about the war or wanting him to tell her about his life when she still had it in her mind this thing was going to end. At least her brothers had gone on ahead and he wasn't sitting there like a liar in front of more of her family.

After Nick paid, the two couples headed out of the Crazy Woman Café. John shook Nick's hand. "I won't say Esther and I are fully onboard with what's going on. Call us prudes, but it's just not the way it was done when we were young. Saying that, you and Michal are more than old enough to do what you want without my permission, and I haven't seen Michal this happy in years. I know I'm babbling, but I wanted to welcome you to the family, Nick."

Nick didn't think he could feel worse than he had in the restaurant until Michal's dad welcomed him to the family. Something the man's daughter hadn't even done.

"Thank you, John. It's an honor."

He watched Michal's face blanch as he hugged her mother. She recovered in time to hug her folks, and they were gone.

"You ready to go?" She nudged his arm.

"Michal I'm sorry, but I better get in a few hours of work."

Her eyes scanned his face. "But you said we'd…"—she cast a glance left then right—"spend the day together."

"Yeah, I'm real sorry, sweetheart, but I need some time. I'll be by your place around lunch."

"My place?" She'd caught he had purposely avoided calling it home. "Nick, what's wrong?"

"Just need a couple hours, Mike. I'll walk over to Jared's."

It was tearing him apart, the torn look in her eyes, and when he called her Mike she'd flinched, but Nick needed time apart. It was like with a foster family when he was getting too attached; that was when he'd start acting up and create some distance. Well, he was a man now, so he wasn't going start acting up, but he needed distance.

"All right." She stepped back from him. "If you need some time."

He cupped the back of her head and dropped a kiss on her forehead. "See you in a few."

Her eyes could have cut iron with the fire there, but it wasn't the fire he liked seeing in those green depths. She stepped around him and opened the truck door. "See ya."

CHAPTER FOURTEEN

"**N**ICK, DID YOU tell Mike you'd be home for lunch?"

Nick shifted a sleeping Eli in his arms and finished typing the last words of his sentence to Hailey about what he'd found in a business needing a significant upgrade in their security. He'd hacked their system in ten minutes. Not a good showing for a company building ships for the Navy. He didn't stop typing or look at Lucy.

"Yeah, why?"

Lucy removed Eli from his arms, and he felt her shadow on him while she waited for him to make eye contact. He lifted his gaze and frowned at her hostile stance. She looked like she was about to go all red-haired wonder on him.

"What?"

"Nick, it's three o'clock."

"Holy shit!"

Lucy cast a glance to Eli and Nick felt extremely lucky the boy still slept.

"Mike called to say she was out on a job. If you decided you still wanted food, she left a plate in the fridge for you. What the hell is going on, Nick? This isn't like you."

He started signing off and shutting down programs. "I needed a break from her indecisive behavior. We had a day planned, but I couldn't go through with it, so she's pissed."

Lucy touched his arm forcing him to meet the wrath in her hazel eyes. "She didn't sound pissed. She sounded destroyed."

"Listen Lucy, I'm grateful for your friendship, but this is me. I had to take a step back. Reevaluate our relationship. I'll go out to her place and make it right."

"First off, you're not listening. She's not at her place. She's working…on her day off, she's working. I understand your need to step back, but did it ever cross your mind who you were taking a step back from? A woman used to men taking a step back and then running away."

He shoved his laptop in its case and tucked it in the space Lucy had left for him. Fuck, Lucy was right. He hadn't thought of anything but his own case of butt hurt.

"Did she say where she was?"

"Over at the Perkins' place."

"That doesn't help me, Lucy."

"Let me get Eli settled at the store with Jared, and I'll take you."

He almost mentioned she didn't need to talk to him like he was an errant child, but sucked in his lip. She cast a final glance his way that warned him he could also end up in the middle of nowhere stripped naked and covered in honey with hungry ants on the march.

"Thanks."

MICHAL CHUCKLED AT the newborn colt as he attempted to strut his stuff and found his wobbly legs weren't built for strutting yet. After a morning spent doubting everything, she was thrilled to get off the farm and away from the memories of the early morning with Nick. She needed something to smile about, and the newborn exploring his surroundings and momma gave her what she needed.

"It always amazes me, however difficult a birth is, after it's done, mom and baby act like it was a walk in the park."

Michal smiled and nodded at the veterinarian. "When is Lindy due?"

He laughed. "Caught red-handed. Guess I didn't hide the worried dad voice."

"Not well. When?"

"Ten days."

"Well anytime you need me to do something, just let me know. I'm not attached."

Dan tipped his head to the side. "Not what I heard."

"Next time check your ears."

"You're not attached because he doesn't want to be attached, or because you're afraid to be attached?"

Dan Paulson was one of the few in town who knew more than she was left by her husband for another woman. Working in professions that often collided in the same region, he'd known Trevor, and he knew about the miscarriages.

"We only went out twice, Mike, because you made the choice. I wasn't the one; that was clear, so things worked out as they should. This Nick guy... just looking at you when I say his name...don't make the wrong choice."

Michal folded her arms on the top rung of the stall door and rested her chin on her arms. She could usually talk to Dan, and he seemed genuinely concerned, but there were undertones when he talked about Nick causing her to tread cautiously. Still, she needed someone who wasn't friends with Nick like the Worrells were—or totally enthralled with him, like her family—to talk to.

"I'm trying, but there are a lot of complications with this one."

"Take our little mare's example and work through the complications, forget 'em and enjoy the rewards."

She scowled. "Are you a vet or a shrink?"

"Both. It's amazing what people tell me."

She laughed, knowing exactly what he meant. "Get out of here and home to your wife. I'll watch our baby and momma for a bit longer and make sure there aren't complications."

He brushed a kiss on her cheek. "Thanks Mike. For coming out here on your day off and for bringing the meatloaf sandwiches. You're a sweetheart."

She heard a truck pull into the yard, but didn't give it much thought. "Yes, just call me sugar."

"Brat."

She stuck her tongue out at him. "You're welcome, Dan. Anytime, really."

He gathered his equipment and started out of the stables. "Oh, I found out our mystery farrier isn't even from around here. He parks his RV in a spot until word of his shabby work gets around then he picks up and heads out."

"Did you tell the sheriff?"

"Sure did. Might help for you to confirm the extent of the damage."

"Will do."

A large shadow started moving toward her from the end of the stables, and she would recognize his shadow if she was two hundred years old and had forgotten everything else. She heard the rumble of men's voices as Dan and Nick introduced themselves. Michal focused on the Blue Roan mare and her new colt.

Heavy footsteps got closer to her and stopped. He leaned an arm on the top rung, and she shifted when his chest brushed her arm.

"Sorry, Lucky Charms, I lost track of time."

"Wouldn't have happened if you had been naked with me as promised."

"True. I wasn't in the right place mentally to have a naked party."

She angled her head to meet his gaze. "Where were you? And why didn't you take me with you?"

"I just needed to step back a bit after breakfast with your folks. All the welcome to the family shit."

"And you don't want to be part of our family?"

"Fuck, Michal, one day you're saying it ends September first, the next you're giving me head and want me to call your parents mom and dad. That's what I needed to step back from."

"Me."

"I'm not gonna win this, and we're talking in circles. A step back is not a full retreat. You gotta give me something, baby, cause I can't live life like every word or deed is a possible IED that blows us to shit."

"It hurt like hell, Nick, when you walked away from me this morning. You should have told me exactly what you told me instead of making me feel like crap. You called me Mike like I was nothing to you." She lowered her voice like she might offend the mare. "Like I hadn't just pleasured you with my mouth and body an hour before. It was my day off, and I wanted to spend it with you after three days apart, and you blew me off. That's more than one step back."

"Lesson learned. I went back to my old ways and wasn't thinking of your past experiences."

"You didn't even call. I know we're not married, but you said you'd be there for lun—"

Michal pushed from the stall, mortified she'd started crying. Nick had the worst habit of forcing her to show emotions she tried to keep hidden and was usually successful at hiding.

Nick reached for her, but she held out her hands. Swallowing gulps of air, she forced the tears back and shored up her spine. "That was a shit thing to do."

"Agreed."

"I know this is frustrating for you. I'll try harder, too."

Nick tugged her into his arms giving her no chance to protest. "We both will. I can't promise it won't happen again, but I'll be more upfront."

Michal sank into his strong arms and held him tight. If it was any other man, she'd suspect this was just the first in an ever escalating series of retreats, but Nick wasn't a runner. He was a doer, and she understood her indecisive behavior and insistence they inch forward must be driving him insane.

He brushed a kiss to the top of her head. "Can you leave?"

"No, I need to stay at least another hour." She tried to escape his arms and the hold he had over her. "You can take my truck if you want to go. They'd let me borrow a truck."

"Interesting, really?"

"Yes."

"It doesn't matter. I'm not leaving until you do. Stop trying to leave my arms, Lucky Charms."

She stilled and finally lifted her gaze to meet his. "I need to check on the mare; it was a difficult birth."

His arms opened. "Oh. Anything I can do?"

"No." She opened the stall door. "Have you eaten?"

He flinched and shook his head.

"There's a meatloaf sandwich and a pop in the cooler. Dan could only eat one."

She heard Nick digging in the cooler while she checked the mare who seemed done with human interference.

"He seems okay. You two ever hook up?"

Michal cringed at the harsh edge to his tone. "We did go on a couple dates." She looked over her shoulder. "No, we didn't have sex. But yes, he's a great guy and good friend."

He nodded and sat on a hay bale. She came out of the stall and sat next to him. He took a huge bite of sandwich. After swallowing, he lifted the sandwich in a salute.

"This is awesome."

"Glad you like it." She bit back the harsh reminder if he'd been there for lunch, he could have had a hot plate with mashed potatoes and green beans. She also bit back more of her pride. "Are you coming home tonight?"

"Unless my gear's tossed on the front lawn."

She moved closer. "I mean, are you coming home, or are you just coming to my farm?"

He cupped the back of her head and pulled her closer, capturing her mouth in kiss. Michal pressed even closer, accepted his tongue as he tasted her, and she tasted him right back. She wrapped one arm behind his neck and caressed his flesh with her fingernails. When he broke the kiss, he pressed his forehead to hers. "I'm coming home to you, Michal."

CHAPTER FIFTEEN

MICHAL STARED AT the ceiling and listened to Nick's soft snores. He had one arm draped over her and a leg draped across her legs as if he thought she might run in the night. She shifted to her side and caressed his face with her fingers. Even in sleep he had a strong face with high cheekbones and a firm, square chin. He'd have made a good cowboy. She smiled as she ran a fingertip along his cheekbones. Most women spent thousands a year to get long eyelashes like his and even more on contact lenses to try to match the indigo blue of his eyes.

She knew he was awake but lying still and letting her explore. She ran her finger over his full mouth that gave so much pleasure whether he was kissing her, pleasuring her, or saying the amazing things that came natural for him. He didn't just say things, he meant them. His mouth could also wound, but she didn't want to think about those times. What a horrible day spent without him.

She pressed close to his broad chest, and her smile grew when his muscled arm curled around her waist, and he buried his face in her shoulder, giving a low growl.

"I'm trying to sleep, woman."

"Do you know how sexy you are when you sleep?"

"It's why I keep my eyes closed, so I'm not blinded by my glory."

Michal laughed, and her body shook against his. He lifted his head and tried to glare, but the expression dissolved into a smile. He scrubbed a hand over his face and turned on his back. Michal followed and stayed tucked under his arm as she rested her head on his chest. He combed his fingers through her hair.

A cool breeze brushed over them and lifted the white cotton drapes. His chest rose in a deep breath, and Michal did the same, inhaling the scent of the lavender plants under her bedroom window mixing with the scents of the country. She couldn't imagine living in a city where a person wouldn't dare leave their windows open, and if they did, the smells wouldn't be so sweet.

She wondered if Nick enjoyed this simple life, or if he was desperate to get back to traffic and bolts on the door. But she didn't want to go there. Not after they'd come to some kind of resolution and enjoyed endless rounds of make-up sex.

"I love you."

His chest stopped rising and falling under her, and she lifted to watch his reaction. "I just said I love you."

"I heard."

"I'm not taking it back, Nick, I love you. I'll love you forever."

He rolled until he was on top of her. "I love you, too, Michal. I've been wanting to say those words for weeks, but I thought you'd bolt. Now we can start planning—"

Michal shook her head, the room closing in on her she struggled under him. "Not yet, Nick."

"Why?"

"Let's just enjoy this step forward."

"Michal stop." His order was sharp, and she froze under him. "Talk to me."

"You're running ahead of me again. Admitting I love you was a huge step for me, now you want to talk about one of us moving and planning a future. I can't make those plans and promises yet."

She closed her eyes as he kissed her forehead. "I'll take what I can get, for now."

"You're an awfully patient man, City."

"Nope, I just want you that much."

"So it's stubbornness?"

"They don't call me Mule because I'm pretty."

NICK AT LEAST got a smile from his lame joke. He gave her some space and rolled to his side. Michal shifted so she was pressed right up next to him, making his heart beat faster. He smoothed his palm over her arm and rested his hand on her hip.

"Do I have permission to at least plan a date for tomorrow night? If I can't plan, the Marine in me dies a little."

"Yes. Although haven't we been having a date every night?"

"No, we've eaten and had sex. I'm talking a date."

Her mouth turned in a wicked grin. "So no eating and no sex on this date?"

"I'm not an exhibitionist, so while we're out, no sex. But when I get you home…oh yeah."

"Good."

"You should get some sleep, Lucky Charms."

"What if I don't want to sleep?"

"Game of Monopoly?"

Michal pushed at his chest and laughed. He'd do almost anything to hear her laugh. He shifted onto his back, bringing her on top of him. Her face hovered over his, and her long blonde waves fell as a curtain around his face.

"You are so beautiful, Michal, and everything I've ever wanted. I'm proud you're mine."

Her smile turned from teasing to tender. "I'm yours." She brushed a kiss over his lips. "I'm yours. It doesn't scare me when I say that."

Nick combed his fingers through her hair, pushing it away from her face. "You shouldn't be scared. I won't say I'll never hurt you. I can be a real jackass as you discovered today, but if you'll let me, I'll never leave you, and I will always love you."

"You make it so easy to believe you."

"That's because it's the truth."

She smoothed her fingertips over his face. "I'm not doubting you, City, I'm just thinking out loud."

Before he could respond, she pressed her lips to his, and Nick didn't give a damn about talking. He took control of the kiss, tracing the tip of his tongue along her mouth until she opened for him and moaned into his mouth and pressed all those great curves into him. He tipped her head to the side and continued to tangle his tongue with hers.

She broke the kiss and moved until she gripped his cock and slid it deep inside her sex. Nick arched until he was balls deep, and her eyes closed then slowly opened, and she smiled. She started rocking back and forth, and Nick kept pace, flexing his hips.

Michal gripped his hands and laced their fingers together, keeping his hands flat on the bed and her face covered by her hair until she lifted her face to meet his gaze. Sweat broke out on her forehead and upper lip, and she licked her lips and smiled at him as she squeezed her inner muscles around him.

"Damn me, Michal!"

"Never, City." She sat back and released his hands.

Nick molded her breasts in his hands, and Michal's mouth opened in a silent scream as she came around him. He ran the pads of his thumbs over her hard nipples, sending her over the edge again, and this time, she took him with her. Nick arched hard and deep. Her hands slammed on his chest and her arm muscles flexed. She panted, continuing their joined pleasure.

Nick dug his fingers in her hair and brought her mouth to his. He kept the kiss tender and kept kissing her long after they came down from their orgasms. Her hands pushed against him and she moved her mouth.

"A little air."

"What do we need with air?"

He captured her mouth again and continued to kiss her until she broke away again.

She flopped on him, and he didn't mind being her mattress. "This is a runaway train."

"Just let it fly, Michal, let it fly, sweetheart."

CHAPTER SIXTEEN

"**I** THINK THIS is about to turn into a double date."

Nick glanced over his shoulder, and when he faced her again, she laughed at his scowl. "What are they doing here?"

Her laughter grew. "The Brewing Co is a popular place, and they have a right to leave their house."

Michal smiled at Jared and Lucy when they made it to their table. She tried to control her laughter since Jared looked similarly ticked about sharing his time with Lucy.

"Hi Lucy, Jared."

"Hey, mind if we join you?"

The men grumbled a greeting as Jared and Lucy took a seat.

"Great music tonight."

Michal nodded at Lucy. "Yeah, the oldies, or as I like to call it, the music we grew up with." She frowned. "Or from my teenage years and early twenties, you all were still in elementary and middle school."

Nick's grip tightened on her hand. "Halt that shit."

She snapped her hand from his. "It's the truth."

"Truth or not, I missed my chance to guide you around a dance floor. I might be a few hours younger, but I can two-step. Dance?"

Jared extended his hand toward her and Michal stared, shocked for a second before she took his hand. He led her to the area where a few couples danced and started leading her around.

"You weren't kidding. You're good."

"Thanks. Mom taught me. Now what's with the shit? What are you tryin' to prove?"

"Who do you think you are?"

"I'm his friend, and I'm trying to be yours."

He turned her under his arm, and she fell right back into step. Jared smiled. "You're good, too."

"Thanks." She shrugged. "I don't know, I guess I wanted to remind him."

"He doesn't give a fuck, Michal. None of us do. So what? You're a couple years older." He dropped his gaze and brought it back up. "You don't show it, woman."

"Should you be talking like that?"

He shrugged. "Lucy's got it in spades; doesn't mean I don't know you're an attractive woman."

Michal exhaled. "A lot of these songs are from when I was younger, too, except those from the 90s."

Jared laughed. "I know. We all do."

They stopped as the band started playing a slow song.

"Can I have my date back?"

Jared hitched his brow and looked at her. "You want him?"

She smiled. "Yes."

"No accounting for taste."

"Hey, why don't you do us a favor and dance with your own wife. If she doesn't just flip you off."

Jared winked and handed her over to Nick. "He's a charmer."

She laughed and stepped into Nick's arms. With a finger on his chin, she moved his face so his gaze met hers. "Why don't you pay attention to me?"

He rested his hands on her hips and tugged her flush against him. Michal wrapped her arms around his neck and swayed with him to the music of Shania Twain's, "The Woman in Me".

"Last time we danced, you ran out on me."

"I won't run tonight. Just hold me tight."

His grip tightened. "You okay, Michal?"

She brushed a kiss on his neck. "I'm amazing, Nick. Keep dancing with me."

They both released a breath when the next song was another slow dance. "You did very well planning a date."

He huffed a laugh. "Kind of easy when the options are limited."

"Limited options or not, you made it special...made me feel special. A man can take a woman out to a five star restaurant, and she goes home feeling like a one star woman."

His arms tightened around her. "He doesn't belong here, Michal, you're mine now."

She lowered her forehead to his chest. "I know."

"What's the memory doing here?"

"It's just so different; you're so different. I think it has me comparing things that can't be compared."

He stepped from her embrace and took her hand, leading her away from the lights around the old barn-turned-brewing company and tap room. "Nick, we're gonna be the talk of the town for years if we keep running out of here." She waved at Jared and Lucy as they passed them.

"Don't really give a damn."

"I noticed. You know we're already top news—you staying at the farm with me."

He kept walking through the parking lot and up the red dirt road a bit until they reached the truck. He almost dragged her around to the passenger side where it was dark. She could barely make out his features when he pushed her up against the warm steel. "I don't give a fuck, Michal, not about the bastard stupid enough to walk away from you and not about town gossip. Do you?"

"No, not about either."

His mouth crashed on hers, and his kiss bruised her lips. He started fumbling with her skirt, and Michal didn't even think to stop him until his fingers brushed her panties aside. She grabbed his forearm and broke the kiss.

He brushed his lips against hers. "Don't tell me. Your family just pulled into the parking lot."

Michal rubbed her cheek against his. "No, but I thought you weren't an exhibitionist."

"I'd make an exception for you."

"Nick, I just can't."

He released a hard breath and took his hand from her. Stepping back, he opened the door for her. "Get in the truck, sweetheart." He adjusted his clothes and Michal stepped up into the truck. She scooted to the middle.

Nick got in and cupped the back of her head, bringing her mouth to his again. This time, his kiss was tender. He ran his tongue over her bruised lips and kept his touch light.

"You mad?"

He smiled against her lips. "No. I wouldn't want to share you or those sweet noises you make with anyone. Trying to cool down. I really need to stop kissing you against trucks."

"I wouldn't go that far."

Michal started to unwind when he smiled and winked at her. He put the truck in drive and pulled out of the parking space.

She sat back. "Is the date over?"

"Negative. Jared says there's a lake not too far up the mountain."

Michal nodded. Neither spoke as Nick drove through town and followed HWY 16 up a few miles through the Bighorns. He turned right and down the small road until they parked right next to the shoreline of Meadowlark Lake. The moonlight skipped across the waves and Michal watched them.

Nick pressed his mouth to her neck. Michal tried to control the involuntary shiver, but her shoulders shook, half in pleasure, half in irrational fear. "What's wrong, Lucky Charms?"

"Nothing now."

"What was wrong?"

"I was thinking why I push you away when all I really want is to pull you closer."

He traced the curve of her face with the back of his hand, and she leaned into his touch. "Like the whole age thing earlier?"

"Yeah, that whole thing that pretty much negates 'with age comes wisdom'."

His chuckle was warm, and as always, made her want to lean closer and share more.

"The age thing and at the truck."

"Lucky Charms, don't give the truck thing a thought. It's pretty early for you to give me that much trust."

She moved from his hand like he'd slapped her instead of caressed her. "I've always trusted you, Nick, but can't you see how it might scare me?"

He cupped her cheek, and she leaned into the power behind the rough palms. "No, I don't see how it would scare you. There's nothing I wouldn't do for you, Michal. There's not a fight so tough I wouldn't fight it, or a place so far I wouldn't go for you. When you understand that, you'll understand there is nothing to be scared of when it comes to you and me and what's going on between us."

Michal broke the connection again, afraid of giving in. She wished he'd turn off the truck so the cab light wouldn't illuminate her face and her eyes where she wore every emotion without the ability to hide them.

"You're too good at making me believe this can work."

He shook his head, and this time, his chuckle served to separate them not bring her closer. Nick turned from her and stared out at the scene before them. Black night faded into dark blue mountains and the dark waters of Meadowlark Lake. "Obviously, I'm not, since there's still a shit ton of fear in your eyes."

"It might take longer than a summer for me to tear down all my walls. Do I only have the summer?"

"You have all the time you need, sweetheart."

Michal settled close beside him and took his arm, draping it over her shoulder. They sat in silence for a few minutes when she smiled, catching him shifting in his seat for the fifth time.

"I trust you now."

He tugged her close and dropped a kiss on the top of her head. "Outstanding."

Michal slipped out from under his arm and reached for the waistband of his jeans.

"Michal..."

She locked her gaze with his as she unbuttoned and unzipped the fly. His eyes slid closed on a deep moan when she released his hard length, then slowly opened and matched the dark blue water of the lake. Michal smiled and lowered her mouth to just above the head of his cock.

"I trust you to keep your eyes open and tell me if you see headlights on the road heading down here."

"Roger."

She pressed her tongue to the tip of his cock, tasting the salt of his precum mixed with the taste belonging to only him and she got to enjoy.

"Michal." Her name was a prayer on his lips. All teasing and smiles faded into his taste on her tongue and his gaze transmitting every ounce of love and pleasure he felt. He pushed back her hair from the side of her face and ran the back of his hand over her cheek as she opened her mouth and took him deep inside, pumping him with her hand.

He sank in the seat, feeding her more as he lifted his hips. His fingers curled in her hair.

"God, Michal, your mouth is…Fuck!" He plunged his cock deep, and Michal hummed around him as she tried to keep her gag reflex in check. She doubled her efforts, determined to keep him under her spell.

His hand molded her breast, and he pinched her nipple. Michal screamed around him and tipped her head to one side and glared as she clenched her thighs together.

"Sorry, Lucky Charms, but you've got amazing tits."

Michal nodded and took pleasure when he slapped his hands on the steering wheel and his knuckles turned white with the grip. She kept the pressure on and continued palming his balls and pumping while sucking until he arched and bellowed.

"Shit, Michal, just one more!"

She followed his orders and was rewarded with her name filling the cab of the truck as he rocked in and out of her mouth, riding out his orgasm. She eased him from her mouth. The heels of his hands where dug into his eyes.

Sitting up, she leaned forward again and brushed a kiss on his neck. "You didn't keep your eyes open, City."

One palm slipped just enough for her to see his narrow-eyed glare as her answer. "Don't even start, woman." She smiled and brushed another kiss on his neck.

"I can't think of anyone or anything I've loved as much as I do you, Nick Walsh. I want you to have everything you've ever wanted."

He crushed his mouth to hers and didn't seem to mind he could taste himself on her lips and in her mouth. He held her head and shifted, opening his door and slipping outside while tugging her to the edge of the seat. Michal didn't hesitate to spread her legs and sucked in a sharp breath when he hiked her ankles to rest on his shoulders and plunged hard and deep into her wet sex.

"Open your blouse and play with your tits."

His voice was hard and authoritative. Michal didn't blink, but started unbuttoning her blouse. She tugged down her bra and molded her breasts with her hands. Nick tugged her closer and bent, sucking one nipple then the other as he continued to rock in and out of her.

Michal didn't last long and arched against him, gripping his forearms. "Nick. Nick." She couldn't control her body or her breath, and his name left her lips as a litany.

He gave as good as he got and sucked her nipple hard until it was almost painful. Gripping his arms, sure she'd drawn blood, Michal came, her back arching off the seat. She gave a soft cry when she felt him fill her. How wonderful it would be to give him the children he wanted. When he would have stood, she tightened her grip on his arms.

"Michal?"

"Why did you have to come to Wyoming?" she whispered.

"So I could find you."

He brushed a kiss over her lips and stood, adjusting his clothes. Michal eased up and opened the glove compartment. She breathed a sigh, relieved Lucy kept wipes in her truck. Blushing, she avoided Nick's gaze as she cleaned up a bit and adjusted her skirt and buttoned up her blouse. His simple statement, *so I could find you*, thundered in her mind like horses hooves on the dry prairie. She lifted her gaze and met his intense blue stare.

Michal smiled. "I thought you said you weren't an exhibitionist and here we are where anyone could come down the road."

He didn't laugh or smile. "I hardly think we were drawing a crowd out here."

Michal slipped on her sandals and slid out of the truck standing before him. "What's wrong?"

"Just restless."

She swallowed hard. "Restless?"

He cupped her face. "Come on, Michal, this is supposed to be a date. We were having fun. Let's have fun."

She nodded, not really wanting to talk or think anymore about things that couldn't be changed. "Walk with me."

Nick dropped his hands and laced their hands together. "Love to."

Michal strolled in step beside him trying to keep his gate slow. The summer was going fast enough and she wanted to keep him with her as long as possible.

CHAPTER SEVENTEEN

T HE SKY LIT up, and Nick ducked into the barn before a thunder-clap shook the ground. The light bulb above him flickered. He swiped his brow with his forearm and narrowed his gaze to focus on Michal.

"Shhh, baby. You're safe. I'm here."

Nick was drawn to her voice as if she'd tossed a rope around him and tugged him step by step to her side.

"What's wrong?"

"Bailey doesn't care for the thunder and lightning."

Another clap rolled through the sky, and the horse shook his head and neighed, pulling away from Michal. She smoothed her palm over the Paint's neck and Nick stayed still, hypnotized by her low voice and tender words. The skin of the horse's neck shivered, rolling down its spine. Nick suppressed his own shiver thinking of those hands on him.

"Hand me an apple slice, please."

Her laughter woke him up. "What?"

"An apple slice, please?" She pointed to a Tupperware bowl with apple slices.

"Aye, aye. Apple slice, ma'am."

She took the fruit and fed it to Bailey, talking him down from another crash of thunder as the barn lit up with the natural light of the storm.

"You were up and at 'em before the rooster could crow this morning." She didn't look at him but kept stroking the luckiest fuckin' horse in the world.

Since their date, he'd been working later in town and running earlier and longer in the mornings. The runs up the mountain had been great for keeping him in shape and shitty at keeping him away from Michal's sweet body. But he hadn't been lying the night of the date; he was getting restless, and it was either screw her until she couldn't walk, or run it off.

"Yep, drills are this weekend. Gotta stay ahead of the younger guys."

"Even in a severe thunderstorm?"

"Was a light rain when I started."

She pushed away from the stall door and sat on her heels, giving some attention to Max the cat that'd been weaving in and out of her legs. "You think I don't know the signs of a man leaving?"

He sat on his heels across from her. "Now I do. I told you, Michal, I'm restless."

"About me?"

"About not knowing where the hell I stand with you. I want you, Michal. I want the whole fucking thing with you including till death do we part. Fact is, I don't even want to stop there. I want you forever. God, woman, it's why I'm desperate to be inside you as much as possible, and always ready for you to say it's the last."

He went to stand, but she cuffed his forearm with her hand. "I want a lifetime with you, too, Nick. I want it more than I've ever wanted anything else. But I'm terrified. What if I can't get pregnant, or worse, what if I do and lose another child…I don't think I could take that, Nick. I don't think I could take losing your child and have you hold me and tell me it's all right. It wouldn't be all right, not for me."

He opened his mouth to set her straight, but her grip tightened on his arm and desperation flashed in her green eyes.

"Just hear me out, then you can go all Marine and bark about how stupid I am. I've truly listened to you, Nick. I know the two of us could be a family, and I know there are other options for children. Adoption would be a wonderful way to help a child who is living as you did. And there is surrogacy and all the other fertility options, but I wouldn't want another woman carrying my child. Do you know how much I want to carry your child? The other night in the truck I never wanted birth control to fail so much in my life when I felt you fill me. I actually begged God that it would. Isn't that crazy?"

He swallowed hard. "Did it...fail?"

Her mouth curved in a sad smile, flashing as fast and dying as quickly as the lightning. "No, I even took one of those early detection tests." Her laugh was bitter and hollow. "Can you imagine? I did that while you were out running yesterday morning. Sitting there peeing on a stick and praying I could tell you the news when you got home." She swiped at tears and pushed his hands away when he tried to comfort her. "I wondered how many years I could sit there peeing on stick after stick, praying I'd have good news for you and listening to your declarations of love before it broke me completely? It's no longer about disappointing you...it's about disappointing me and about that disappointment being the thing that kills us."

They sat there staring at each other and listening to the storm raging outside the barn, which was nothing compared to the ferocity of the storm raging within.

"Why didn't you tell me what you were doing yesterday?"

"It wouldn't have made any difference."

"I would have been there; that's the difference."

"I know. I was wrong not to tell you."

"Is that why you asked about me coming to Wyoming and acted all weird as you wiped yourself off?"

She moved forward and knelt in front of him. "Yes. I was ashamed of my thoughts. We haven't even settled anything, and there I was, hoping for a baby."

He tried to laugh, but it came out a strangled choke. "Shit, I thought you were ashamed; pissed I screwed you outside again."

"No, I was never ashamed. I'm not ashamed of any time we've made...had sex."

"Made love. Say it. I'm sorry I didn't."

"Anytime we've made love."

"Lucky Charms, you're right; this is about you, not me. I'll admit it does a heart good that you mentioned a few times I'd stick like desert sand to you no matter what, but you know what your body and mind can stand."

"I also know what my heart couldn't stand."

"What's that?"

"Not being yours."

"That day won't ever come."

"What if you're restless?"

Nick locked his jaw and absorbed the blow. He stood and she followed him to her feet.

"I'll grouch around like an ass. Work more. Run earlier in the morning and eat up some pavement."

Michal turned back to feeding Bailey apple slices. "And today, are you restless today?"

Nick rubbed the top of his head and released a deep breath. "Not as much as I was."

"Are you going to work?"

He glanced outside to the pouring rain. When he turned his focus back to Michal, her mouth was curved in a seductive smile. He leaned a hip against the pole of the stall door and crossed his arms over his chest. "You have another suggestion?"

"Well, the rain has made it a little chilly this morning."

"Yep."

"And it's my day off."

"It is?"

Her smile grew. "Yes, but you knew that."

He smiled back, relieved she was moving on from the tense conversation of before. "I vaguely remember you mentioning it."

Her gaze dropped. "Those are some pretty short shorts."

He laughed. "Are you mocking my greenies?"

"Not mocking...admiring."

"So, back to the plans for today."

She walked toward him and stopped so close he had to tip his head to look down and meet her gaze. The tease put her arms behind her back, elevating her amazing breasts and stretching the t-shirt she wore.

"There are some Westerns on the TV, and I was wondering if you'd spend the day with me?"

He hiked a brow. "Watching John Wayne? That's the plan?"

"It's just a part of the plan."

"The other part better not be the Hallmark Channel the other half of the day."

She laughed and rose on the balls of her feet pressing close her hands cuffing his forearms. "No, I wouldn't even suggest it. I was thinking the other part would require a lot less clothes and a lot more heating up."

"What if I wanted to start the second part here?"

Michal glanced around. "I know it's silly, but not in front of Bailey and Max. I don't think I could meet their eyes after they witnessed what you do to me."

Nick responded with a full throttle belly laugh. "Roger. We'll save the innocence of your horse and cat." He tossed her over his shoulder and started for the door.

"City, put me down. I'm too heavy."

He swatted her ass and tore across the farmyard as the rain and her curses pummeled him. The second they entered the house he set her on her feet, turned her around, and cut off any rant by capturing her mouth. He only allowed her to breathe as he tugged off her t-shirt and sports bra. He tugged her close and walked to the bedroom. Their bedroom. Their bed.

At the edge of the bed he stopped and hooked his thumbs in her shorts, tugging them and her panties down as he trailed kisses over her breasts and belly.

"Step out."

She did as he ordered. With a slight push, she sat on the edge of the bed, and Nick buried his face between her legs.

"Oh sweet mercy, I love when you do that." She moaned, and her head fell back.

Nick smiled and continued using his tongue and mouth on her. He reached and molded her breast with one hand and closed his eyes against the ecstasy of hearing her scream his name as she came apart.

"You are so beautiful when you orgasm, Michal. Now turn around and put that sweet ass in the air."

Again she did as instructed without even a glare at his harsh command. She moved to the edge of the bed and knelt with her ass in the air, her head flat.

Nick stripped then moved behind her but didn't slide his aching cock into her tight sex. He smoothed his hand over her back and caressed her cheek with the back of his hand.

"What are you thinking, Michal?"

"You know."

"I don't want you thinking of anything but the pleasure of me being inside you."

"Then get inside me, so I can forget everything but how much you belong there."

He stood and ran the head of his cock over her sex until she squirmed back, then slid balls deep, his moan matching hers. Gripping one of her hips with one hand, Nick, grabbed her ponytail and tugged, losing control as the rainwater from her hair rolled over her back, causing her to shiver. He pounded into her. The sound of his skin slapping against hers drowned out the storm as white noise filled his ears.

What he focused on were the moans, grunts, and pants coming from Michal. She fisted the quilt until she twisted at the waist and gripped his forearm, her nails digging into his muscles. Her forehead was wrinkled, and her mouth was open as the sweetest sounds of pleasure echoed around them.

"You feel so good, sweetheart."

"Oh god." She turned and reached between her legs stroking him and her clit.

With a deep thrust, Nick came hard and barely heard her gasps as she climaxed. The muscles of her pussy clamped down around him and milked him. Nick returned to earth.

He eased from her and turned her to her back before lying between her legs. He was relieved to see the smile on her face as she ran her fingers over his.

"I'm fine, Nick, really. I don't want you to worry I'll break every time you fill me."

"What are you thinking now?"

She smiled. "What time *McClintock* starts?"

He brushed a kiss on her forehead and smiled. He hooked a hand under one of her thighs and lifted it to his back. "How much time do I have?"

"I thought you said forever."

"Don't joke about that, Michal."

"I'm not, Nick." She cupped his face. "I can see the planning going on in that wonderful mind. I'm just taking one more step to you. Don't go calling the preacher or picking out white fences."

"Oh I've already picked everything out, and the preacher is number one on speed dial. The planning is done, I just need the woman to give the marching orders."

"Nick, it's only been two months."

"And you're already wanting my child. Who's already a million steps ahead?"

"I don't want to talk about that."

He nodded. "Get up and let's have some breakfast before you make me watch a man say 'howdy pilgrim' a thousand times." He sat up and slapped her ass.

"Nick!" She glared and rubbed her ass as she rolled and started gathering her clothes. "For that, I'm going to let you make breakfast while I shower."

He winked, and flopped back on the bed folding his arms under his head. "It was worth it."

She stared at him, her gaze tracing him, not like she was getting ready to continue their fun, but like she'd never seen him on her bed before.

"Lucky Charms, you okay?"

Her gaze snapped to his. She smiled, but it never reached her eyes. "Yes. I expect lots of bacon with breakfast."

She turned and left the room. Nick wasn't going to push, she'd given a lot today. He pushed off the bed and dumped his wet clothes into the laundry basket before tugging on sweats and a fresh t-shirt.

"Save some hot water for me," he hollered as he passed by the head.

"I don't smell bacon," she tossed back.

Nick shook his head. He was sinking fast into the illusion this was his home and they were a family. His cell rang as he passed the coffee table where he'd emptied his pockets the night before. He glanced at the name and groaned as he glanced at the head.

"Hey, Hailey."

"Nick. You workin' today?"

The bathroom door opened to reveal Michal wrapped in a towel. Her gaze darted from his phone to meet his gaze, and she couldn't hide the disappointment there. He turned from her.

"Wasn't planning on it since I worked Sunday. You need me?"

"Not necessarily today. Just checking in. But tomorrow for sure."

He wanted to give Hailey the biggest bear hug on the record. "Aye, aye."

"How's everything going with that other project?"

"Subtle, Hail, real subtle. Don't go SpecOps, or anything."

"So you can't talk right now, because she's there...Eww...You're not..."

He hit *end*, but he could almost hear her hysterical laughter. He'd hear about hanging up on her the next day. Nick put the phone on the counter and started getting out pans, eggs, bread, and, of course, the bacon.

"I'll have your chow ready in a flash."

Michal touched his arm and Nick stopped. "Thank you for staying."

"Sure, sweetheart."

Her grip tightened on his arm. He liked how she always held onto him whether they were talking or he was balls deep. She reached for him.

"I'm not going to let you sweep this off. You knew how much today meant to me, thank you for making it happen."

He rested his hands on her hips and tugged her close. "Really, Michal, spending a day with you isn't a hardship."

She wrapped her arms around his neck, and he lowered his mouth to hers, savoring a slow, easy kiss. Them making out in the kitchen while the rain pounded on the roof overwhelmed Nick with the sense of being home. Michal pressed her sweet, warm body closer, and he *was* home. He brushed his tongue against hers in an unhurried stroke, and she responded in kind. Her arms tightened around his neck as he secured her to him with his arms linked around her.

Michal broke the kiss, but not the connection. "There's something romantic about kissing you with the storm raging outside."

"There's something outstanding about being with you anytime, Michal."

"What am I going to do with you, Nick Walsh?"

He let his gaze drop to her body pressed against him. The towel had long since dropped to the deck. "I have a few thoughts."

"Tell me?"

"I'd rather show you."

She brushed a kiss on his neck. "Maybe we could skip a movie or two."

He ducked out of her embrace and scooped the towel up off the deck, dropping a kiss on one of her breasts as he stood before wrapping the cotton around her. "Negative. You wanted a cuddling on the couch movie day."

Nick captured her mouth again, unable to resist the temptation. "Go get dressed and I'll get the chow going."

Her frown and the disappointment in her gaze made him smile. "Thanks for the offer though, Lucky Charms." He rested a hand on her breast.

She held his hand still in one of hers. "I would do anything to make you happy, Nick."

"Then marry me."

Like she'd made eye contact with Medusa, Michal turned to stone. "I…"

He didn't move, just waited.

"I would love to be your wife."

He almost smiled until he saw the tears cutting trails down her cheeks. "But?"

"But nothing. I want to be yours forever."

Nick tried to keep his cool. He cuffed her upper arms. "No stipulations?"

"Well, just…not yet, please. Give me until the end of summer."

He tipped his chin in a short nod. "End of summer, I can concede that."

He gripped her hair and gave a tug lifting her face so their gazes met. "Then you're mine."

"Yes." It came out as a broken whisper as tears continued to fall.

"Why are you crying, Michal?"

"Because I love you so much, and can't believe I get to keep you. But I'm terrified of what it means for you."

He gave her hair another tug. "You just be honest with me, Lucky Charms, about everything. Meaning no more hiding in the bathroom peeing on a stick, or silently praying for me to impregnate you. You come to me with everything; you be my family, and I will live and die a happy man with the love of my life."

"Yes. Where…"

"No more right now." He took a page from her book, for once not wanting to jump to planning ahead. He just wanted to enjoy the word yes on her lips. He captured her mouth, kissing her with all the love and passion he felt for her.

He stepped back after what seemed days. "Go get ready. This time I really will get breakfast."

"Yes, sir."

"Don't give me ideas."

She frowned before her eyes rounded until she smiled and wrapped the towel back around her.

"Don't get used to being called sir. Don't forget: lots of bacon," she tossed back over her shoulder.

"I'm marrying a bossy one, for sure."

"Right, I'm the *bossy* one."

Nick chuckled and started breaking eggs in a bowl. As soon as the door shut, he dropped the false humor. Michal Dunn had just agreed to be his wife. His *wife*. He had no illusion any of it was going to be easy from getting her to the I do's to the years after.

CHAPTER EIGHTEEN

"**I** DON'T KNOW why people keep using this asshole."

Dan finished giving the horse the shot of antibiotics as Michal secured the poultice to the bruised hoof. She shook her head at the sickening sight of a horse in pain.

"He didn't move far, just down the road to Cody. I've never had to pad so many shoes in all the years since I started."

"But still one of your usual clients."

Michal frowned. "What are you implying?"

"I feel like this is personal. Maybe you, maybe me. Hell, I even checked where Trevor was to make sure it wasn't him trying to screw you over."

She ran her hand down the gelding's leg mumbling little bits of nothing meant to soothe. "Trevor could be a sonofabitch to people, but he'd never hurt a horse. You should've known better."

"True. I was grasping at straws. Thinking with you and Nick getting close."

She chuckled. "Trevor is happily married with five children. He doesn't care about me or you, or who's sharing my bed. Hell, he'd probably feel sorry for Nick more than anything."

"Well, I feel better you're not on the farm alone. Something doesn't feel right."

Smoothing her hand down the gelding's neck, she bit her lip. "I am alone for a couple nights. Nick's at drills."

"Can you stay with Lucy?"

She shook her head. "No, I have Bailey and Max, and I don't need to. I'm fine. Whoever is doing this is obviously a bit of a coward since he moved on from Ten Sleep."

He opened his mouth and Michal intercepted. "How's Lindy?"

"Overdue and grouchy. Nice block."

"You better be getting home. I'll finish up here."

"You've been the one staying late on all the appointments."

"That's because I'm not waiting for a baby to arrive." As soon as the words left her mouth she felt a sharp pain cut through her heart.

"Mike." Dan rested a hand on her shoulder.

She shook her head and forced a smile. "It's fine, really. Go on home."

"If you're sure?"

"I'm sure. Go!"

MICHAL ROLLED HER eyes, but smiled when she pulled into the farmyard. She slid out of the truck.

"How long have you been here?"

Lucy smiled and pushed out of the porch swing, holding a sleeping Eli. "Only about five minutes. Dan called and filled me in."

"Yeah, and if his theory is right, do you honestly think you being here alone was a good idea? Jared would kill the guy and then me if anything happened to you."

Lucy shrugged. "I sent him a text we'd be staying with you. And told him why."

"Noooo!"

She yanked her phone from her pocket. She'd put it on silent a few hours ago. Sure enough a slew of texts and two voicemails met her.

"What's wrong?"

She showed the screen to Lucy. "You didn't think Jared would tell Nick?"

The younger woman tucked her head in her shoulders. "Sorry. I had my own mountain of texts to get through followed by a conversation. I guess I wasn't thinking."

Michal's shoulders slumped. "It's fine, but please go home. I'm fine."

"Mike, I know it's hard to accept help, but we're friends, or at least, I hope so."

Michal caved. "Well it is late and Eli should be in bed. Come on in. I can only offer the pull-out sofa bed, or mine."

"Sofa bed works for us."

"I need to take care of Bailey, so make yourself at home, and I'll be right back."

Lucy laid Eli on Michal's bed until they could get the sofa bed ready. "Tell Nick to chill."

Michal gave a nervous laugh. She headed to the barn. Ignoring the texts, she checked the time. Hitting the send button to call. Eight o'clock. Maybe he'd be at supper…

"What the hell's going on, Michal? You didn't answer my texts or calls."

"Nick, nothing is going on, and I was working, so I put the phone on silent."

"Nothing is going on? Bullshit! Why does Lucy have to stay with you?"

Michal rubbed her forehead. "She doesn't. Dan jumped the gun. I think his wife's hormones are rubbing off on him. Lucy doesn't have to stay. Please reassure Jared."

"Reassure Jared, my hairy ass. I'm coming back tomorrow."

"No, no, no." She stomped her boot to complete the four-year-old affect. "I'm going to kill Dan. You will stay at drills like you need to. Lucy will go home tomorrow like she needs to. And I will be fine. Now I need to feed Bailey. Love you."

"Michal."

"Please."

"Fine. Love you, too."

Michal ended the call and leaned back against the wall. Stupid Dan. Why did he have to get everyone stirred up, including her? She'd been jumpy the rest of the afternoon with every sound in the old barn.

She hit the send button on her phone again.

"Hey, City, talk to me."

"What's really going on, Lucky Charms?"

"You know. Some douche is doing shitty work on horses. Like I said, I think Dan went too far and put too much thought into it. Not all the ranches impacted are clients. He even looked into Trevor."

"But you're sure there's no connection to you?"

"Is this ass shady? Yes. Disgusting? Yes. But no, I don't think he has me in mind. That being said, Dan's stupid theories have me jumping at everything."

"Then be glad Lucy is there for tonight, but I'll have Jared call her off for tomorrow."

"Are you out on the town?"

"At a bar with Tim and Jared, yes."

"You're nice to talk to when you're not bellowing at me."

"Yeah, well, I'll still cut out early."

"No, but call me tomorrow night."

"Roger."

"Goodnight."

"Goodnight."

NICK HIT THE end button and took a long draw of beer. "Hey, Worrell, I appreciate Lucy doing what she thinks is needed, but if you could get her to stand down tomorrow, that would be best."

Jared nodded. "I'll talk to her."

Tim took a drink. "You don't think there's a threat?"

Nick shook his head. "Other than the veterinarian hitting the panic button and getting this shit stirred up?"

"You and this Michal seem to be making some headway."

"Yeah, Mike calling you back is a huge step."

Nick sat back on the chair at the high top table. He scanned the bar. He brought his attention back to the table and met the gazes of his buddies. "She agreed to marry me."

"What the fuck? You're just telling us now."

"I keep waiting for her to recant."

"So you're moving to Wyoming?"

Nick scowled at his beer mug. "I don't know. We haven't discussed that."

"You haven't discussed where you're living? That's a bit fucked."

"Well, life is a bit fucked."

"She really worth all this shit? I mean she's twisted you up from the get-go."

"Yeah, Hayes, and when Hailey kneed you in the balls the first time you met and led you around by them for a year, was that worth it?"

"Stand down, Walsh, I was just looking out for you."

"Who the fu—"

"Both of you knock it off. We're all working on high alert and saying shit we'll regret."

Nick nodded. "You're right, Worrell."

"Yeah. Sorry, Walsh."

Nick waved Tim off. "Let's just let it go." He signaled the waitress. "I'll buy the next round."

"I can get behind that."

Nick ordered the beers then flipped off Jared. "Why are we listening to this sonofabitch anyway? Didn't Lucy practically beg his sorry ass to marry her?"

"Yeah." Tim chucked a pretzel at Jared.

"Knock it the fuck off. She didn't beg." He smiled around his beer mug. "But she was awful close to my dick at the time."

Nick joined Tim in throwing more pretzels. Jared batted the incoming missiles away. When the waitress returned to the table, Nick cleared his throat and gave her an innocent look. "Thank you, ma'am."

Her cheeks turned red, and her smile told him he didn't have to be alone that night. But there was only one woman he wanted to be with, and no other even came close.

"You're welcome." She winked and Nick glared when a pretzel hit him in the face.

Jared shook his head. "The days of using 'ma'am' to get free beers are over, asshole."

Nick lifted his mug. "I'll drink to that."

CHAPTER NINETEEN

NICK MOVED HIS legs, rocking the porch swing back and forth. A blanket of stars cut the black night, and Nick was reminded of the clear skies in the desert. But the desert didn't have cool breezes rustling the leaves of aspens and cottonwoods. He tipped back the beer bottle and let the cold brew wash the invisible sand from his throat.

He'd done everything they suggested when he got back from his fourth tour. Even visited the Marine Corps psychiatrist, Captain, now Major, Lydia West, at the Naval Hospital San Diego. It ended up she unloaded about her three tours as much as she expected him to talk. He didn't care; she was fun to hang out with, had been since they'd both been in Iraq. And for the most part, he avoided the dark side, but sometimes, the shit crept back in.

That night, while driving back, he'd thought of Michal running out to meet him, but she wasn't home, and Lucy didn't know which ranch she might be at. He should have stayed for a bit at Lucy and Jared's, but he wanted to get home and away from their happy reunion.

Headlights illuminated the farm yard like spotlights. Nick continued to move back and forth and took another swallow. The swing stopped for a second as Michal took her place beside him and hugged his arm.

"Welcome home."

"Thanks, Lucky Charms, it's good to be back."

She rested her chin on his arm. "Sorry, I wasn't here. Dan was supposed to stay late this time with you coming back, but his wife went into labor."

He huffed a laugh. "Can't argue with that. The man had a great excuse."

"You ticked?"

"Not at all."

"Nick?"

"Just thinking, Michal. Really about nothing to do with you or us."

"Everything has to do with us, City. That's why I poured out my fears to you about the guy causing all this damage. You listened to me for an hour. I can listen to you."

"Michal, I really appreciate the offer, sweetheart, I do, but I don't need to hash it all out. I think it's just working with some young Marines and things kicking off again in Iraq. Sent my mind off on a mission doomed for failure."

She pushed out of the swing. "You want to come inside? I made a coconut cream pie."

He chuckled. "That's it?"

She sank back down. "I'm sorry, I'm not very good at this; I never have been. You said you didn't want to talk and why; I took your word for it. Did you need to talk?"

Nick's chuckle rumbled into a full blown belly laugh. "You really are bad at this shit."

He took Michal's hand and tugged her toward him, capturing her mouth. He cupped the back of her head and held her to him. He shifted on the seat so he could guide her mouth and head. He stopped trying to control it and just enjoyed tasting Michal and swallowing her sweet sighs.

Nick smiled against her lips when she pressed closer, smoothing her hand over his abs. He tapped her thigh and shifted again so she could straddle him. Michal complied and straddled his lap, her hands drifting under his t-shirt.

Gripping the ends of her t-shirt, he leaned back a breath. "Lean back, sweetheart." She did and stretched her arms. Nick tugged the tight fitting cotton over her head and tossed it on the porch.

"Let your hair down."

Her mouth curved in the sexiest smile he'd ever seen, and she bent forward, brushing a kiss on his neck. "You are so damn bossy, City."

He smiled. "Yeah, now let your hair down."

Nick braced his feet so the swing wouldn't move as she pushed back and unraveled the thick rope braid of pure honey colored silk. She arched her back, giving him a spectacular view of her bare from the waist up and her hair lying in thick waves as she shook the heavy locks loose.

While she was busy, Nick unhooked her bra and filled his hands with her breasts. Michal's belly contracted, and she flopped forward digging her fingers into his chest.

"Nick…oh god!" She gasped when his pinched her nipples.

Nick grabbed a fistful of hair and tugged her face up so their gazes locked. "Rub your clit, Lucky Charms."

Unbuttoning and unzipping her jeans, she reached inside and started rubbing her clit. He brought her lips back to his and molded her breasts while sucking the tip of her tongue. When her orgasm hit, she pushed away from him, her forehead wrinkled and her lips parted as she continued to rub her clit. She dropped her head forward and panted until Nick removed his hands from her breasts. He cupped her face and kissed her tenderly.

She broke the kiss and sat back on his lap, crossing her arms over her chest. Nick peeled her arms away and stared at the sight of her bared to him from the waist up, her hair mussed, looking like she just woke up. Her tits were round and full with gorgeous pink nipples. Her belly was flat except for the slightest curve. He smoothed his hands over her muscled arms and down over her collarbone. She captured his hands before he could cup her breasts and moved his hands to her hips.

"You're like a child told not to do something, so it becomes the only thing they want to do."

He laughed. "All I want to do is you, Michal Dunn, and I want to touch because God blessed you with the finest pair of tits I have ever seen, touched, or tasted." He brought the fingers she'd used to pleasure herself to his mouth and sucked. "Mmmm…you taste so good everywhere. Now just sit there for a second and let me enjoy the view I've only dreamed about for three days."

He smoothed his hand from her belly button to between her

breasts, and cupped the side of her neck. He caressed her jawline with the pad of his thumb. When he caressed her lower lip with his thumb, she pressed a kiss to the pad. Her chest rose and fell in heavy breaths.

"I want to taste you, too."

"Do what you want, Lucky Charms."

She captured his mouth in a burning hot kiss, and his abs flexed when the back of her fingers brushed across his belly while she unbuttoned and unzipped his jeans.

Breaking the kiss, she slid off his lap and gripped the waistband of his jeans and boxer briefs. She lifted her gaze to his, and he winked. She smiled and ran the tip of her tongue along the top of a cut line. His hips flexed, and she chuckled against him.

She slid his pants and underwear down, and kneeling between his legs, she pumped his dick then ran her thumb under the head, hitting his sweet spot. "No orders, First Sergeant?"

HIS BLUE EYES flashed and his grip on her hair tightened. "Now, Michal."

Michal opened her mouth wide and took his length as deep as she could without hitting her gag reflex. His hips rose, feeding her more, and she willed herself to take all of him. His grip tightened in her hair, and she held onto his thighs as he moved her head, her mouth moving from the root to the tip. She lifted her eyes to his and sucked harder at the fire burning in his gaze as his nostrils flared. His lips parted, and he moaned.

She couldn't believe how much she loved being controlled by Nick, craved his orders and command. Had any other man wrapped her hair around his fist and demanded she deep throat him, she'd have shoved an iron up his ass. With Nick, she felt her belly burn and her sex clench as he almost willed her to orgasm with him.

Just as his balls contracted and Michal prepared to swallow him deep, he pulled her mouth from him and used his hand on his cock rough and hard. Michal watched entranced and gasped when he released his cum over her breasts.

"Aw... Michal!" he bellowed as he painted her chest.

She stared at her breasts and then lifted her gaze to his. His mouth curved in a devilish smile. "Damn, that's beautiful."

Michal ran her finger through a trail on her breast and put the finger in her mouth.

"Damn me."

She repeated the action at the pleasure in his voice. "You liked that, marking me?"

"What was your first clue? Take off your jeans and lie back."

"You want…with this?"

"Use your t-shirt."

Michal nodded and wiped her chest and belly. She stripped and laid back on a pile of clothes. Nick didn't waste a minute before he moved between her legs. He captured her mouth in a kiss and pressed his muscled torso against her.

The warm night air turned to a thermal blanket, covering them as their bodies turned slick with sweat. After minutes of kissing and stroking, Nick slid his hard length deep inside her. Michal arched, wanting more. She inhaled the scents of lavender, freshly mowed grass, the farm, and Nick, all ordinary in their own right, but made exotic by the feel of him hot, heavy, and thick deep inside her and his big body surrounding her.

Her inner muscles quivered as his thrusts turned harder and deeper, and he rubbed her clit with the pad of his thumb. Michal locked her legs around him and gripped his biceps, digging her fingernails deep.

When he pushed deep on his orgasm, Michal opened her mouth in a silent scream. He rolled so she was on top and cupped the back of her head, bringing her mouth to his for a lazy kiss. Michal melted against his body and into the kiss. His hand moved from her head, and he smoothed his rough hands over her body, cupping her ass and squeezing. Michal wrapped her arms around his neck and pressed closer.

She lifted from the kiss. "I missed you, City." She brushed a kiss on his strong jaw, tucked her head under his chin, and used him as a mattress.

"I hate leaving you, Michal, but I have to admit, the coming home does not suck."

She laughed. "No, it doesn't. But I'm being serious. Going through that shit this past weekend, it was such a relief talking to you. I've come to depend on you being here for me, having my back."

"No matter where I am, I'll always have your six, baby."

"Nick, when you asked me to marry you, was it just a heat of the moment thing?"

He sat up forcing her to sit on his lap, her legs wrapped around his waist. "Absolutely not."

"You haven't said anything since."

He breathed a laugh. "Neither have you."

"Where did you see us living?"

"Would you move to San Diego?"

She glanced at the barn where Bailey and Max were probably curled up asleep in the fresh hay. Her tools were in there. She pressed her palm to his chest. "I don't know."

"You don't know?"

"It would be a big move. And what would I do out there?"

"There are horses in California."

Michal hated she'd brought up the topic at all. "I don't want to argue, I'm just being honest."

He gripped her waist and tried to lift her from him, but Michal tightened her thighs.

"What the hell?"

She cupped his face. "Are you pissed off?"

His grip tightened. "You ask that a lot. Whatever lame ass man you've had in the past, I can promise you this: You'll know when I'm pissed. You said there was pie, and I'm starving."

"You want pie?"

"Michal, we're not going to settle where we're going to end up tonight. It's late, I want pie and then to screw you some more." He gripped her hips. "Now, can I get up?"

Michal scanned his face. "Yes." She let him help her stand and followed her up. They gathered their clothes.

When they stepped inside, she turned to go to the bathroom, and he yanked on his jeans and turned toward the kitchen. "You've got to learn to trust me, Michal."

"I do trust you."

"You trust I'll have your six, and you trust me with your body, but you're still letting your mind hold us back."

"I'm trying."

"That's why I'm still here."

CHAPTER TWENTY

N ICK FOLLOWED THE sound of iron pounding on iron to the barn.
He handed Bailey an apple slice as he walked past and into the
back where Michal had a forge set up. The coals burned hot, and she
had a piece of iron inside, glowing red, yellow, and orange as it turned
to butter in the fire.

He leaned a hip against the frame of the doorway leading from the
main barn to her work area. Michal pounded a piece of iron, shaping it.
Her skin shown with perspiration, and she ran her forearm over her
forehead, then went back to work, the muscles in her arm flexing. Some
men might be intimidated by a woman with her physique but Nick
found her muscles damn sexy. Thick locks of hair fell from her braid
and curled under the heat.

Damn, she really was everything. Strong, sweet, gorgeous, humble,
smart, and talented. She had it all, and she was his.

She turned and startled. "Shit, Nick."

And a mouth like a Marine...perfect. He pushed off the frame
while she retrieved the chunk of iron from the fire and turned back to
the anvil.

Nick wrapped his arms around her waist and tugged her close.
"What ya makin'?"

"A horseshoe hat rack for Jared's shop." She nodded to the rack.
"Thought I'd add some decoration on top. He asked for it a couple
months ago." She angled her head so she met his gaze. "But I got
sidetracked."

"Really? I can't imagine anything throwing you off your game."

She narrowed her gaze at him. "Well, you see, this big Marine came struttin', all six foot six of himself, in my face, and I had to have a bite."

Nick tucked a lock of hair behind her ear and ran his fingertips over her jawline. "He's been known to indulge in a taste or two as well."

She chuckled. "Exactly." She started pounding the metal, forming something amazing out of bar stock. She swiped the back of her hand under her nose. "How was your day?"

He shrugged. "Good. Helped a company fill in a few holes in their system. Tim, Jared, and I hashed out what we'd like to see from our men in the next drills. Oh, and Eli kept us in stitches explaining his personal training program. The kid is outstanding."

She smiled. "He is."

He leaned back on the wood workbench. "Yes, ma'am. Poor Lucy, her boy is bound for the Marines. He's following in his father's footsteps for sure."

"Any father would love that."

She returned to shaping the iron and submerged it in water to cool it.

"He can already do three push-ups…modified, but still."

She chuckled, but it sounded forced, and pain wrinkled her forehead. "He's a little sweetheart."

He rested a hand on her shoulder. "Michal."

She shrugged off his hand and used tongs to pull another piece of iron from the fire.

"Wouldn't know it by how you treat the kid…"

Her gaze snapped to his, and her green eyes sparked with more fire than her pit. "What?"

"You barely look at Eli when he's around. Hell, have you even said two words to him? He sure doesn't act like you've ever given a fuck. Barely even knows you when we bring up your name."

"He doesn't? But, when they stayed the night I fixed him hot chocolate and everything. I don't try to ignore, Eli."

"Michal, when you made the hot chocolate did he know it?"

Her forehead wrinkled. "I gave the cup to Lucy, so she could make sure it wasn't too hot."

"Do you say hi? Grab his foot? Even ask Lucy about him?"

"Why are you being cruel?"

"I'm not, Lucky Charms, but just because we might not be able to have a child doesn't mean we should ignore every little one out there. I know it hurts…"

She slammed the iron hammer down on the anvil. "Stop saying that! Stop saying *we*, like anything is wrong with *you*. *You* can have children. *You* can have a hundred of them with whatever woman you choose…*I*…*I* can't have children. I don't ignore the little ones, at least I don't mean to. Maybe I just don't care about the stinkin' Worrells and their day-to-day affairs or how many push-ups their son can do!"

She turned on her heels and started to stomp out. "That's right, run away like always. Anything gets tough and you run."

Stopping, she turned and faced him standing toe to toe. "Why are you being an asshole?"

"Because you're being a real ass. You asked about my day, so I told you. Yeah, you don't have to like my friends, but you damn well better respect their place in my life just like I respect that jackoff vet you hang with. And I use *we* 'cause I kind of thought that's what the fuck we are, but maybe my definition of being engaged and being married is different from yours. You're the fucking woman I want, so if you can't have children neither can I, and we don't even know you can't. But I'm not going to punish Eli and every couple with children because of your insecure shit. And just so you know, Lucy is pregnant again, so don't act like a shit about it. Maybe act like you give a fuck, 'cause she seems to care about you."

This time he didn't give her time to stomp out, but about-faced and left her where she stood. He ran a hand over his head and tried to cool his blood. He'd had tough fights before when things went to shit and he was sure he wasn't walking out of it, but this with Michal was his toughest fight, and every time he kicked through one door, she put up a fucking wall.

Nick got into the truck and peeled out of the farmyard. He glanced at the barn and caught Michal at the doors, but kept on going.

MICHAL WATCHED THE truck tear out of the farmyard and down the road. When he'd told her a few nights ago she'd know when he was pissed, he was right. His face had been so hard and eyes dark as he spat hateful words…true words. She sank on a hay bale; they hurt, because they were true. She had asked him how his day was and proceeded to punish him because he knew how to enjoy Eli's antics. Pushing off the bale, she took care of the forge and cleaned up her work space.

After washing up, Michal glanced at the clock and frowned. She dressed in her yoga pants and a t-shirt and started a late supper. When the hamburgers were done, she ate, and still he wasn't back. Michal checked in the room to confirm his seabag was still there.

She startled when her cell phone rang. "Lucy?"

"Yeah, Mike, I wanted to let you know Nick will be staying at the shop tonight."

Her stomach twisted. "Is he okay?"

"He's drunk. Jared brought him home from the Big Horn Bar."

"Drunk?"

"Don't worry about it. It's not like he gets that way often, hasn't in forever. Must have been really upset about something."

Michal nodded to the empty room. She didn't doubt it was a rare thing. She felt a pang of guilt for driving him to a drunk. "Thanks for letting me know."

"Sure thing. Goodnight."

"Goodnight…Oh Lucy."

"Yes."

"Congratulations. Nick told me you were pregnant. That's wonderful."

"Thank you. That means so much."

"Well, goodnight."

"Oh, and Jared says when you get done being pigheaded and decide to sneak in to be with Nick, he put an extra key behind the sign on the door."

Michal crossed her legs and tried to sound normal. "Thanks."

She sat there on the sofa and stared at the old movie, *The Cowboy and the Lady*. The black and white movie reminded her of her and Nick, only she'd be in the role of the cowgirl, played by Gary Cooper, and Nick would be the city slicker, played by Merle Oberon. She glared at the hallway leading to the bedroom. Sitting here watching movies and avoiding their bed was something she reserved for his time at drills. Who cared if Jared and Lucy did know she wanted to go to him.

Uncurling from the couch, Michal closed up the house and checked on Bailey and Max before getting in her truck and heading toward Circle Dub Chocolates. She tried to be stealthy as she closed the pickup door and headed to the shop, but somewhere, she knew the Worrells knew she was there and were laughing at how she hadn't even lasted two hours after finding out where Nick was.

Patting the wall behind the sign, she found the small box holding the key and let herself inside. Letting her eyes adjust to the darkness in the shop, she found the door to the backroom and slipped inside.

Nick laid on his side, dead to the world, or so she thought until she curled against him. He draped his arm over her waist and pulled her closer, flopping a leg across hers. He nuzzled the back of her neck.

"Mmmm, you smell outstanding."

"You smell like smoke and beer."

He laughed. "Sorry, Michal."

"No, you were right. I was letting my self-pity keep me from enjoying my friends and their families."

"Yeah, but I didn't have to be such a motherfucker in how I talked to you."

"I wasn't very nice, either. I was an ass."

"Michal, let me apologize for shit sake."

Not wanting to fight again, she nodded. "Okay."

"I'm sorry, too, that I can't treat us both to a make-up fuck."

Michal shifted and rested a palm on his cheek. "Why?"

His forehead wrinkled. "I'd hurt you, sweetheart. Alcohol is not my friend, and I'd pound in you forever and never come, leaving you raw and both of us aching and unsatisfied."

Her hand dropped, but he caught it and brushed a kiss over her knuckles. She winced at his admission. "Oh, I'm sorry, too." She snuggled close. "But I just wanted to be with you."

He nodded and hugged her close. "Thanks for coming to me."

"Always," she whispered, his soft snores alerting her he'd already passed out. She pressed closer, tucking her head under his chin. "Always."

CHAPTER TWENTY-ONE

N ICK KEPT HIS eyes narrowed, allowing just enough sunshine through to see his surroundings, but not enough to kill him with the spears of light. He used to be able to hold his liquor and spring from his rack ready for PT at 0600. He shifted and groaned at his stomach twisting and the loss of his youthful abilities.

"Are you going to be a bear today?"

He frowned. Somewhere in his beer-filled dreams he remembered Michal joining him and pressing that sweet ass right against his groin. If he was right, they'd made their peace. Raising one eyelid higher, he growled at her smiling face hanging over his.

"Probably."

She nestled closer and rested her head on his chest. "Can I help?"

He shifted under her and stood. "Gotta hit the head, sorry."

Her chuckles followed behind him. Nick made quick work of emptying his bladder and came back into the room to find Michal sitting on the bed, her knees up to her chest and her arms around her knees. He gave what he hoped was a friendly smile and not the cringe he was sure it looked like.

"We did make up last night?"

"Yes."

He swiped his forearm across his forehead. "Whew."

She patted the bed. "Come lie down."

Nick bent to see under the blinds. The sun was starting its ascent, but not fully engaged.

"Better get back to the farm, change, and get my run in."

She frowned. "Stay with me a bit."

Nick shrugged and lay back on the bed. Michal curled along his side. "Lucy said you don't get drunk often."

"I don't anymore. I used to own stock in Coors, but those days are gone."

"I need to admit something to you."

He tossed an arm over his eyes. "God, Michal, I don't want to fight anymore."

"Neither do I, and I pray it won't be the cause of one."

Nick lowered his arm and held her gaze. "What?"

"Yesterday, I meant to tell you something, or ask you something…well whatever, then we fought, and I didn't get it said."

"Are you going to get it said today, Lucky Charms?"

She frowned. "I made an appointment to get my IUD taken out."

He raked his gaze over her. "Holy fuck, when did you do that?"

"I haven't yet, I made the appointment for a week from yesterday."

"Why?"

"Well, it takes a few months to get my system back on track, and so I thought…but I wanted to talk to you about it."

He sat up. "And what if I'm against it?"

"Are you?"

"I don't know, Michal. You make everything hinge around a child, and there's so much more to us. At least I hope so. I hope I'm not just some stud in line to see if it works with me, and if not, that's it, it's over."

Michal sat back on her knees. "I'm sorry I come off as this crazy woman determined to reproduce; it's not how I mean it. It's not how I feel about you…about us. And you're not just a stud to check off the list and move on. I thought we need to be making some firm decisions. Like, how long are we going to try the old fashioned way before we look at other alternatives, and what are those alternatives going to be? Or is it just going to be you and me, Bailey and Max forever? You've got me thinking of the future, City, but only a future with you."

He combed his fingers through her hair tucking a lock behind her ear. "Michal, are you shootin' straight with me right now?"

"Yes. I understand how you might doubt it, but I mean every word."

"Uncle Nick!"

A chubby toddler came strutting into the room. Nick smiled and swung Eli up onto the bed, but pinned Jared with a glare he hoped melted the man's balls.

Jared held up his hands. "Sorry, man. He knew you were here. We've already had one tantrum when we wouldn't let him bust in earlier."

"It's fine."

"Hi, Mike."

Her cheeks turned a light pink, but she didn't back down. "Good morning. What's for breakfast?"

"Huckleberry truffles."

"Yum."

Eli reached out and grabbed a small fistful of rich, golden hair. "Do I know you?"

"Eli, don't be rude." Jared admonished.

"He's fine." Michal smiled. "You know me. Remember I put shoes on horses."

The little boy's eyes brightened. "Yeah. Horse lady."

Nick shifted, sitting Eli on his lap. "Her name is Michal, Buddy."

"Mike."

Michal laughed and tickled his stomach. "That's right, just plain old Mike."

"Okay, son, you've seen Nick, and seen Mike again. Let's get to work."

Eli hugged Nick around the neck and turned and wrapped his chubby arms around Mike's neck, hugging her close. "Nick's." He pointed to Nick then back to Michal.

Nick mussed Eli's hair. "You got that right."

Jared swung his son into his arms. "We'll be back over in fifteen. Sorry it's all I can give you before I have to start working."

"We'll be gone."

Michal tipped her head to the side. "Sorry about last night."

Jared glanced at his son as if he wanted to say something completely rude about Nick; instead, he shrugged. "Not a problem. Glad you came over."

Jared shut the door behind him and Nick stood. He scrubbed a hand over his head. "You ready to go?"

Michal stood and he noticed she only wore her yoga pants and tank top. "What the hell, Michal?"

She lowered her gaze and cringed. "Not what I usually go out in, but I'm just going to the truck and then the farm. You coming?"

"You're not walking out of this place with that tight tank top and no bra. I feel like gouging Worrell's eyes out."

She slipped on her flip-flops. "Nick, don't be ridiculous. There's nothing wrong with this. I'm not fighting with you."

Nick wrapped his arm around her and over her chest. She glanced down and laughed. "Yes, that's so much more inconspicuous. I knew you were the possessive type, but this is going too far." She shrugged off his arm, and Nick opened his mouth, then shut it when her hand shot up. "Stop. The longer we fight, the later it gets, and more people will be up. If we go now, no one will even be out."

She turned, but he rested a hand on her arm. "Lucky Charms, keep the appointment next week."

She tipped her head to the side, and her eyes narrowed. "Are you sure that's what you want? Not just what I want?"

"It's what I want, too, I'll come with, and we can discuss other options with your doctor."

"Are you serious? You'd do that? Come with me?"

"Affirmative. It's our decision; I need all the facts, too."

Michal wrapped her arms around his waist and hugged him close. "Thank you, Nick."

He refrained from asking if Trevor ever went with her on any appointments, because her tight hug told the story. He didn't want any ghosts anywhere in his relationship with Michal, but the thoughts popped up like an enemy ambush.

"I'm thanking you, City, because you're thoughtful and sweet. Don't go there."

He squeezed her back in a silent thank you for reading his mind. "We better get out of here before Jared sends the whole damn family in to interrupt us."

He scooped her up and carried her to her truck. She smiled. "That's one way to keep me shielded I won't complain about."

Nick leaned in and pressed his mouth to hers kissing her thoroughly. "See you at home." He leaned away and closed her door.

"See you at home."

Nick got into Lucy's truck and frowned. He needed to get his own truck. He needed to get all of his things moved out to Wyoming. She'd never answered him about moving to San Diego. He felt the tug of his frown deepening. Michal hadn't answered him about a lot of things; instead, she started talking about going off birth control and focusing on making a family. Their whole relationship was ass backward.

MICHAL GLANCED BACK in her rearview mirror. Nick was right behind her. She was driving the poor man insane, and she knew it, but didn't know how to stop. He must have been longing for the days of dealing with insurgents in Iraq compared to the crazy Wyomingite he'd hooked his star to.

She pulled into the farmyard and met Nick at the front of the trucks. "I better check on Bailey."

"Yeah, I'm gonna change and head out on my run."

"Okay."

They stood still, and Michal held her breath, waiting for him. When he didn't make a move, she stepped closer and tipped her face to his. Nick ran the back of his fingers over her cheek, and she closed her eyes. When his mouth touched hers, Michal stretched so there was more pressure to the kiss.

His hands slid down her back and cupped her ass, pulling her flush against him. He pressed his mouth to her neck by her ear. "Why is your hair in a ponytail?"

She chuckled. "Because you were incapacitated and didn't take it down."

"Mmmm." He kissed her neck. "Let me set things right." He

smoothed a hand up her back and released her hair, digging one hand in her hair and the other in her ass. "You have to see about Bailey right away?"

She brushed a kiss on his neck. "Can you...are you able?"

He gave her hair a slight tug brining her gaze to his. "What the fuck does that mean?"

She felt the tug of her forehead wrinkling in confusion at the hostility in his voice. "Last night you told me when you drink you can't come...that you..."

"I told you that? Shit, I must have been more wasted than I thought."

She curled her fingers around the belt buckle separating her from the ultimate fire of being molded and melted into Nick. "So?"

The hand on her backside and the one in her hair tightened, keeping her pressed close. "Let's find out."

Nick's mouth crashed on hers, and he feasted on her. Vibrations shot up her thigh, and she moaned when another shot of vibrations tingled up her leg. She pushed back and laughed.

"Is that your phone, or something kinky you're trying?"

"Shit." He kept his hand tight on her ass, but pulled out his phone. "What, dammit?"

Michal watched as the creases in his forehead grew deeper and deeper.

"Yeah. Roger. Out."

His gaze dropped to her and the regret in his eyes reflected her own.

"You have to go?"

"Affirmative. But believe me, Lucky Charms, I do not want to."

She lowered so she stood flat on her feet allowing inches to separate them. "Well that really sucks."

He laughed and let her go. "You summed it up perfectly."

"Guess Bailey gets fed and cared for now after all."

"Lucky horse."

She lifted back on her feet and brushed a kiss on his lips. "See you tonight?"

"See you at supper."

"Even better."

Michal hugged his neck and gave him one more kiss before letting him go and heading to the barn. As always, she couldn't resist one last look and lifted her hand and smiled when he looked back and waved at her.

CHAPTER TWENTY-TWO

MICHAL DASHED FROM the bedroom to the ringing of a cell phone. She eyed Nick's phone on the table. He'd showered, dressed, and headed out before she was done with Bailey earlier that morning and must have forgotten his phone. She hesitated through one more stanza of the Marine Corps Hymn.

"Nick Walsh's phone?"

"First Sergeant?"

The woman's voice surprised Michal. She held the phone away from her and returned it to her ear. "No, this is Nick's fiancée. He left his phone."

"Nick has a fiancée? Oo-Rah!"

"May I ask who this is?"

"Oh, Roger. This is Major Lydia West. I need the First Sergeant's help with IT. Can't get shit done with NMCI. Do you have a number where I can reach him?"

"Yes, he's at Jared…I mean First Sergeant Worrell's…"

"Copy that. I'll just give the Chocolate Sergeant a call. Thanks…Oh, and good luck with Nick. He's a sweetheart, but a handful."

Before Michal could respond the cell phone beeped; Major West had ended the call. She frowned at the phone. Something in the major's voice didn't sound like a Marine major calling a first sergeant, Lydia West sounded like a woman who knew what a *handful* and then some Nick really was. Shaking her head, trying to rid it of the green-eyed monster, Michal tucked Nick's phone in her jeans pocket, grabbed her thermos of coffee and cooler with her lunch, and headed toward the Worrell's to return Nick's phone…and maybe get a little information on the good Major.

Michal raised her hand to knock on the Worrell's front door when it swung open, startling both her and Lucy.

"Crap, Mike, don't do that."

Michal dropped her hand from where it was clutching her chest. "I won't need coffee now."

Lucy laughed. "Come on in. You looking for one of us, or Nick?"

"Nick for now, but would you want to do lunch this Saturday?"

Lucy quirked her mouth in disappointment, and her shoulders fell. "I can't Saturday. Jared and I were going to the fair in Billings." Her hazel eyes rounded, and her smile returned. "Hey, you and Nick want to tailgate? Mom and Dad are watching Eli, so it'd just be the adults."

"Sounds fun."

Michal joined Lucy in turning her attention to the baritone voice behind them. She really had to pull it together when it came to the man. Just the sight of him did all sorts of magical things to her body, starting on the inside.

"You'd want to go to a fair?"

He leaned his shoulder against the entrance to the hall. "Absolutely."

Michal turned to Lucy. "It does sound fun. You guys staying the night?"

"Yep."

"Okay. I'll get reservations at the Boot Hill for Nick and me. I'll see if Dan can check on Bailey and Max."

Lucy's smile spread. "This is going to be so much fun!"

Michal cast a glance to Nick whose grin was pure devil. She smiled at Lucy. "I agree."

Lucy started around her. "Well, I'll leave you to your man while I track down my men. See you Saturday. We'll leave departure time to Nick and Jared."

Michal waved at Lucy's back and let the screen door shut behind her as she edged toward Nick. She tugged his phone from her pocket.

"You forgot this. Thought you might need it."

He hiked a brow, and instead of taking the phone, his hand covered hers, and he tugged her close. "Bullshit. You want to know who Lydia is."

She tilted her head and gave a *you caught me* grin. "A little bit curious, yes."

Nick pushed off the wall and framed her face with his hands. "God, you're beautiful, you know that?"

She smiled. "She was that good, huh?"

He laughed. "Lydia, Major West, is one of the best damn head docs in the Marines. Affirmative, I visited her in a professional capacity after my fourth tour. Affirmative, we dated after I stopped seeing her in the aforementioned capacity. Affirmative, we did what I see playing out in your eyes. Affirmative, Lydia is beautiful woman, reminds me of the actress Emayatzy Corinealdi. She gets the comparison a lot and hates it. But hell no, she doesn't hold a candle to you in any capacity. We served a purpose for each other; that purpose is over, but we are good friends. You satisfied, Lucky Charms?"

She felt the tug of her frown. "Did she help you?"

"We helped each other. Lydia was feeling pretty down herself after she was severely burned from the neck down during a mortar attack in Iraq."

"How horrible. That must have been so painful."

"It was. We okay?"

"Yes."

"We okay because you feel sorry for Lydia, or because you know how I feel about you?"

"Because I know how you feel about me. You already said she's beautiful, so I assume she'd be competition anyway..."—he opened his mouth, but she shook her head—"if you didn't love me."

"Exactly."

His hand dropped, and she felt the tug of her ponytail and then her hair falling loose. She sighed. "You know, I had my hair fixed for work?"

"I thought so. I just wanted it fixed for me for a few minutes." He tugged her behind him into the room he was using as his office. Before she knew what he was up to, he tugged her t-shirt and bra down under her breasts and bent, kissing the top of each one.

Michal laughed and pushed away from him, laughing harder at his frown when she adjusted her clothes. She nodded to the large print of Jared. "No way can I do that in here with that"—she pointed at the poster—"staring at us."

"Damn Worrell. He ruins all my fun."

"Nick, what if I would have been in a jealous rage about Lydia?"

"I would have stepped way back. It's one thing to question me because of your past experiences. It's another to question my past experiences."

"I can understand that. You've never questioned my past choices."

"Never will. Because that's what they are—the past. Now what about our near future and finally finishing what we've started about ten times this morning."

"You know, funny you should mention our interrupted morning fun." She pulled her hair back and fastened the elastic band around the thick ponytail, smiling as his frown deepened. "I'll be working in the north field at the Killeen's ranch around lunch. No one for miles and miles. Just ask them to point the way and drive out to see me."

Nick hooked her waist and pulled her to him. "What time?"

"Twelve thirty."

"I'll be there."

"I'll warn you. I'll be dirty and sweaty."

"I'll warn you, you'll be a lot dirtier and sweatier when I'm done with you."

She chuckled. "Yeah, I figured."

NICK SMILED AROUND Michal's flesh as she came apart while he left one last hickey on her breast. She'd given him full access to her body in and outside the hot truck. Making love with her spread wide in the ninety degree sunshine was a hot, sweaty, steamy, fuckin' dream come true. He released her breast and brushed kisses on her belly, bringing her back down to earth.

"You are the tastiest lunch I've had in forever, Lucky Charms."

She pushed off the seat of the truck and wrapped her legs around him where he stood outside the truck door. Wrapping her arms around his neck, she captured his mouth in a hungry kiss. Nick let her guide the kiss until she dropped her head under his chin, her thick honey locks draping her face.

"Lord, City, how am I supposed to move after all that?"

"That's what you get when you ask me to reapply your sunscreen."

She lifted those amazing green eyes to meet his gaze. "You'll have to apply some more now."

He wagged his eyebrows. "My pleasure."

She shifted and knelt on the seat. Nick took the opportunity to pull up his shorts and jeans so his ass didn't burn. When his gaze met the sight of her kneeling naked before him, he swallowed hard. "Get dressed, Michal."

Her eyes widened, and he knew she recognized the command and the meaning behind it. If she didn't cover her ass, he was going to have it again.

Michal tugged on her bra, panties, and t-shirt, and with each layer, Nick cursed the need to work and wear clothes. If life was fair, his reward for years of service would be Michal naked and under him twenty/seven. He'd give her some time to eat, sleep, and just chat with him.

She wrapped her arms around his neck, and Nick rested his hands on her hips. She bent and brushed a kiss over his chest where his purple shirt still hung open. "I love the taste of you on my tongue."

He closed his eyes and tightened his grip. "Do you know how much I love when you say things like that?"

She lifted her head and smiled. "Yes." She sat back. "Do you want some actual food?"

"I'd love to stay, sweetheart, but I've gotta get back to work or Hailey will beat my ass."

"Yeah, I better get back to work, too." She slid from the truck, but turned and grabbed the cooler on the floorboard. "At least take a water with you."

He tried not to smile like an idiot as he buttoned his shirt, but having someone give a shit about him felt better than being personally pinned by Chesty Puller.

She turned and was so close her body brushed against his. She matched his groan and handed him the water. "I might be a little later than I originally thought. They've added a few more horses. I'll also need to ride Bailey. He missed his ride last night, and I didn't have time this morning."

He downed the water, and she handed him another. He glared at the horses in the field.

"It's not their fault, City."

"I know. I'm just pissed 'cause I'll be later, too."

She canted her head to one side and her forehead wrinkled.

"Hey, what's up?"

"We sound like a married couple."

"And that's bad?"

"No, it's great. Sometimes, I worry I'll screw this up."

"You can't, Michal; honest to god, you cannot screw this up." He brushed his lips across hers. "But you can screw me anytime." He wagged his eyebrows and got the smile he was after.

She pushed against his chest. "Go. You're a bad influence on me."

"I'm trying my damnedest to be."

Grabbing fistfuls of his shirt she pulled him close and kissed him. "Thank you."

"Anytime, Lucky Charms. Anytime, anyplace, you just call."

Nick swallowed the last of his water and tossed the empty bottle in the sack she kept in her truck for trash. He kissed Michal and turned.

"How old is Major West?"

"Don't even, Michal. I am not going there with you. Not after being inside you a hundred ways to Sunday and feeling good."

"No, I don't mean it like that. I just wondered how old a major was."

He lifted an eyebrow. "About my age, I'd guess."

"You don't know for sure?"

"Nope. I really don't give a shit, Michal. And she obviously didn't either. We didn't share our driver's licenses for all the stats."

"Don't get all pissy. I was reading one of the books Lucy let me borrow and wondered about the rates and ranks, officer versus enlisted, and everything."

"Stop reading all that shit. Why do you need to know any of it?"

"Nick, you're a Marine. I want to know about you. What? You don't plan on me ever being around your Marine buddies except Jared?"

He honestly hadn't pictured her at a barbecue held by one of his buddies, or hanging around an installation. It was hard picturing Michal outside of Wyoming. She was like a wildflower, once picked and placed in a new location, it would wilt and die. He groaned at his thoughts. What a bunch of poetic puke. He must be in deeper than even he realized.

"We can talk about all that later. I really gotta go."

"Okay. Sorry I brought it up."

"Not a problem. I had premature e-jackass-ulation."

He stepped into the truck and leaned out. "Oh, we thought we'd head to Billings by seven for a whole day of fair fun."

"Sounds good. We'll see you tonight, City. Thanks again for a yummy lunch."

"Ditto."

Nick put the truck in reverse, flipped a uey and headed across the field toward the dirt road. He glanced in the rearview mirror and lifted the hand hanging out the side window in a return wave at Michal. He turned his gaze to the road, but his thoughts remained with her. Why hadn't he ever pictured her among his Marines?

"HEY, MAN, NO shit on this, but did you picture Lucy hanging out with us from the get?"

Jared stopped adding up the till and lifted a brow but didn't smile or give Nick crap. "Not from the get, but by the time I was sold on marriage."

"And you knew she'd fit? Like bringing her to active duty training, you knew she'd be Marine approved?"

"I knew she was mine, and you guys would accept that and accept her because of it."

"Yeah, I get that. But did you think she'd fit, I mean really be accepted like she is as one of the family."

"What's this about, Walsh?"

"Lucy gave Michal some of those books on OIF in all its evolutions and glory. She's been reading some and asking me more. I don't care about her knowing, but she's asking about Marine rates and shit, and it got me thinking... I've never pictured her hanging out with the wives during active duty training. Lucy and you here in Wyoming, yes, her hanging out at a Marine social? I'm not sure I see it."

"Well, keep that shit to yourself if you're serious about marrying her."

"Fuck, I know that. I'm not a dipshit."

Jared shook his head. "You can't compare my relationship to Lucy, or Tim's relationship with Hailey, to what you have with Mike. And if I were you, I wouldn't give a hot damn if she fit anywhere else but in your arms, brother."

"Thanks."

"Anytime."

"I was being sarcastic."

"So was I."

Nick refrained from entering a battle of insults with Jared. Something like that, if done properly, could take hours, and he didn't have that kind of time.

"See ya tomorrow."

"Not if I can duck and cover soon enough."

"Asshole."

"Just stay out of the bars, buttmunch; I need my beauty sleep."

"Yeah, too bad it won't help with your face. A baboon's butthole is better looking."

"Wouldn't know, I've never fucked a baboon."

Nick opened the door. "No, as I recall, you preferred goats." He shut the door before he could hear Jared, knowing his buddy had responded despite the oak barrier separating them.

He'd have to admit it someday, but it'd be when they were both deep into a few beers, when he told Worrell the man was right. He needed to get his head dislodged from his six and stop giving a shit if Michal fit with anyone else except him.

CHAPTER TWENTY-THREE

NICK HANDED OVER the money and took the deep fried Milky Way, handing it to Michal with a smile. "You're going to be sick for days eating all this crap."

She wrinkled her nose and stuck out her tongue. "What good is going to the fair without sampling the food?"

He shook his head and draped an arm over her shoulders as they continued walking the carnival midway.

"How can you be satisfied with a Philly steak sandwich and onion rings?"

"I'm saving my craving for something sweet for later."

"What about my impending stomachache?"

"I'll pick up Pepto on the way to the hotel."

She took a bite of the fried candy bar and moaned. "Oh, this is almost as good as sex."

"Wow, my competition is a fried lump of chocolate and nougat. I need to step up my game."

Michal hip-checked him. "If you win me one of those stuffed bull-dogs over there, you'll surpass the chocolate and nougat as first in my heart once again."

Nick turned toward the shooting game she'd nodded to and smiled. Sure enough, one row of stuffed animals was comprised of bulldogs of various sizes. Nick eyed the largest size.

"Deal."

He reached for his wallet, but she covered his hand. "Don't go overboard. I know you can win the largest, but I just want the size before."

Nick nodded and smiled at her faith in his ability. He slapped down his money and listened to the guy give unneeded instructions. He winked at Michal and stepped behind the toy rifle.

When he handed her the stuffed bulldog she frowned. "I said not the biggest." But she hugged the prize.

"Sorry, Lucky Charms, but what if Worrell played this game? No way in hell was I walking back to the parking lot with him and Lucy and her holding a bigger bulldog than you."

She drew a circle in the air with her eyes. "Is everything a competition?"

"Except who has the finest woman. We don't go there."

Taking his hand and lacing their fingers together, she fell into step with him. "Really?"

"Worrell, Hayes, and I will talk shit about every little thing, but not our women. It's just not done."

"That's sweet."

"That's us...sweet."

She squeezed his hand. "Thanks for being patient with me while I looked over every horse like they were mine."

"That's what we sweet guys do."

She nudged his arm. "Yes, it is. And thank you for going to the rodeo."

"Michal, it's what we're here for."

"Did you enjoy it?"

"I did, but I kind of liked the one in Ten Sleep more."

"I just fell in love with you a bit more."

They fell into silence as the bright lights of the midway swirled in front of them. The place was overrun with teenagers and couples of all ages as most of the families with children had left after the rodeo.

Michal rested her head on his arm. "I'm tired."

"Yeah, I'm ready to call it a night, too. I wonder where the Worrells are?" He pulled out his phone to call Jared.

"Mike?"

Her body stiffened, and she squeezed his hand like it was her last tie to earth. "Don't leave."

"I wasn't going to."

A tall cowboy came up to Michal's side. The man had a full head of gray hair and deep wrinkles carved in his face, appearing not much younger than Michal's father. Nick had a sick feeling.

"Trevor."

On Michal's confirmation of the man's identity, Nick slipped his phone in his pocket.

The man gave Nick a visual inspection, and Michal cleared her throat. "Trevor, this is Nick, my fiancé. Nick this is…"

"Yeah, I know." He held out the hand Michal wasn't clinging to and shook Trevor's hand as much as he wanted to drag Michal away. When she realized he was done talking to her ex-husband, Michal stepped closer to him, but kept her gaze on the asshole who'd treated her like shit and cheated on her.

"What are you doing here?"

Trevor nodded to a woman talking to a group of teenagers and preteens. "Staci and I moved to Montana a couple years ago. We're here chaperoning the two oldest and their dates.

Nick watched for pain to streak through her gaze or for her to cringe. Instead, she nodded. "That's nice. We've gotta go."

"Hey, Mike, I'm glad everything worked out for you."

Her gaze narrowed. "You can be such an asshole."

"What?"

"You've got a lot of nerve coming up to me and acting like you give a shit. Like you ever did. All I ever was to you was a young body you could use to get what you really wanted. When I couldn't give you what you wanted, you didn't even comfort me, or maybe take precautions so my body could heal. I don't give a fuck if you're glad."

Nick started walking, tugging her along with him and leaving the motherfucker gaping after them. "I am so damn proud of you Michal Dunn, I'm about ready to burst. You are so fuckin hot."

"I'm glad you're proud. It makes me sick when I think of all the times I lay under him hoping…" She shoved the bulldog in his arms and dashed to trash can. Her heaves could be heard for miles, he was sure.

He stepped in front of her, shielding her from those who tried to gawk. When the retching subsided, he reached in his pocket and handed her a peppermint.

She gave him a small smile. "Thank you."

He smoothed the back of his fingers over her cheek. "You're welcome, Lucky Charms. Let's get out of here."

She took back the stuffed dog, and her mouth curved in a small flicker of smile. "Yeah."

"Hey guys." Jared and Lucy stepped from the crowd. Jared's gaze shot from Nick to Michal. Nick couldn't even find humor in the fact Lucy was indeed holding an equally large stuffed bulldog. "Everything okay?"

"Yeah, we're heading to the hotel."

"You sure? We were just going to see if you wanted to head somewhere for food and drink?"

Nick shook his head. "Naw, we're calling it quits."

"See you tomorrow then."

MICHAL SNUGGLED INTO Nick's side when he draped his arm over her shoulders and started out of the fairgrounds. "You sure you don't want to get a drink with Jared and Lucy?"

"Yep. Did you? I guess I did just speak without asking."

"No, I didn't want to."

He hugged her close and dropped a kiss on the top of her head. "You feeling better?"

"I am. Just ticked off I let him get to me."

"Honestly, I think you needed it. You never got a chance to look him in the face and tell him to fuck himself. Now that door is closed."

"Is that what your psychiatrist girlfriend would say?"

Nick stopped short and tipped her face up to meet his with a finger under her chin. She tried to hold onto her frown, but she couldn't keep from laughing at his sour face.

"You're a brat."

He kissed her forehead before opening the door on her side of the truck. She set the bulldog in the center between them and waited, biting her lower lip.

"Oh hell no."

She laughed and looked around the stuffed animal to find Nick's face folded into a frown to rival the bulldog's. His eyes narrowed, and she looked into the face of First Sergeant Walsh. "Don't even play, Michal."

With another laugh, she slid over to the center seat and put the dog on the passenger seat. "Despite running into Trevor, tonight was a lot of fun."

"Affirmative."

She studied him as he checked the mirrors and backed out of the parking spot and drove the short distance to the Boot Hill hotel in the section of Billings known as the Heights. It hit her how much she'd gotten used to him being around. When he stopped the truck, she caressed his cheek with the back of her fingers as was his habit with her.

"You didn't say anything to Trevor."

He lifted an eyebrow. "I didn't have anything to say to the man. Did you want me to say something?"

"No. That came out accusatory, and it's not how I meant it. I admire your ability to remain cool, to know when to speak and when to let someone else handle things. Like the night at the Brewing Co what seems like years ago, you could have told me to stick it. Instead, you went with Charlene and let me figure things out."

"The tactic worked out for me that is for damn sure."

She smoothed her fingers down his face again. "Worked out for me, too."

He opened the door and slid out. "Glad you think so."

Michal followed him out the driver's side and turned back to retrieve the dog. They didn't speak as they made their way to the room. Michal took a quick shower and was a bit disappointed when Nick didn't join her, but got in after her. She slipped on one of his clean t-shirts and sat on the bed waiting for him. Glancing at the clock when the water stopped running, she nodded, five minutes. The man could wash down quicker than it took her to wash her hair.

He stepped out of the bathroom with a white towel wrapped around his waist and Michal swallowed around the lump of pure lust. His tanned skin contrasted with the white of the towel, and his hard muscles seemed harder.

The fire in her belly turned cold when he flipped on the TV and flopped on the bed beside her using one of his arms for a second pillow. She glanced at the movie playing and back to him.

"Nick?"

His gaze didn't flash to her. He hadn't even glanced her way since entering the room. "Yeah, sweetheart?"

She straddled his waist and forced eye contact. "We're in a hotel room, City, the place made for nights to do all the illicit things you usually reserve for the cab of my pick-up truck. You'd rather watch *SportsCenter* than have your wicked way with me?"

He slipped his arm from behind his head and gripped her thighs with both hands. "I didn't think you'd be in the mood."

She sat back and shook her head to clear the crazy thought. "In the mood for you? Always...seriously always. Because of Trevor?"

"Before you puked, you said something about lying under him and hoping...you've used the same words in regard to me at one time after that night at the lake."

She framed his face with her hands. "God, Nick, not even close. I didn't finish." She gave a harsh laugh. "With him, I rarely did." He frowned and she pressed her lips to his forehead. "I meant lying under him, hoping he'd finish quickly because it was just a duty. And yes, hoping I'd become pregnant, because then he'd stop berating me and leave me alone. With you..." She rested her forehead against his. "With you, I'm complete and filled with everything a woman should feel when a part of the man she loves. And yeah, I hope, because I want a child with you not because it's your dream, but because it became mine, too. That's the huge difference, City. With Trevor, it was his dream, and I wanted to see it done for him. With you, I want it because a child will be something else we share."

His rough palms smoothed up her thighs and continued up her

sides, and Michal leaned back and lifted her arms, wrapping them around his neck after he stripped her. He lay back and ran his palms from her belly to her breasts where he molded her flesh. Michal pushed forward to fill his hands more and moaned.

"You are the only man who has brought me pleasure like this."

He lifted and replaced his hand with his mouth on one breast while continuing to pleasure her other breast with his hand. Michal's body began to tremble, and she hugged him close. She pressed her lips together to keep from crying out, but he didn't bring her to full orgasm.

He gripped her waist and rolled. Moving between her legs, he kissed her sex and Michal compressed her lips harder as he licked and sucked and kissed, but once again, he stopped when she couldn't suppress a deep grunt as her orgasm started.

He moved over her and captured her mouth as he slid his cock deep inside her sex. She tore her mouth from his and pressed her mouth to his ear. "Say something, Nick." She arched back as he rocked, keeping his strokes slow and steady so she felt every part of his length inside her.

Nick rocked back into her. "What can I say to you, Michal, that my body hasn't already?"

She locked her ankles on his back and kissed his neck. "Nothing."

When her orgasm hit, Michal buried her face in his shoulder, screaming at the intensity he'd been building since he first touched her. Nick captured her mouth and used the kiss to buffer his bellow when he rammed deep as his climax consumed him and moved through her.

He didn't move to roll from her, and Michal continued to cling to him. "There is one downfall to hotel sex."

"What?" He nuzzled her neck.

"I just can't scream. I've never understood those who could cut loose and let the whole place know what's going on."

He moved lower brushing a kiss on the top of a breast. "You don't?"

Michal gripped his shoulders. "Please don't."

He stopped and slid back up, capturing her mouth in a slow, soul-stealing kiss. When he broke the kiss, he hovered above her and scanned her face.

"You realize September is right around the corner, Lucky Charms?"

She squirmed under him. "Yes."

"I'm not trying to be a shit and ruin tonight, but I gotta get back to San Diego."

"You do?"

"Yeah, sweetheart, I do."

Michal hooked a leg over his back and he laughed. "You gonna hold me here, Michal?"

"You asked me to marry you."

"And you said yes."

"Nick, please don't do this tonight."

Fire flared in his blue gaze. "When? Either you're coming with me, or you're staying in Wyoming."

"I can't go." She couldn't get enough oxygen past the pain in her chest to push the words out in anything but a small whisper.

Michal braced for his anger, or disappointment, or both. It was so much worse than what she could have ever imagined. It wasn't anger, disappointment, or any hostility; it was resignation settling in his eyes and he nodded. As though he expected to be rejected. She remembered the same pain in his gaze after they'd first had sex, and he told her about his foster parents cutting him loose just like she planned to do.

"Nick..."

His mouth covered hers as his hand slid down her side and under her thigh, hiking her leg higher as his erection grew inside her. He took his time with his kiss and his lovemaking, bringing her close so many times only to bring her back down and using his cock and tongue to bring her to boil again.

Michal ran her hands over any part of him she could reach, desperate to feel every part of him inside and out of her body. She opened her eyes to find him staring at her, his eyes the color of the blue in the center of a flame. She hoped he could see through her to what she really wanted, how she really felt. She prayed he'd give her just a little more time; she was so close to being whole. He was so close to breaking through the last pile of bricks still standing from the walls she'd erected for ten years.

He tore his mouth from hers and, bowing his back, roared her name as if he truly wanted everyone, not just those in the hotel, but for two states to hear him and know who held him. Michal clung to him as her own orgasm rolled through her. He rolled to his back, and she dropped kisses over his face and down his neck and chest.

"Nick…" He tugged her up so they were nose to nose.

"I don't want to talk about it, Michal. If I have to leave you in a week, I'm not spending time rehashing shit…"

She pushed away from him. "A week?"

"Hailey needs me on site on a job. I might have been able to push it back if we needed to pack your stuff, but if it's just me, I really need to get back."

She scanned his face. "But we have that appointment next week."

His forehead bunched. "You don't think that point's kind of moot, sweetheart?"

"No, I don't."

"Then I'll make sure to be there and leave next Saturday."

"Next Saturday." She mumbled.

He cupped her face. "Come on, Lucky Charms, that gives us six days of debauchery."

She lay on top of him and wrapped her arms around his neck. He roped his arms around her and hugged her close. She pressed closer. "I just want to hold you for a bit."

"That works, too."

She wanted to scream at him for being so calm and ask if his heart wasn't exploding in his chest, but she didn't. She didn't need to, as his arms tightened around her and his heart beat fast under her ear.

CHAPTER TWENTY-FOUR

"H EY, WALSH." JARED stood outside the dorm room he'd been assigned for drills at the University of Utah.

Nick tossed his ruck on the rack. "Worrell. How's everything with you and Lucy?"

"Outstanding."

He pushed down the lump of pure hot jealousy. "Everything all right with the pregnancy?"

"Affirmative. How's everything on the coast?"

"Runnin' around like a one-legged man at a butt kickin' contest."

"That why you haven't talked to Mike?"

"Haven't talked to Michal because, honestly, I don't know what the fuck to say. I said it all a month ago when I left, and she pretty much shoved it in my face. You want to go for some chow and a beer?"

Jared stepped in front of him. "Fuck you, Walsh. A beer? I'm not letting you brush this off. You gave her a fuckin' week to decide…"

Nick shoved his fellow first sergeant. "Fuck you, I gave her three months asshole, three months of telling her every fuckin' day how much I wanted her, loved her, would give anything for her. So don't give me shit about a week. I asked her to marry me; she said yes. I even sat in a fuckin' doctor's office talking about a baby that's never going to happen. When it came time to put it on the line, she folded."

Jared didn't budge and neither did Nick. He was nursing a hurt, and if Worrell wanted to step forward as punching bag of the day that would suit him just fine.

"What the holy hell?"

Nick didn't even glance at Tim. "Nothin' Hayes. Just step down. I'm not in the mood for you to pile more shit on the mountain Worrell here built."

"Don't be a fucktard, Walsh. And Worrell, back the hell down. We have incoming and they don't need to see their first sergeants measuring dicks."

Each nodded and stepped back, the tension deflating to a level where fists wouldn't be introduced to jaws.

"Sorry, Walsh. I overstepped."

Nick waved Jared off. "We both did. Let it go."

Tim cut a look between the two. "This about Michal?"

Nick glared. "Drop it, Hayes. I'm not askin'. Drop it."

Tim held up his hands in surrender. "I don't even know the woman. I know you weren't such a bastard when you were with her." Before Nick could take Tim out, Hayes spoke again. "Stow your gear; Colonel wants to meet with us for five about tomorrow's drill.

After the briefing with the colonel, Nick joined Jared and Tim at a local sports bar. By mutual unspoken agreement they talked Marine business and memories. Nick knew it was coming though, so he tried to steer the conversation for as long as possible.

"Marksmanship tomorrow, huh, not sure it required the level of briefing we just endured. None of us have seen Maggie's Drawers in fucking ever."

Jared snorted. "Hell no. I expected death by PowerPoint at any minute. *This is the stock, this is the barrel, don't point it at the privates of Darryl...*"

Nick almost spewed beer. "You've been saving up that one, buddy?"

"I've had it in the arsenal for a few years."

Hayes shook his head. "My friend, you don't amaze me much, but you've got a talent with the lines."

"That would mean so much more coming from someone else."

Nick coughed to cover his laughter and in an attempt to stay out of the insult machine.

"All right, I have to ask or Hailey is gonna kick my ass, and I don't want my baby son seeing that. What's going on with this Michal? Hails says you don't give her grief anymore and take any she dishes out in the balls without response."

He wished he would have joined in tossing the bullshit as Jared and Tim both locked in on him. He took a deep draw of beer then lifted his hands and shrugged. "I honestly don't know, man. But I'm done begging for a woman to give a shit. I wanted her and a family." He gave a harsh laugh. "Screw that, I wanted her as my family."

"Thought you were going to settle down in Wyoming, though?"

"Kind of wanted to discuss the options. I know this makes me sound like a real shit, but after a bit, I kind of wanted to see if she was willing to give up everything for me like I would for her." He turned to Jared. "You or Lucy tell her any of this shit, and I swear you won't have to worry about fathering another child."

"Don't be an ass, Walsh, you know we wouldn't."

"I know, I just wanted to say it out loud."

"So, what's the next step?"

"Don't know if there is one. She still having trouble with that shit-head farrier?"

"Some. Looks like he might be wreaking havoc around Kaycee."

He rubbed the back of his neck. "She doesn't go out to those jobs alone? Right?"

"No, Dan always goes with her and stays late if it's needed even though he and his wife have a new little one, and Mike fights him tooth and nail."

Nick pushed back from the table and stepped off the high top chair. "I'm headed back and hitting the rack."

"You okay, man?"

He tossed a couple bills on the table. "Affirmative. Just thought I better find me a manual or something describing the various parts of an M-16."

His friends laughed, and Nick tossed them a wave before heading out. He stepped out into a cool September night and cringed. September. He was supposed to have been skipping drills that month because he would have been newly married. Instead, he'd be spending the weekend listening to his brothers talk about their wives and children and ask him if he was all right every time they talked about their families. What really bit it was, after this weekend, Michal wouldn't be waiting for him, or driving up late and joining him on a porch swing. He'd be headed back to an empty apartment on a busy boardwalk. Even a busy boardwalk would be paradise with Michal.

"Mike?"

Michal came out of her trance. "Shit!" She pulled the iron out of the fire and submerged it in water. "Sorry."

Lucy and Dan shared a look. Michal frowned and turned to attach the horseshoe to the horse's hoof. Straddling the horse's leg she started nailing the iron to the hoof, ignoring her friends. She finished and swiped her forearm over her forehead.

"Did Jared get home okay?"

Every day, the pain of missing Nick grew more unbearable, but the other night, when he should have been pulling into the farmyard and showing her in a million ways how much he missed her, it had almost doubled her over.

"Yes. You want to know about Nick?"

"Yes."

"He's been kept hopping with onsite work. But he misses you."

"He said that?"

"No. It was other things he said."

Michal nodded and took in Lucy in a big sweater hiding her baby bump. All Michal had to do was go with Nick or, hell, ask him to stay, and instead of pounding hoof, she could be on her honeymoon. She knew the second he drove away, a simple *please stay* would have kept him by her side forever.

"Hooves look like they're healing up nicely, Dan."

"Yep. Thank Gerry for letting us board these horses here at the Circle W."

Lucy nodded. "I will. What happened?"

"That jerkoff really messed the mares up. A couple had to be euthanized; they were too far gone. The guy who owned 'em was so torn up, he lost it. We'll have to find homes for them all."

Michal fit the corrective shoe to the horse's hoof with a pad between hoof and shoe while Dan recounted the mess they'd found on a ranch between Buffalo and Kaycee. It was another rancher who reported it to Dan since he'd known him from when Dan worked that area.

"Why do people keep hiring him?"

Michal shook her head and stood. "I don't understand it either. His prices are a lot lower than mine, but you'd think word of mouth among the ranching communities would have stopped him. I'm wondering if he's not someone known or from a known family and people keep giving him a chance. Although, I was up at Hyattville the other day and no one up there has had a problem."

Eli came scampering into the barn with Patty Thomas close on his heels, the smile of a loving grandmother spread on her face. He stopped short in front of Michal and pointed.

"Nick's." Michal's breath caught and she froze.

Lucy swung the toddler up. "Enough of that. She has a name, and you know it."

"Michal."

Michal grabbed his booted foot. "Just Mike remember?"

The boy's forehead scrunched in a frown, and he shook his head. "Nick says Michal."

She let go of the foot and stepped back. "He does, doesn't he?" Michal met Dan's gaze.

"I need to ask a big favor." She cut her gaze back to Lucy. "From you, too. From all of you."

CHAPTER TWENTY-FIVE

"THANKS FOR DRIVING me down, Lucy."

Her friend's hazel eyes sparked with mischief. "I wouldn't miss it for the world. I hate I couldn't tell Jared."

Michal cringed. "Sorry, I swore you to secrecy. I just didn't want anything said to Nick until I was one hundred percent sure I could do this."

Lucy rested a hand on her shoulder. "You can."

Michal cut a look to the cover sheltering her suitcases in the truck bed. "I'll leave those there just in case."

Lucy nodded. "It's ten to four, you better head on over. Jared said they're dismissed right at 1600."

Michal inhaled a deep breath and slipped from the truck. She tugged her black wool coat closed as a few sugary snowflakes danced in the late October sky. A few days ago she'd driven into Sheridan and bought a beautiful peach Western skirt and matching blouse for this moment. Now she realized why she'd gotten such a great price. It was most definitely a summer outfit. That's what she got for filling her wardrobe with jeans, flannel, and t-shirts. At least the buff new cowboy boots fit her like a glove and kept her feet warm.

She smiled when she stepped into the portion of the parking lot where Lucy told her Fox Company 2/23 mustered and was dismissed. Her internal conversation kept her mind occupied until she made it to a sea of Marines in utilities milling around, most heading out until they saw her.

Tugging the coat closer, she started through the ocean of camo searching the faces of the tallest and most muscular to find Nick. She bit her lip when she caught sight of Jared, and his eyes grew big before he slapped the arm of the big Marine standing next to him.

Nick gave a look like he might deck Jared before his gaze connected with hers. She bit her bottom lip to keep from smiling at how damn hot he looked in his utilities. She bet he made women wet with a look in any of his service or dress uniforms, and suddenly, she desperately wanted to see him in those uniforms, wanted to see her City in jeans and Western shirt, and wanted to coldcock the first woman who looked at him.

He didn't move toward her, but remained glued to his spot next to Jared. She wondered if he was waiting to see if she'd walk all the way to him or turn tail and run. Jared stepped away from Nick, but only went so far. Lucy must have followed. Another big Marine kept his place by Nick, but he was smiling like a fool. She recognized him as Tim Hayes, but didn't spare him even a nod. It seemed everyone wanted to see the show. She should be used to making a fool of herself for Nick Walsh; only for him would she walk through crowds and declare her heart.

In a flash, everyone else disappeared as she stood in Nick's shadow. He still didn't move, giving her all the time she needed to say what she needed to say. She decided to keep it simple.

"I love you, Nick. I'm sorry I let you go, and I want to be where you are always. May I go home with you?"

"Where is that home, Michal?"

She squeezed her hands into fists fighting the tears threatening to close her throat. "Anywhere you are." She tossed a quick look back at the parking lot. "I brought some things. I can be happy in San Diego. I can be happy anywhere with you. I want you."

"What about Bailey, Max, the farm?"

She frowned, frustrated he'd made no move to touch her, or act the least bit pleased. "Nick, don't you want me?"

His eyes flashed blue fire, and a look of pure possession transformed his face into something that set a fire in her belly and had her stepping back at the same time. He gripped her coat and pulled her flush against him as he bent and captured her mouth. It was a kiss that left no doubt just how much he wanted her, how frustrated he was that she'd let him squirm for two months, and how much he'd kill the first man who thought she wasn't his.

Michal pressed closer, happy to oblige and announce she didn't want anyone but him. She gasped when he broke the kiss and grabbed her hand, leading her through cheering and catcalling Marines.

When they got to the stairs inside, he tossed her over his shoulder and started taking the stairs two at a time. Michal slapped his ass in a half-hearted protest trying to hide her smile. Once inside his dorm room, he set her on her feet. Her smile dropped. There was no play in his eyes, no tug of a smile on his mouth.

She backed up as he stepped forward until she was forced to sit on the bed with him towering over her. "I've answered your question, Michal, now answer mine."

"Bailey is boarded at the Circle W until I can make arrangements in San Diego. Max is there, too, in their barn. I sold the farm."

"You did what?"

Her neck hurt from staring up for miles. He stepped back, allowing her to stand, with deft movements he had her up against the wall with him still towering over her.

"I sold the farm. I told you I want to be where you are."

"Who'd you sell it to?"

"I don't know. They went through a broker. It sold quickly."

He cupped her neck and ran the pads of his thumbs over her jawline. She sank into his touch. "Finally."

"Finally?"

"You're touching me."

His face broke in a smile. "Thought I was doing a good job of touching you before?"

"No, you were punishing me, possessing me, and telling everyone I'm yours. Now you're touching me, and it feels so good."

"Yeah, it does, and damn I'd love to touch more, but not here."

Michal laughed more in relief it was going so well than in humor. "You've made love to me in a truck, by a lake, on my porch, and a hundred other places, but a room with a bed...yeah, that would be too convenient."

"I expect the door to rattle any minute with my ass-chewing for PDA while in uniform. Plus the added infraction of you being in here with me. No, sweetheart, I'd just soon get out of here still a Marine and with at least part of my ass intact.

She eyed the door waiting for it to be kicked in. "Should I leave?"

"You take one step toward that door and I'll tie you to the bed."

She frowned but cuffed his wrists. "So, I can go to San Diego with you? I brought plenty of clothes for a few months until we can get my things."

"Yeah, I'm taking you home. What about all your other things?"

"My parents said they'd see to hiring movers and getting the house ready for the buyers. Dad will keep my equipment until I get settled and find out if a farrier can make a living in San Diego."

"Aw shit, are they there now?"

"Yes, they came to see me off. Why?"

"Call 'em off, Lucky Charms."

"What? Why?"

He slammed a cell phone in her hand. "Call them the fuck off, Michal, I'm the buyer."

"You..." She shook her head. "But...how...Why?"

"Jared said you were selling the farm. I figured I'd buy it."

"Why would you want it?"

"Call 'em now."

His tone kept her from arguing further. She dialed her mom's cell. "Hey, Mom."

"Yes, I'm with Nick and going with him."

"Yes." She lifted her gaze to his. "I'm very happy."

"Mom, Nick is the one who bought my farm. I don't know the details, but just don't do anything, and I'll call you later."

"Okay, love you, too, bye."

Michal hit end and handed his phone back. "Now will you explain?"

"I was headed home to get you after this weekend drill. So, I figured you had something like this in the works and didn't want you selling our home, or you were making a run for it and I was going to hunt you down and bring you home."

"*Our home.*"

"It's been that way since the first night."

"Yes. So, we're not going to California?"

"Yeah, we are. I have to finish a couple jobs there and want you with me. We'll be home by Christmas."

"Are you sure this is what you want, Nick? I meant it; I'll move to California and I'll be happy."

His mouth curved in a tender smile, and he brushed his mouth over hers. "I'm positive." He stepped away from her. "I better get changed and we get out of here."

He started stripping and Michal watched the show just for her. "Tonight?"

His eyes turned hot again. "We're finding the closest hotel and I am working off two months."

He tugged his t-shirt over his head and Michal licked her lips. "Maybe I should wait outside if there's a no-touch rule?"

"Hell you will. The hall is crawling with half-naked Marines."

She smiled. "Doesn't sound bad."

"The only half-naked Marine you get to see is me, Ms. Dunn."

She sank into a hard university-issued chair. "Not a hardship at all."

"Not hard for you maybe, but a part of me is hard as the damn iron before you put it to fire."

He continued to undress. She admired the body she'd ached for weeks to touch only to have him dress again. "Thank you, Nick."

"For stripping? You can have a free show anytime."

"No, I'm being serious, thank you for not making me squirm or beg or humiliating me. You could have made me pay for how I acted when you left."

"I'd never do that to you, Michal. I love you. Love doesn't do that. Besides you came for me. You don't know what that means to me."

"I shouldn't have let you go to begin with."

He squatted on his heels in front of her and took her hands. "Let's look forward from now on, Lucky Charms. Looking behind lets the enemy catch up."

"I like that idea."

He stood pulling her up with him. "Now, let me go bend over so my commander can plant his foot up my ass about kissing you. After I dislodge the boot, we'll find the nearest hotel."

"Can it be one with room service? I couldn't eat earlier today, I was so nervous about seeing you again. Now I'm starved."

Nick tossed his seabag over one shoulder and draped an arm around her shoulders. "Least I can do is feed you before I tie you to a bed for hours."

Michal gave a nervous laugh, not sure if he was teasing about tying her to the bed or not. The gleam in his eyes said not.

CHAPTER TWENTY-SIX

"WELCOME TO YOUR temporary castle." Nick pushed open the door to his condo. He let Michal enter first and watched her reaction just like he'd watched her reaction to everything after leaving Salt Lake.

She slipped her hands in her jeans pockets and inspected the living room. Like most people, she was drawn to the deck to overhead windows looking out over a stretch of beach and beyond the sand, the vast ocean. Working in IT had been good to him; he couldn't deny it.

She turned and smiled. "It's beautiful, Nick. I'll admit, I pictured a small, dark closet of a place when you said apartment. This is amazing."

Framed by the ocean, wearing a yellow cotton blouse and her hair down in waves, he nodded. "Amazing is what I was thinking."

She ignored the cheesy compliment, but her hands slid from her pockets in a gesture Nick recognized as her relaxing. "You want to see the bedroom?"

Her green gaze locked with his and sparks shot through her eyes. He'd made good on his promise in Salt Lake, he'd fed her then bedded her for hours, and yeah, he'd made good on the tying up promise, too. The following day he'd driven practically straight through from Utah to San Diego, forgetting his passenger wasn't used to long hours on the road. Luckily, she spoke up in Nevada and asked if she could get out and stretch her legs. Now, he wanted to help her work off some of those kinks.

She'd come for him. Fuck. He still couldn't believe he'd watched her walk through his Marine brothers and stand there bold as hell, declaring her love and asking if he'd take her home. She'd chosen him over everything. He was glad he was in a position in life where he could give some of it back.

Michal's smile turned sly. "See the bedroom, or test out the bed?"

Nick sauntered toward her taking her hand and tugging her close. "I might let you catch a glimpse of the room."

She stepped back and glanced out the window, and her gaze dropped down to her cowboy boots. "Do you think I'll fit in here, Nick?"

"Absolutely." He spoke with conviction and authority. "I won't lie; there was a time I questioned it, but you being here…"—he held her left hand to his lips and brushed the place where her wedding ring circled her finger—"…and being my wife, I know you fit wherever I am."

A Vegas wedding on the fly had never been in the cards, but when she asked to stretch her legs, he'd offhandedly popped off about stretching her legs to a wedding chapel. When she said *yes* he'd nearly run the truck into one.

"I think so, too. And I love you're my husband and agreed to a wedding at the Venetian. Even if the lady where we got our license had to mention our age difference. Could have done without that."

He frowned. He'd never wanted to slap someone as much as he had the woman when she looked him up and down like a boy toy and told Michal *good job*.

"Yeah, that wasn't cool."

"In a way it was, though, because it didn't bother me. I could have done without it, but it really didn't bother me. Guess I want you too much now to care."

"Other than you walking across that parking lot and saying you love me, nothing has sounded as sweet as those words."

She smiled and toed off her boots. "Now, do you know what I want to do?"

"I hope."

"I want you to take me down to the beach."

"Or we could do that."

She smiled and pressed a kiss to his neck. "Please. You can have me a hundred ways to Sunday after."

"So, I'm going back to the truck and bringing up your bags so you can change."

"Yes."

He heaved a sigh. "Guess the honeymoon is over?"

She smoothed her hand down his chest and just above the bulge in his jeans. "You play your cards right, City, and the honeymoon can last a lifetime."

Nick cleared his throat and covered her hand. "I'll get the bags."

"YOU MIGHT BE blending in too well, Lucky Charms." Nick scanned Michal from head to foot for the hundredth time. She'd packed a swimsuit, and even though it was a one-piece, it highlighted her assets. His gaze dropped to her backside, and the assets were barely covered by a nice pair of cut-offs that showed the curve of her ass and led to her muscular thighs and long legs.

She hip checked him. "Oh, and no one's looking at you in swim trunks all huge Marine muscles and tanned." She stopped and stuck out a leg. "I mean look at my legs; they're blinding."

He stepped in front of her as a low whistle from somewhere around them almost cost a man his life. "Put that away, Michal. God, I went and married a knockout."

"Stop." She rested her palms on his chest. "I'm not lookin' at any-one but you, City." She raked her gaze over him. "It's a view that rivals any in Wyoming."

He took her hand and led her toward the water. "You ever been to the Pacific Ocean?"

She shook her head. "Never been to any ocean." He lifted a brow, and she shrugged. "You married a country girl. My big trip last year was to Denver with the Wyoming Farriers Association."

He wanted to kiss her senseless when she gave him one of those I'm-a-shit-kicker-deal-with-it smiles. "It's cold as shit, but kick off your sandals, and let's go in."

She stepped out of her shoes and slid off her shorts, but narrowed her eyes at him. "Just a warning, Marine, if you're planning to dunk me, remember, I pound iron for a living."

He nodded. "Message received and understood." She screamed when he scooped her over his shoulders and beat a retreat to the waves. When he was deep enough, he tossed her into the water. He cringed at her scream.

When their gazes connected, he actually pushed back, but she wrapped her arms around his neck and her legs around his waist. "You better be glad I don't want to be a widow a day after our marriage."

"Somehow, I believe you."

Nick used his arms to keep them above the water as Michal seemed content to cling to him, and he was content to let her. "You cold?"

She pressed closer. "I'm getting warmer."

"Roger."

A wave crashed over them and Michal gasped and narrowed her eyes at him. Nick laughed. "That was not me, sweetheart; old Poseidon's trying to get me in trouble."

"Why don't you take me home and warm me up?"

Nick stood and started carrying her to shore. Her gaze dropped then flashed to his.

"You could have stood the whole time?"

"So could you."

"I didn't know it though. It was your evil plot to get me all cold until I'm begging for you."

He lifted both eyebrows. "Begging, that sounds promising."

He set her on her feet, and she slipped her shoes and shorts back on. Once dressed again, she took his hand and linked their fingers together. She pushed her hair back out of her face. "I should have tied it back."

"I would have yanked the tie out."

"Yeah. I know." She glanced around them as they walked. "You didn't even bring towels, City; what kind of beach bum are you?"

"The kind who loves seeing you wet."

She hip checked him. "Stop."

"You know what I love?"

"Me?" She smiled up at him as they continued their walk back to the condo.

"Oh yeah." He leaned closer. "But along with the obvious, I love that you came with me even knowing you could have gone back to Wyoming and I'd be there in a couple months."

She cupped his face. "I meant what I said, Nick; I want to be with you wherever you are. You had to come back here. This is where I wanted to be, too."

He laced their fingers together. "Michal, did you have your IUD reinstalled?"

Her laughter had him glaring her way. "It's not a computer program, City." Her smile faded. "No, I didn't. Does that bother you?"

"Negative. Just wanted to know."

"I wasn't trying to hide it from you."

"I know." He started up the ladder to his condo, keeping their hands locked together.

"Then why are you frowning?"

"Didn't know I was."

"Nick, if you want to use protection tonight and until I can…"

"Fuck no. I don't know what the frown was, except thinking."

"Thinking about how many times we went at it the other night and what you have planned when we finally get up to the room?"

He shifted and traced her face with his fingers. "You're my wife now, Michal, and while I want children with you, it scares the shit out of me to think of seeing you like the morning in the barn, broken and sobbing. If it doesn't happen, or it does and…"

She covered his mouth with two fingers. "I was thinking of that, too. I can't promise there won't be days when I need to lean a little harder on you about all of this, but I'm more sure of us than anything. I know we can get through it together, whatever the outcome."

"Do you really believe that?"

"I really do, Nick. I think you finally got it through my thick head and hard heart."

"Your heart has never been hard, Michal, just cracked like Mable's hoof. You needed a little loving care to see how strong it is."

"Did you use a horse reference to explain something to me?"

"I believe I did."

"I thought I couldn't love you more, but right now… Husband, you just scored major points." She brushed a kiss over his knuckles.

CHAPTER TWENTY-SEVEN

NICK LET THE door close behind him and turned the dead bolt. Michal's gaze never left his hands as she stood looking like every man's dream in the living room of his place...their place.

"You okay, Lucky Charms?"

Her gaze snapped to his, and she nodded. "Still a little weird being here."

"Makes sense. You've only been here for a few hours and even less in the condo."

"It's more of a waiting-to-wake-up feeling. Where I'll still be alone in my bed watching the snow fall."

Nick hooked a finger under one of her swimsuit straps and pulled it over her shoulder. He smiled when she helped him get it over her arm.

"You were alone in our bed." He slipped the other strap off with her help. "And that was a damn shame." Nick tugged the front of her swimsuit over her breasts and ran the tip of his tongue over the top of each mound.

Michal arched, feeding him more, and his smile grew at her complete trust in him. "And you were alone in that bed." She nodded to the bedroom. "Equally a damn shame." She cupped his face, lifting his gaze to hers and tipped her head to one side, narrowing her gaze. "You were alone in that bed, right?" Her smile belied any real concern.

"Just your ghost haunting me every night."

Michal took his hand and led him back to the bedroom. She nodded to the bed. "Sit, please."

"Please, huh? How can a man resist such a polite order?" He sank onto the bed. His smile faltered when she stripped off her shorts and swimsuit then grabbed his waistband.

"Lift up…"—she winked—"please."

Nick winked back and lifted his hips. He held her gaze as she slid his swim trunks from his legs and over his feet. Kneeling before him, she rested her hands on his knees and gave a gentle push. Nick complied and spread his legs.

"Take off your shirt."

He laughed. "No please?" He tugged the t-shirt over his head.

Michal brushed a kiss on one of his inner thighs then the other. He moaned when she wrapped her hand around his cock and started pumping. The strength in her hands got him every damn time, and she knew just how hard to squeeze to make him sweat.

"Does that feel good, City?"

"God, Michal, it's fucking outstanding."

"Lie back and let me pleasure you for a bit." She nipped his thigh and chuckled. "Please."

"Only because you said ple—sweet fuck!" He flopped back when she wrapped her mouth around his cock and sucked him deep. Gritting his teeth against the tension threatening to end the sweet torture early, Nick arched his neck and back, taking deep breaths through his nose. He tried to block out Michal's sweet moans, the loud smacks, and guttural groans as she used her mouth and hands bringing him close to a heart attack.

His stomach muscles flexed, and he started sweating like he'd completed a twenty mile hike with a one-hundred-pound ruck on his back. "Michal."

"Mmmm, you taste like the ocean." She licked under the head of his dick, and Nick's back bowed as she swallowed him right as he exploded. Her hands smoothed over his thighs, belly, and chest as she soothed his racing heart.

He draped an arm over his eyes. "You should do that, like, a hundred times a day…every fuckin day."

Michal crawled on the bed. "I would have done it the other night, but you seemed preoccupied with driving me insane."

Nick cupped her neck caressing the tender skin with his thumb. "Not preoccupied, Lucky Charms. Desperate. I'd been craving you for two months. Correction, two months and two hours since you made me sit through dinner with the Worrells and Hayes."

"I craved you, too. And then, to have a taste of you one night and the long drive yesterday…"

He pulled her to him, covering her mouth with his. He swept his tongue in her mouth, tasting her like he'd been denied food for months. Smoothing his hand up her side, he cupped her breast, and she screamed into his kiss. Nick released her breast immediately, and she sank into his kiss again. He'd learned her body, was an expert, and recognized a scream of pleasure and one of pain. She'd been flushed after giving him head and was still too sensitive to appreciate an orgasm from him fondling her, but damn, he loved that.

Shifting, he rolled her to her back and knelt between her legs, admiring the view. He tugged her down so her thighs rested on his, and she was spread wide. Gripping her waist, he slid his cock deep. Her eyelids lowered so her eyes were green slits and her tongue traced her lips, tasting him again.

Nick dropped his gaze to the outstanding view of her body taking him, and he didn't hold back, but kept up a steady pace, pounding into his wife. He smiled at the thought. Michal moaned and gripped his forearm as her breath came in steady pants.

"Just…please…"

He moved a thumb to her clit and rubbed, pleased beyond measure when she molded her breast without him having to ask…or order her to do so. Her fingernails dug into his arm, and her back and neck arched. Her mouth opened in a beautiful O, and she panted his name while her inner muscles clamped down around his dick.

Nick pumped a few more times, before the pleasure of her body milking him took control, and he came deep inside her. Michal arched her hips, and her knuckles on his arm turned white. She grabbed his other arm and held on like they were lifelines. He stayed inside her wet heat, feeding her what she wanted. When he could, he sat back on the bed, bringing her with him. Michal wrapped her legs around his waist and buried her face between his neck and shoulder, nuzzling him with her mouth and nose.

With a smile, Nick brushed her hair back from one shoulder and nipped on her neck, then licked and sucked the area. Instead of pushing him away, she adjusted, taking his length inside her again and ground against him while he left his mark on her neck.

Being tangled with her so close nothing could come between them was a dream he'd started to doubt when no word came from Wyoming. She wrapped her arms around his neck and pulled him closer as if thinking the same thing.

"I love you, Nick. I crave you, too."

He bit a little harder, and her body jerked around him. He continued to bite and suck until they came down from their orgasms.

He kissed the spot where he'd caused pain. "I know you do. I've felt it every time we're together."

"That must have been frustrating for you."

Lifting his head, he met her gaze. "It was worth everything, Michal; this is worth everything."

He lay back and Michal stayed on top of him, resting her head on his chest, moving only her arms to lace their fingers on both hands together. He felt her mouth curve against him.

"What are you smiling about?"

"This. Being with you. The look on your face when the guy asked for the ring."

He chuckled under her. "Not my finest hour."

"I don't know, it was sweet when that little old lady offered hers and hoping it blessed us with as many years together as she and her husband had, and you insisted on paying for her night at the slots."

"I don't think we need the good luck charm because, lady, I am never letting you go."

"I kind of got the message."

"You hungry?"

"No. I just want to stay like this for a bit. Am I too heavy?"

"Negative."

She laughed. "This is driving you crazy, isn't it, just lying here doing nothing?"

"What makes you say that?"

She lifted her head. "Your legs are moving—along with other things—and your heart kicked up the pace like you started to think about all the things you need to do tomorrow." She lifted an eyebrow. "Or want to do to me tonight."

"Two months, Lucky Charms. Two months, and I've only had two nights so far."

"I suppose you have paid your dues listening to me ramble on about all the news about Ten Sleep from Utah to California."

He squeezed her hands. "I appreciated the debrief, except the part about the bastard still hurting horses."

All teasing left her voice and features. "Yeah, I hated leaving when…" She shrugged.

"Michal, I'll help you find him when we get back."

"Are we really going back?"

He sat up so they could face each other. "Affirmative. Why would you question that?"

"I guess it's hard to believe. I left everything, understanding I wouldn't be back."

"Well you will…we will."

"And you're not moving there because you're afraid I won't be happy here?"

"You trying to piss me off, Lucky Charms?"

"No. I just want to make sure…" Nick half groaned half growled and she stopped. "Do something to shut me up, husband."

"Aye, aye."

CHAPTER TWENTY-EIGHT

M ICHAL BURIED HER face deeper in Nick's chest at the sound of the "Marine Corps Hymn". "Don't answer it. I'll do wonderful things to you if you don't answer."

He untwisted from her and chuckled. "Tempting. But I have to."

Michal tugged the comforter over her head. She'd always been a morning person, but that was before Nick kept her up until three in the morning giving her mind, body, and heart a real workout.

"Yeah, Doc."

Michal's ears perked up at the name. She peeked over the top of the thick blanket. Nick scrubbed a hand down his face. When he caught her staring, he tugged the blanket over her head and swatted her backside. She yanked the covers back and glared.

"Sure, I'll be there. See you soon."

He hit *end* and hooked an arm around Michal's waist and hauled her close. She wrapped her arms around his neck and enjoyed a long good morning kiss. She rubbed her cheek against his when the kiss ended.

"The call wasn't for today?"

"It was for ASAP." He kissed her again and trailed kisses down her neck. "Shit, you were so hot last night."

"So were you. And this morning. Ummm, Nick…"

"You trying to get rid of me?"

"No."

He leaned back from her. "You're right, I better get going. You wanna tag along?"

"Lydia wouldn't mind?"

"If you're going to scowl at her like that, yeah she would."

Michal tried to train her features. "Yes, I'd like to come along."

"You want the shower first?"

"No. You can go first."

He tossed back the covers and Michal watched him gather some clothes and head into the master bathroom. She shifted to her back and stared at the ceiling. Why she was going to the Naval Medical Center escaped her. She frowned at the lie she was telling herself. She knew damn well why she was going, it was to get a look at Lydia. Sure, she was Nick's wife, and she had no doubt how he felt, but she wanted to see the woman who'd come close to being in her place. Nick hadn't said as much, but he didn't have to.

"Shower's all yours."

Michal stretched and stood, even with stretching she walked like she was eighty-five. She'd thought she was in good shape until she met Nick.

"You okay there, grandma?"

She snagged some clothes from a drawer. "If I could hobble over there fast enough, you'd be sorry."

Hearing his laughter, she straightened her back. "Don't laugh. I might be out of commission."

"Hey, sweetheart, I'm sorry."

It was her turn to laugh, but it didn't last when she saw her wreck of a reflection. She needed a year to look close to respectable.

"Hey, Michal, hustle up. We want to miss traffic."

NICK REACHED HIS hand back and Michal took it as they walked toward the hospital. She glanced at everyone in their squared away uniforms or professional dress and down at her simple t-shirt, jeans, and boots. Even Nick wore dark wash jeans, a button down shirt and blazer.

"I should have dressed nicer."

He dropped his gaze. "You look outstanding. What are you talking about?"

"Everyone is dressed for business."

"You're not here on business."

"Never mind."

At the desk, Nick flashed his security clearance. He gave them her name and since he had such high clearance she could get in with just her driver's license as his guest. He'd kept his fingers laced with hers through it all.

She almost groaned when a gorgeous woman in a Marine Corps uniform stepped from her office. Lydia West was the kind of woman who made the spring Service A uniform look like it belonged on a fashion runway.

"Good morning, Mule."

"Was till you called, Doc." He tugged Michal forward. "This is Michal."

Michal held out her hand and Lydia didn't hesitate taking it. "Outstanding. I'm glad you came with Nick."

Lydia had and open smile, and her handshake was firm. Michal returned the smile. When Lydia turned her head to smile at Nick, Michal saw the evidence of the horrible burn Nick told her about. From her jawline until her collar hid it on the left side, the smooth, dark skin was puckered where it had healed and she supposed skin graphs had been placed. Michal took her hand back but kept her smile, hoping her face didn't give away anything.

"It doesn't hurt anymore."

"Sorry, I didn't mean to be rude, but I guess that ship sailed."

"Not at all. It's natural to look. You want some coffee?"

"Sounds good."

"Mule, you know the problem." She smiled at Michal. "I'll bring back some coffee and we can compare notes while Mule works on the beast."

Michal nodded and followed Nick inside the office. She lowered her voice. "She's gorgeous."

His forehead wrinkled. "I suppose."

"She's gorgeous, City, it's just fact."

He shrugged and started typing a bunch of codes or whatever on the computer. Soon, he had about eighteen windows open at the same time, so Michal stood back and let him work.

Lydia stepped back into the office and handed Michal a cup of coffee and set another by Nick. "Sorry if you take something in it, I'm used to the Marine way, thick as oil and black as tar."

"It's fine. Thank you."

They sat on the opposite side of the desk from Nick. He continued to work and ignored both.

"So you two met in Wyoming?"

"Yes, through Jared and Lucy."

"How is First Sergeant Worrell?"

"Great. They're expecting another child, and he's still working his magic with chocolates."

"And you two met here?"

Nick glanced back with a glare. Lydia either ignored him or didn't see. "No, we met in Iraq during Mule's third tour, my second"

"Oh, I thought..." She let the comment drop.

Lydia's gaze cut from Nick back to her. She lowered her voice. "We got used to keeping it close hold. You know fraternization is against Article 134 of the UCMJ."

"Against the what?"

"Means we were hanging our asses over a fire and hoping not to burn. Move the conversation on, Doc."

Michal didn't want to move on, but she also didn't want to fight in front of the psychiatrist and Nick's former lover.

Lydia shifted in her seat. "So, are you staying long in San Diego?"

"She's my wife, Doc." He barked without looking at them.

"Holy shit!" She covered Michal's hand with hers for a second. "I'm sorry. That's outstanding. Really. Guess I could have looked at the left hand. Congratulations and good luck with this one. Really...Mule, finally...holy shit."

"You already said that."

Michal relaxed again at the sincerity she felt from the Marine and shared a smile at Nick's grousing. "Thank you."

"Maybe I should take a trip to Wyoming. Seems to be the place for old Marines to find someone. Any cowboys out there with a taste for chocolate, and I'm not talking about the chocolates in Worrell's shop."

Michal laughed. "I'm sure you'd have a line of cowboys from Wyoming and Montana. Seriously, you're welcome to visit."

"Might take you up on that."

Michal nodded and, like always, Nick drew her attention, and she watched him work. "Did he help with computers in Iraq?"

"When he could during some endless downtime. But he was there to kick in doors and kick ass more than systems management."

"*He* is kind of sitting right fucking here."

"And *he* never talks to me about those years."

"Really? Why not, Nick?"

"Doc, I don't need you shrinking my head." He angled his face over his shoulder. "I'm fine, really. Just hasn't come up."

"Roger."

Michal watched their interaction. There was so much being said between the two Marines she'd never understand. They shared their service, the hell of war, and the days of helping each other get through returning to the States.

"Is there a restroom...?"

"Affirmative. Take a left and it's down the passageway about four offices down." Michal stood and Nick stood with her.

"Okay, Doc, looks like I finally have things up and running again."

"Oh, I..."

"Go ahead. I'll wait."

Michal hurried in the restroom. She smiled at the doctors as she made her way back to Lydia's office keeping her back straight and her head high. She might not be in business dress, but she'd learned a long time ago if you act like you belong people will think you do.

Lydia's laughter joined with Nick's deep chuckle, and Michal swallowed against the irrational jealousy. She stuck her hands in her pockets and stepped inside.

Nick stood from where he'd been sitting with one hip on Lydia's desk. The doctor stood in front of him. "You ready?"

Michal nodded. "It was nice meeting you, Lydia."

"You, too, Michal. If you have time, maybe we could do lunch or grab drinks while you're here."

"I'd like that."

"We'll see you later, Doc."

"See ya."

Nick took Michal's hand and guided her out just as he'd guided her into the building. When he closed the door to the truck he shifted to face her. "Okay. Get it over with."

"What?"

"You're pissed about something. What? You don't want to meet up with Lydia?"

"No, I do, I really like her."

"But…"

"Well, I suppose I am a little jealous."

"Because she's attractive?"

"No, because she shares something with you I never can."

"Bull fucking shit."

"Nice, Nick."

Her phone started ringing. "It's Dan, I'll call him later."

"Yeah, like you share something with your little veterinarian friend."

"Oh talk about your bullshit. We went out on two dates, City, two fuckin' dates. Dan was never inside me; hell we barely kissed. We certainly didn't hook up in a war zone against the UCMJ or whatever."

The flash in his eyes confirmed he and Lydia had more than met in Iraq. "Don't even try to stare me down, Nicholas Walsh. I've told you everything about my past…every damn thing from my worst day to my best. You give me snap shots of only what you want me to see. And you didn't want me to see everything about Lydia…" She stopped and rested a hand on his arm. "Or you did and that's why you wanted me to come along today."

He turned and started up the truck. "Fuck, do all women have to analyze every detail?"

"Nick, don't. Was that the point?"

He turned onto the freeway. "You hungry?"

"Yes."

"Burgers okay? I have another appointment."

"Yes. Can you drop me off at home before you go to your next appointment?"

"Affirmative."

"Can you talk to me?"

"I suppose in a way it was, Lucky Charms. I knew if you met it'd all come out."

"You couldn't tell me?"

"Not really, and don't ask me why not, because I don't have a fuckin' clue."

"Any other girlfriends I need to meet while here?"

"Oh that's nice."

"That was for the crack about Dan."

"Okay, I deserved that. Just don't talk about another guy being inside you. That was a punch to the balls."

He swung into a parking space and put the truck in park. Shifting in the seat, he locked his gaze with hers.

"Lydia never had my heart, Michal. She's always been a friend, one of the best, a sister Marine, and for a time, what anchored me when I needed that and she needed that. She never had my heart. That's just you."

"I know, and I really do like her, but I can't lie knowing you and she...that she knows...well it bothers me, it's not something I plan on dwelling on, and I do look forward to getting to know her. She never had your heart, but she did have a part of you." She half-snorted, half-laughed. "Couldn't you hate her like I do Trevor?"

"No."

"Why does she have to be one of those truly kind, wonderful people a person can't hate or even dislike a little?"

"You still hungry?"

"Yes."

"If it makes you feel better you can introduce me to some guy you actually still like that you slept with when we get back to Wyoming."

Just when she thought she couldn't blush. "I'm afraid you've met him and you kind of know my feelings toward him when I told him to fuck off."

"What?"

She stuck her hands in her pockets and rocked back on her boot heels glancing left then right. "I hadn't had sex yet when I met Trevor. After thirteen years with him, and all the...well, you know, I just...until you..." Why couldn't she form a sentence today? "Let's go eat."

"Halt, halt, halt. You're telling me Dan was the only guy you dated in ten years?"

"There were a couple others, but like Dan, I kept it to two or three dates and cut out before it could go anywhere."

His mouth curved in a slow smile. "So I was so damn irresistible..."

"You are so damn annoying."

He draped his arm over her shoulders, and she took the hand hanging over her chest as they walked to the restaurant. "You know, there was another reason I wanted you to come with me today."

"Really? Why?"

He dropped a kiss on her head. "I like being with you. I've missed having you near."

"Lord, City, you are good at making a woman feel special."

He held the door open for her and winked. "Only one woman whose feelings I care about."

"Maybe I don't have to go home while you go to your next appointment."

"Good we'll have time for dessert."

She lifted an eyebrow and he laughed as he followed her inside. "Actual dessert, Lucky Charms. Sweet as you are we'd be late for sure."

CHAPTER TWENTY-NINE

"**Y**OU GOING TO drills this weekend?"

Nick carried his plate over to the sink and dumped it in. "Affirmative. You wanna come along?"

Michal took her plate and glass and stood in front of him. "Anyone else bringing their wives?"

Her heart still kicked up a beat when he gave that little smile at hearing her call herself his wife.

"Don't think so. Lucy's seven months along and Hailey will be getting ready for Thanksgiving. It's a rare thing for any of the wives to come to drills. Active duty training, yes."

"Then no. I'd just be in a hotel alone." She set down her plate and glass and turned, leaning back against the counter, gripping the side. "You want to do the whole turkey, dressing, pie, eat until we pop, Thanksgiving?"

He moved in front of her and rested a hand on each hip. "Sounds good. You?"

"Yeah, I'd really like that."

"You missing your family?"

"A little, but you're my family, and I can't wait to celebrate the holidays with you."

Nick brushed a kiss over her lips as his thumbs stroked her bare belly. "Gotta get back to work."

"Wish I could say the same."

"Sorry no one's answered your ad, Lucky Charms."

She shrugged. "I figured most real horse people already had their farriers, and who wants someone just in town for a few months?"

"They're missing out on an opportunity to have the best."

Cuffing his wrists she smiled at the sincerity in his voice and gaze. "Thank you. Speaking of the best, didn't you say you needed to get back?"

"I said that, but now I'm reconsidering." He tugged out the hairband holding her ponytail and combed his fingers through her hair, the telltale sign he meant to have her.

He ducked his head and brushed his lips to her neck. "No bites, husband, I'm meeting Lydia for drinks this evening."

His head snapped up, and he raked his gaze over her. "Not dressed like this."

She gripped his wrists tighter and tried to frown. "What's wrong with how I'm dressed?"

He stood back, and his frown turned dark as she watched him take in her way too short sweat shorts and tank top revealing more than it concealed. She wore the less than attractive ensemble to clean house, but her husband had been giving her hot gazes since he came home for lunch. So shoot her if she bent over a few extra times to get things she didn't need out of the fridge, and stretched for glasses she never planned on using. Turning Nick on was one of the hottest things she'd ever known, because bringing a six foot six tower of muscle to his knees was something she'd never grow tired of feeling. That and when the tower decided it was her turn to kneel.

Just thinking of it had her mouth turning in a quick smile; she groaned when it wasn't quick enough, and he lifted an eyebrow in recognition of her ploy. "Not a damn thing is wrong with the way you're dressed, sweetheart, but you're not going to be dressed at all in about five seconds." His grip tightened. "So you wanna do this on the counter or the couch?"

"Don't sweep me away with a bunch of sweet words, City."

"Couch it is."

She laughed, but let him lead her to the living room. She cut a glance to the windows when Nick's hands fisted the hem of her tank top. "Nick?"

"No one can see, sweetheart, and I'm going to be covering you in a breath."

She nodded, trusting him. He slid the top off, and Michal reached for his shirt, but stopped when his hands slid over her. Then his mouth was on hers, hard and hungry, as his hands ran over her in rough strokes. She wrapped her arms around him and held on tight. The thought crossed her mind she might have teased the man a little too much as he covered her on the couch, his big body pinning her to the soft leather. He only lifted a sliver when she slid her hands between them and worked the belt and button and zipper of his jeans.

She arched under him when he started kissing, biting, and sucking another love bite on her neck. With a hitch in his breath, he only stopped for a second when she released his cock and started stroking the thick length.

Blood rushed to her ears and her heart thundered against her chest until, with a crash, she faintly heard the distinctive ring of his cell phone.

Nick's growl was almost terrifying. "Fuck, something better have exploded. I mean G.D. exploded all to hell."

He grabbed his phone from the coffee table, but didn't move from her. "What?"

"Yeah, I've got it under control, Hailey. Hold for a sec."

His mouth curved in a wicked smile as he pressed the phone to his chest. "Could you remove your hand from my dick, Lucky Charms? Kind of hard to concentrate."

She snatched her hand away. "Sorry." He turned back to his conversation, and Michal didn't bring up the fact him between her legs and one hand a centimeter from her breast was a bit distracting, too.

"Roger that. I'll be fine. I'll let you talk to Michal about the other later."

He hit *end* and returned to Michal's neck. "We're still doing this?"

He moved his hand the final centimeter and squeezed her breast. "Affirmative."

Shifting under him, she moved her shorts over and felt his mouth curve against her neck. "No skivvies, I'm shocked."

Gripping his cock, she arched, sliding him inside her wet sex. "No you're not. I've given you enough previews; none of this was a surprise."

Michal locked her ankles around his waist and moved with him. Their days and weeks in San Diego had been like a honeymoon, even with his work. In these moments, she'd refused to let the thoughts that threatened their happiness enter in, so why were they intruding today?

Nick's hands turned rough as he willed her to look at him. "Don't, Michal."

She nodded and pressed her mouth to his neck as he brought pleasure to her body and soothed her mind. She arched, taking him deep, and gripped his shoulders as he came. Michal bucked under him, riding out her own climax until his instincts kicked in, and he removed his hand from her breast. She continued to kiss his neck and hold him close.

"You okay?" He caught a few tears on her cheek with his thumb.

"Dammit. I'm sorry."

"Stop, Michal. Are you okay?"

She nodded. "Yes. Thanks for staying."

He chuckled and brushed a kiss to her forehead. "That was as much for me as it was for you. We were way beyond stopping. What's with the tears, Lucky Charms? And no shit."

"I don't know, I haven't let all that crap get in the way. Maybe it's with the holidays coming up, and like you said, Lucy is getting ready for another baby and Hailey has her little ones." She shrugged. "And you…"

"Oh no, you don't. I'm fine. I'm fucking outstanding. Everything I want is under me right now."

"I was going to say, and you and I don't have that, but I don't even know why it's bothering me today."

"You need me to cancel this afternoon?"

"Absolutely not. I don't need a babysitter."

He pushed off her and stood. "Well then, I better get cleaned up and head out."

Michal sat up, catching her tank top when he tossed it. "Yeah, you've taken care of my awesome girls' night out outfit."

Nick held her gaze, his blue eyes turning to a deep indigo. "You really good to go?"

"I am." She yanked the tank top on. "What am I supposed to talk to Hailey about?"

He pointed to their bedroom with his chin. "Come on while I change." She followed him into the room and sat cross-legged in the center of the bed. Nick tossed his pants and grabbed a fresh pair of jeans and a new shirt and headed into the master bath. "Hail wants to know if we want to have Thanksgiving there. It's where I spent it before us." He hollered back to her.

She wrinkled her nose. "Oh."

He sauntered back in buttoning up his shirt and hitched an eyebrow. "Oh?"

"I'd rather spend it just us. Did you want to go?"

"No."

Michal rose to her knees and smoothed his shirt. "Good. I'll tell her no."

"I can tell her next time we talk. I thought you might want to, or I'd have told her."

Michal smiled. "I'll call and tell her. This is a very husband-and-wife conversation. I like it."

He chuckled. "Me, too. Now to complete the effect, I'll see you later tonight, sweetheart. Have fun."

"We're going to The PB Shore Club if you want to join us when you're done."

"We'll see. I don't know if I'm in the mood to be picked up by sailor boys."

She rolled her eyes. "Maybe there will be a blonde there just waiting to hit on you."

He wrinkled his nose. "A blond sailor…no thanks. I'm really more into brunettes…"

Michal shoved his chest. "You are a menace. Please come."

"I'll try."

She nodded. "Are you working on computers this afternoon, or breaking into a place."

He wagged his eyebrows. "Wouldn't you like to know?"

She sat back and winked. He was definitely getting to break into a place. "You know there's no place to break into in Ten Sleep."

He gripped her chin between two fingers and brushed his mouth over hers. "Got a key to where I want to be there."

"See you tonight."

"See ya."

"I THINK I lost you?"

Michal shook her head and swallowed another drink of her beer. "Sorry, Lydia. This place is packed. I thought the brewery back in Ten Sleep got busy, but this is ridiculous."

"Well, Friday night. And you being a knockout, brings all the men hovering."

"I think you're drawing a fair share."

"Anyway, how are you settling in?"

"Better than I thought I would. I'm adjusting to all the traffic. And I have to admit the views around here are amazing, and seventy degrees beats twenty any day. Can I ask you something?"

"Of course."

"Do you think Nick will be happy in Wyoming?"

"Have you asked Mule?"

"He says yes, but I think it's because he doesn't think I'll be happy here."

"Mike, I really can't answer that, but I've never known Nick to be anything but straight up. Have you?"

Michal thought for a second about anytime she'd asked him something. "No, he's always been honest, sometimes brutally so."

"Well, there you go."

"Does it bother you, talking about him?"

Lydia laughed. She was open and approachable in her uniform; in a red cotton dress and her short bob fluffed for an evening out, she was even easier to talk to. Maybe a little too easy.

"Not at all. I hope you won't give what's past a thought. Mule and I were always more friends than anything. Nick is outstanding at making a woman feel like a woman. I needed that, and he gave it to me. I care for him, always have, but he belongs with you."

"No, the past doesn't get to me…well maybe a little." She cringed. "I didn't want to be one of those friends who bores you with my life."

"Remember I'm a psychiatrist; I love hearing about other peoples' lives."

"So, are you dating anyone?"

"No. I was seeing another doctor, but it was a ships-passing-in-the-night thing. He transferred to Walter Reed in Bethesda, and I knew he wasn't the one when I wasn't at all disappointed."

"You should come out to Wyoming." Michal held up her hands. "I'm not promising hot love, but just to relax."

"Might take you up on the offer. That is, if I don't end up on an extended vacation to the Middle East."

"I hope you can avoid that particular trip."

Lydia shrugged. "It's all part of the job."

Michal nodded. She'd thought about possible deployments more with Nick, too, being out here with the evidence of troop movements in front of her. She was aware of it in Ten Sleep, but being in the heart of Navy and Marine Corps country it was a stark reminder he could be called up as more troops were heading back to the Middle East.

"On to happier topics. Is Nick taking you to the Marine Corps Ball?"

"I don't think so. When…"

She stiffened as a large hand cupped her ass. Only when Lydia laughed did she shoot her husband a frown. "When did you get here?"

"A few minutes ago. I spent some time shooting death rays at the men buzzing around my wife. Though I don't blame them." His gaze swept over her. "You look particularly hot in that dress."

She'd worn the white sundress with splashes of green, hoping he'd take her up on her offer and join them. "Thank you." She cleared her throat. "Your hand is still on my ass."

He didn't move his hand, but turned his attention to Lydia. "You're looking beautiful tonight, too, Doc. Hope you don't mind me showing up?"

"Negative, First Sergeant. I was just asking Michal if you two were going to the Birthday Ball."

"Yeah, I thought we would. You going?"

"Absolutely."

"If you're flying solo, you could join us."

Lydia caught Michal's gaze. "Would you mind?"

Michal shook her head. "Not at all. I didn't know we were going though."

"Sorry, Lucky Charms, I always go and took it for granted."

She nodded. "Your hand is still on my ass, City."

"I know."

Lydia's smile grew and she waved over a waitress. "What you drinkin', Mule? My treat."

Nick swung onto the picnic table style bench next to Michal. The man who'd been edging closer did the smart thing and let him. "Whatever's on tap. What are you having, Michal?"

"Fat Tire."

"Sounds good, I'll have a Fat Tire."

"Just one?" Lydia winked at Nick.

Nick laughed. "Yeah, I lost my shit in Wyoming and suffered the next day."

"You have an episode?"

Michal tensed until his hand moved to her lower back and his thumb caressed her back through her dress. "Jared talked me down. Stop calling it a fucking episode."

"What was the trigger?"

Michal swallowed hard, trying not to look guilty. She hadn't even known he'd almost had an episode. Jared and Lucy just said they brought him back to the store to sleep it off.

"Just shit, don't worry about it."

Lydia shrugged. "Sounds like you got it under control."

His thumb dug deep into her back as he took a drink of the ale the waitress set in front of him. "And I do."

"So you want to go dress shopping tomorrow, Mike?"

"I'm not much of a shopper especially for a gown."

"Good, I'm not either. We'll make it quick. Just look for something red."

"Red?"

"Yeah, when in doubt as a Marine wife, go with red for all official functions."

"And you're going to wear a gown, not your uniform?"

"That's why I want to go shopping through you. I'll be in my Dress Blue Alpha as required. Though if I find something just so, I might change after the ceremony."

Michal met Nick's gaze. "Did you have anything planned for to-morrow?"

"Negative. I have a few things to tie up from today."

She turned back to Lydia. "Then it's a go."

"Outstanding. Now, if you two don't mind, I'll leave you and see if I can get that Marine at the bar who keeps looking over to buy me a drink."

"Happy hunting." Nick gave a mock salute and Lydia saluted back.

Michal lifted her glass. "See you tomorrow."

"See ya then, honey. I'll pick you up."

Nick moved to the seat Lydia vacated so they could visit easier. "Sorry to break up ladies' night."

"We were almost done anyway." She reached across the table and took his hand. "I'm glad you came."

"Even if I grab your ass?"

She narrowed her gaze. "Yeah, I'm getting used to you staking your claim. What that says about me, I don't know."

He brushed a kiss on the inside of her wrist. "It says you like being mine. I like that."

"You didn't tell me you almost had and episode. That I triggered that."

"I didn't tell you because I was shitfaced and didn't know what I was saying, evidenced by me telling you about my issues. And you didn't trigger anything, sweetheart; don't even think that shit. Old memories brought on by too many beers triggered it."

"But if I hadn't been an ass."

His grip on her hand tightened. "You didn't do shit, Michal, except come to me that night and let me hold you so close you must have almost suffocated. Do you know how many so called episodes I've had since meeting you?"

She shook her head.

"One…almost episode on a night I fucked up and got drunk. I'm not saying love conquers all, or your pussy is a magic cure, but you coming for me, yeah, that helps. You letting me get lost in your sweet body…yeah, that helps. So let it go and don't get mired in bullshit thoughts."

She didn't care if anyone heard their conversation, so she kept her gaze locked with his. "Will I know if something is a trigger?"

"Affirmative."

"Will I know what to do?"

"Affirmative. You just keep doing what you do."

"But I don't know what Jared did."

He laughed and his grip loosened. He brushed his lips over her palm and her wrist. "Jared uses a different method than what I need from you, thank God."

He sat back and took a long draw of beer. "I think it's one of the reasons Wyoming is good for me. The animals help a bit, too, and the wide open spaces. I can run for miles and work shit out. Michal, it's not what you're imaging. I don't need meds, or get sweats or chills, or anything like you've heard on TV or like some guys and gals go through. I just get quiet, and sometimes, things haunt me a bit. That's it."

"Well, Bailey has enjoyed the extra apple slices." She smiled around her glass. "Don't think I haven't noticed. Both my horse and cat have gained a few pounds since a certain man showed up on my farm."

"Guilty." He swung a leg over the bench. "Let's get out of here. It's a madhouse."

Michal nodded. He stopped by Lydia. "You good to get home, Doc?"

"Affirm."

He turned his gaze on the younger Marine, Lydia was talking to and the man gave a sharp nod. Michal smiled and wrapped her arms around his as they stepped out into the cooler night air with a breeze from the ocean rustling her skirt. "I'm so proud your mine."

"Where did that come from?"

"How you see to everyone. I noticed that night with Charlene. You didn't leave her standing there, you made sure she was going to be okay. And just now, you checked on Lydia and gave some kind of silent message to that Marine, which I can only imagine by the look of fear in his eyes, said he'd regret it for many years if anything happened to her."

He shrugged and Michal let it go. Nick wasn't going to agree with any praise no matter how much she tried.

"You want to take a walk? It's nice out."

He nodded. "Let's walk on the beach."

They strolled down to the beach and Michal slipped off her sandals. She smiled when Nick took off his socks and shoes, too. She laced their fingers together as they started walking in the sand.

"This is cool."

He nodded. "Glad you're enjoying your time here, Michal. This is nice away from the crowds."

She ran the back of her fingers down his face. "And you need to be away from crowds tonight."

"Need to be alone with you." His gaze swept over her. "You really do look outstanding, Michal."

"Thank you. I thought you'd like this when I picked it up."

"You thought right."

Something changed and his grip turned tight on her hand. "Nick, come over and sit with me."

They sat in the sand. Michal slid close to his side and ran her fingers over his face. His eyes didn't glass over and she knew he was present in the now, but he was also thousands of miles away.

"The appointment this afternoon?"

He gave a sharp nod.

"Then seeing Lydia again?"

"Didn't help. Just be quiet for a bit, Lucky Charms."

She caressed his forehead with the pad of her thumb, humming softly.

"Are you using the same tactics with me as you do with your horse?"

She had to chuckle at his incensed tone. "Yes." She continued the motion and the humming.

"Holy shit, I can't believe it's working." It didn't take long before his grip loosened. She ran the pad of her thumb along his upper lip.

"Bailey doesn't talk back though."

"I can't wait to get back to Wyoming."

She brushed a kiss on his cheek. "Me, too."

"Glad you're here, though."

She smiled and brushed another kiss on his cheek. "Me, too." She nuzzled her nose behind his ear. "And just think, I get to wear a red dress next week. Do you want it low cut to my belly button and high cut to my hip?"

"Hell, no."

He was completely with her again, and she laughed at the horror on his face that had nothing to do with war and everything to do with the image she'd painted and the thought of her wearing such a dress in public.

"Good, because I wouldn't wear such a thing." She nipped his neck. "At least in public. And at a Marine Corps Ball. I don't need your ass getting chewed again on my account. But for you, anytime."

He rubbed his thumb on the spot where her neck met her shoulder. "There it is."

It was Michal's turn to sweat, and her clothes tightened as arousal flooded her body when he wiped the cover-up makeup off the dark purple bruise his mouth had left there. She pushed back her hair on the other side exposing the second love bite he'd given her behind her ear.

"I say not to and get two while you have me drugged on your lovemaking." She let her hair drop, but he combed his fingers through the locks, pushing them back.

"Thanks for the distraction, sweetheart."

She leaned forward. "You want some more?"

NICK CUPPED HER neck with one hand. "Right here?"

Her eyes grew round, and the clouds of lust parted a bit over the green orbs. "Nick…Not here."

"Good. I can do without the ass sand." He took her hand and lifted her when he stood. "We'll save our outdoor fun for Ten Sleep."

She chuckled. "Well not until next summer. I don't want you losing anything important to hypothermia."

"Roger that, Lucky Charms. There's always the heater in the truck, though."

She shook her head and rolled her eyes. Nick felt his heart rate kick up and his breathing became rough, but it wasn't in some damn episode.

CHAPTER THIRTY

NICK SMILED AT Michal's dramatic toss of her high-heeled shoes when they entered the condo. For not enjoying shopping for dresses, she'd sure done a damn fine job of finding one. It was a beautiful deep cranberry color with just the right amount of sparkle, and while the front didn't plunge to her belly button, there was a sizable slit up to her thigh. Keeping it Marine approved, the flowing skirt kept the slit hidden, but Nick knew it was there, and that made it even sexier.

She let the matching wrap drop on the deck, and he chuckled and picked it up. "Tired?"

Her gaze didn't meet his for a few minutes as she checked him out for the thousandth time that evening. He tossed his cover and white gloves on the table. Wearing the Dress Blues Alpha uniform paid off this night. Her eyes turned the sexy shade of jade green signaling she was up for anything he wanted to do to her and with her.

"Long night, and my brain hurts from trying not to embarrass you." He frowned, and she held up her hand. "Okay, embarrass myself. I wanted to get all the ranks and protocol correct and not stick my foot in my mouth. Although right now, I don't think I'd feel it."

Nick shot a glance to her shoes and back to her. "Why the hell did you go with the three-inch heels?"

"Because your dear Major West told me how amazing they made my legs look, and like an idiot, I fell for the flattery."

Nick stalked toward her, and Michal was stopped in her retreat by a wall. He rested a hand on one side of her head and ran a finger of the other hand up and down her exposed thigh. "Your legs did look outstanding. I was having fantasies of you keeping those shoes on while doing some dirty things."

"You can't mean you want me to put those things back on?"

He gave a strangled laugh and shifted his gaze. "Guess not."

He laced his fingers together with hers and led her to the bed. Michal flopped on her back and Nick smiled. Sinking onto the mattress, he took one of her feet and started massaging deep into the sole and ball.

Michal arched, her face reminding him of when she climaxed. "You really needed a foot massage."

"Oh god, Nick, that's amazing. Are you really going to massage my feet?"

"Um…" He cut his gaze from his hands working over her foot and back to her. "What do you think?"

"I think I'm more in love with you right now than I've ever been."

He chuckled and caught her smile. "What?"

"You have the best laugh. It's so low, it rumbles through you and into me. It makes me smile." Her neck arched back when he added more pressure to the massage. "I take it you don't want to talk about all the things I love about you?"

He shrugged and started working on her other foot. "You think you might be pregnant, Michal?"

Her eyes glistened with moisture, and he never wanted to kick a man's ass more—even if it was his.

"No. Why?"

He kept massaging her foot and up her leg a bit. "Just wondering. I saw the pregnancy test while getting a new razor."

"Oh, that."

"Yeah, that."

"I bought it Saturday thinking I might be. I've just been so tired and blah, and feeling a little off. But I remembered you asked me not to take those tests alone, so I was waiting. You got home Monday, and well, there wasn't time."

He smiled, and her mouth curved in a sexy smile, but she continued. "Then Tuesday I had that job Lydia set up with her friend and went back Wednesday, and I realized I was tired because I was bored." She gave his leg a light kick. "And my new husband has been keeping me up until three every morning. I forgot about the test. I'm sorry."

He shrugged and brushed a kiss to the inside of her ankle. "Nothing to be sorry about, Lucky Charms. Thank you for respecting my request about the test."

She slipped her foot from his hands. "And that's it."

He frowned while lifting a brow. "That's it. I just wanted to make sure you're okay."

She rolled to her knees beside him and cupped his face. "I love you."

"Love you, too."

"You don't understand, Nick. That you asked because you cared about me...me...not that you wanted to know so you could start in about how I need to take more vitamins, or lie still with your semen inside me longer, or quit working so hard so I can get pregnant for you. I know you're nothing like my past, I've known since minute one, but every day, every hour, every minute, you prove how much you meant it when you said I was your family, and all you needed."

"That didn't take as long as I thought."

She pressed closer, and her hands clamped tighter. "Don't joke. Not about this. I'm desperate for you to know how much you mean to me. How much loving you has changed me for the better. You're the one thing in life I wanted more desperately than anything else and never thought I could have. Tonight, I walked into a ball as your wife...your family...you're everything to me."

Nick couldn't form any other words, just the one that meant most to him. "Michal."

Leaning forward he brushed a kiss over her lips. The brief taste wasn't even close to quenching the fire she'd started with her words. He sank his teeth into her bottom lip then suckled the full flesh. Her hands dropped from his face, and she roped his neck, a small gasp escaping her lips when the sound of him tugging the zipper of her dress filled the otherwise silent room.

He nipped her lip once more and reached for her hand, tugging her up to stand before him. He finished unzipping the dress, and his gaze followed the material sliding over her body and landing at her feet. Nick sank to his knees before her.

"Nick, what...?"

"Red lace underwear, nice." He brushed a kiss on her belly, running a finger underneath the curve of her bra.

"I thought you'd like those."

He ran the tip of his tongue along the waistband of the panties. "I appreciate the thought."

Her hands gripped his shoulders. "Well, tomorrow it's back to jeans, t-shirts, and cotton panties."

He nipped the inside of her thigh, enjoying the shudder that ran through her body. "Good."

Smoothing a hand down her leg, he admired the muscles of her thighs contrasting with the silk of her skin. Hard and soft, like every part of Michal. He lifted her leg and hooked it over his shoulder.

"City, you don't have to...oh god!" Her fingers gripped his head, and the sweet moan from her lips was reward enough as Nick pushed her panties aside and feasted on her sex. He kissed her, using his tongue deep inside her and his nose against her clit. Nick held her to him, lost in her taste, the feel of her sex on his tongue, her flesh under his hands, and the sounds of him sucking on her and her deep sighs and sharp catches in her breathing.

He lifted his gaze as her head dropped forward, and their gazes collided. She caressed his cheek with her thumb. "Nick."

Nick doubled his efforts, smoothing a hand up her belly and tugging down her strapless bra, molding the firm flesh of her breast. Her body started to tremble, and he latched onto her clit, sucking and licking. Her body bucked against him, and she held onto his head to steady herself as he continued sucking her through her orgasm.

In a swift move, he stood and cradled her in his arms laying her on the bed. Capturing her mouth, he shared her taste with her. Michal's fingers brushed the ridge of his hard-on as she tried to undo his pants. Nick reared back and tore off his coat. He unzipped his trousers and released his hard cock. Michal spread her legs, and he didn't worry about taking anything else off, but thrust deep into her hot, wet, sex. Gripping her hips, he roughly tugged her farther under him and thrust hard and deep, over and over.

Michal gripped his hips, and he groaned at the action she knew turned him on. Nick held onto the headboard as each thrust took him deeper and made him more a part of Michal. Their bodies grew slick with sweat, and Nick inhaled the damp heat of a room turned hot with sex. Michal ran her tongue over his neck and then sucked and licked, leaving her mark on him for the first time, and her grip tightened on him as he threatened to send her through the headboard. With a primal grunt, Nick plunged every last inch inside her and emptied his cum deep. Not satisfied with his own release, he fondled her breast until she arched her hips, keeping him deep, and her inner muscles held him locked inside her as she fought for breath. He tipped his head, catching her gaze with his, and she lifted and brushed another kiss on his neck. His shirt hung open where she'd ripped the buttons from the Mandarin collar on down. He smiled, having not even heard the material tear.

"You are one fuckin' hot lover, Michal Walsh."

Draping a leg over his waist, she nestled back into the bed looking drunk and beyond content. "Mmmm…Lydia was right; you are the master at making a woman feel like a woman."

He frowned. "Only one woman I care about making feel good and gorgeous."

Her mouth quirked in a smile and she winked. "I know." He couldn't help laughing when Michal sounded drunk off her ass.

He shifted, her leg tightened, and her eyebrows formed a V above her nose. "What are you doing?"

He kissed her forehead. "Thought I'd get a little more comfortable, if you don't mind?"

"Oh. That's a pity. Did I tell you how off-the-charts hot you looked in uniform?"

"Only about a hundred times."

Nick rolled from her and sat on the edge of the bed, peeling off his shoes and socks. He glanced back at her still lying where he'd left her, but her gaze was locked on him.

"You have lots of medals."

"Guess so."

When he stood to take off the blue trousers, she ran a finger down his thigh. "What's this red line mean?"

"That's the Blood Stripe."

She frowned, and he kissed her forehead. "Tradition says it's to commemorate the blood Marines spilled at Chapultepec Castle during the Mexican War. Truth is it's something the Marines borrowed from the Army around 1840. It's still a proud day when, as and E-4, you can wear the Blood Stripe. Found out the real story at a visit to the Marine Museum near Quantico."

"Historians ruin all the great stories."

He shook his head and laughed. "You okay, Michal? I didn't think you had that much to drink tonight."

Her frown returned, and she shoved his thigh with her foot. "I'm not drunk, except maybe drunk on you. Are you okay?"

He shed the rest of his clothes. "Fuckin' outstanding."

Michal lifted and disposed of her bra and panties. Nick caressed her belly with his hand. "Much better, huh?"

"Yes. The only thing that would make it perfect is if you'd get back on top of me."

"That's the plan, but first, I need to hydrate."

He kissed the top of a breast and left the room. He'd lifted a bottled water to his lips when Michal stepped out of the bedroom wearing his shirt. He swallowed hard at the vision walking toward him. Her hair hung loose and heavy over her shoulders and down her back. When she stepped into the light, the shadow of her body was outlined to perfection. She held his shirt closed since she'd ripped a few buttons tearing it open. Her gaze shot to the windows and her gaze ran over him.

"You just walk out here in all your glory?"

He laughed. "If someone wants to see my glory that bad, who am I to deny them?" She smiled and started slipping off the shirt. Nick caught it and held it closed. "Your glory, on the other hand, would draw attention and is for my eyes only."

"What's wrong, Nick? You've seemed a bit out of sorts since you got home?"

"I'm thinking of separating from the reserves, Michal."

Her gaze searched his face. "And transferring back to active duty?"

"No. Focusing on you and our life together."

"City, don't feel like you have to…"

"I don't, sweetheart, it's just something I've been thinking about, well, really since I met you, but since we married, it's been on my mind a lot. What do you think?"

"Nick, don't do that to me. The Marines are so important to you."

"You're more important to me, Lucky Charms, and you're my wife, I want to talk things over with you."

She held his gaze for a minute, like she was giving him time to back down and say he didn't want her opinion. He waited.

"When you think of not going to drills every month, does it bother you?"

"Some."

"When you think of continuing, does it bother you?"

"Some."

She slammed her foot down. "Dammit, Nick, I'm being serious."

"Sorry." He dropped a hand to her ass and squeezed.

"I think you've already decided."

"I didn't think so, but now I have."

"You're giving up everything."

"No, I'm not, Michal. I'm holding everything, and I'm letting go of some things so I can hold tighter to what means most to me."

"But you can keep the job with Hailey?"

"Of course, and I'll be keeping this place cause we'll have to come back a couple times a year for onsite jobs."

"And you won't miss hanging out with Jared and Tim at drills?"

She was going to beat this to the ground until he could convince her it wasn't something he was doing just for her. "I'll be living too damn close to Worrell most of the time, and if I need to see Tim's ugly mug, I'll have Hailey point the computer at him during our Skype chats."

"Nick…"

"To be straight with you, I already talked to them about it. Sounds like they might be getting out soon, too, with their families and everything." He held up his hand. "Which is not why I'm looking at that option. Michal. I've given seventeen years to the Marines, and I'm proud of every second. Wouldn't change it for the world. Now, I want to focus on my new family."

"I'm proud of you, too, City. So, whatever you decide, I'll support you one hundred percent."

"Thank you. That's all I needed to hear."

"Can we please go back to bed now?"

"Affirmative, ma'am. I think you mentioned something about me covering you."

"Affirmative, Marine. Full coverage is required."

"Full coverage will be provided."

CHAPTER THIRTY-ONE

MICHAL OPENED THE door to the farmhouse and smiled at the fire blazing in the fireplace. "Look what Jared and Lucy did so we wouldn't come home to a cold house."

Nick crowded behind her and nodded. "The gesture would mean a lot more if I could get in the damn house."

"Oh, sorry."

She stepped all the way in and continued to the bedroom, setting down the luggage she carried. Nick followed and set down even more bags. She caught him taking inventory of the small house—not nearly as big as his condo in San Diego—coupled with the snow piling up outside the door, promising a white Christmas in a week.

"You still good with all this?"

"Don't start, Michal. I'm dragging frozen ass here."

"Sorry. Knowing Lucy, I bet there's food."

"Yeah. I've gotta find a place for a computer and where we might hook up what I'll need for work."

She scanned the room and the living room. "Could you work out here for now? Come spring we can look at building on."

"Guess that'll have to work. This is creepy as hell."

She stepped back. "What?"

He waved his hand to encompass the house. "This. Last time I was here it was about a hundred degrees, and you were giving me the kiss off."

"I was not." She shifted her gaze from his. "I didn't give you the kiss off. I was devastated. But I agree it is a little weird being back standing across the bed from each other like we did the last morning."

He grunted and headed back into the living room. "At least Worrell got the internet set up. Guess I could use the kitchen table for a temporary desk."

Michal released a breath and tossed her coat and scarf on the bed. Since the night of the ball, they'd shared days of afternoon delights when he was home for lunch and nights of tender lovemaking turned to rough play and back to the slow, easy exploration like they were learning each other's taste and touch for the first time.

Even packing up what he wanted moved to Wyoming had been an adventure. She'd never made love on bubble wrap before, but she couldn't say that now.

"You want something to eat, or what?"

She glared at him. Then came the drive to Wyoming and prince charming changed to the beast in a whirl of snowflakes. "What's up?"

"Not a fucking thing. I'm asking if you want a late lunch." She followed him into the kitchen. "When do we pick up Bailey and Max?"

"Not until we decide this is where we're staying."

The refrigerator door shut in slow motion and Michal almost took a step back, but held her ground.

"What the hell does that mean?"

"It means you've been an ass for two days of driving, and now you're stomping around the house like it's a piece of shit. Sorry, it's not up to your California standards anymore."

"Hand me your phone."

"What?"

"Hand me your damn phone."

Michal slipped her phone from her back pocket and handed it over. He scrolled through a screen and hit a button.

"Yeah, Mr. Thomas this is Nick Walsh. Thank you, sir. Okay, Gerry. Michal and I just pulled in and wanted to get settled tonight, but we wanted to pick up Bailey and Max tomorrow morning."

Michal tried to keep her mouth from dropping open. She closed her hands into fists.

"That would be outstanding, but we don't want to put you out.

Well, thank you, Gerry. See you tomorrow."

He hit *end*, pried her hand open, and slapped her phone on her palm. "They'll bring Bailey and Max back at 0700."

She held onto her tears trying not to give into the hopelessness of another marriage destined to end because she couldn't get past the honeymoon before it all went to shit.

His lips brushed over hers, and she opened her eyes. "I'm sorry, Michal. I've been acting like a shit because I'm pissed off Hailey scheduled that last job, and that put us behind in getting back here. There's not even a damn candy cane in the place and your folks are coming in just a few days. I wanted our first Christmas to be special."

"So you've been growling like a bear and snapping at me because you wanted Christmas to be special?"

"It's my first with my family."

Just like that, the anger boiling her blood froze only to warm at his tenderness. Sometimes it was easy to forget Nick had never known a real family because, when he wasn't acting like a real bear, he was amazing at taking care of those he loved. Even when he was in a mood, it seemed it had to do with things not going right for his family.

Michal scanned the house. "We can get a tree tomorrow. I have some decorations in the barn. Mom will bake like it's the last Christmas when they get here. Day after tomorrow, we can go into Worland and get the turkey and all food items needed."

He leaned back against the counter. "How about presents?"

"Presents?"

"Yeah, you know things wrapped with paper and bows. You have nieces and nephews, brothers and sisters-in-law, plus your parents."

She frowned as the weight of shopping weighed heavy. "You have them, too." She snapped. Her chest rose and fell as her breathing became erratic thinking of all that needed to be done. She pressed her hands in the air as if stuffing the rising tide of panic.

"Okay, okay. We'll go to Billings instead, and we can go to Sam's Club and hit the stores for gifts." She narrowed her gaze at him. "Why didn't you bring up gifts while we were in San Diego?"

He shrugged and let his gaze leisurely wander up her body. "Had other things on my mind."

"You're calm now? My panic is making you calm? What an ass!"

His laughter followed her outside to bring in a couple boxes. Instead, Michal passed the truck and went into the barn, a new panic rising when she remembered Nick arranged for Bailey to come home the next day, and she didn't have fresh hay or oats.

She sank onto a fresh hay bale when her eyes adjusted to the dim light as evening settled. A muscled figure sank next to her, and she scooted over to give Nick room only to be hauled close again.

"Jared and Lucy are life savers, having things ready in here."

"They're the best."

She cupped his face so he was forced to make eye contact. "You arranged this didn't you. The hay? The oats? The fire in the fireplace?"

He just nodded. "I told Jared to forget it though since Lucy had their baby girl early. But the Thomases helped out."

"Oh, their baby girl. We still owe them a gift for Anna's birth. Another gift."

"Did you ever get Dan's little one a gift?"

"Now you're just being cruel. But yes, I did that before I left, thank God."

"Have I really been that bad?"

She huffed a laugh. "Worse. When I asked to stop for a coffee this morning, I thought you were going to kick me out into the snow."

"When are you going to tell me, Michal?"

Her breath caught, and she dropped her hands from his face but held his gaze. "How?"

"I know your body, and while your breasts have always been sensitive, it's intense pain or instant orgasm when I touch them. When?"

"I think the night of the ball, which is kind of funny since we'd had that whole conversation and all."

His scowl was dark. "I don't find it fuckin' funny at all that my wife, who knows how concerned I am about this, keeps it from me."

"I didn't want to ruin Christmas."

"Ruin Christmas? Finding out you're having my baby is ruining Christmas?"

"Nick, having a part of us growing inside me is at once the happiest news of my entire life and the most terrifying. I can't even let myself think about what your child will look like, will be, without breaking down in torrents of tears. Me crying all the time, yes, that will ruin Christmas. If it helps at all, I didn't take a test. I thought we could go to the doctor together after the holidays."

"You wouldn't be able to get in before?"

"Do you want me to try?"

"Yeah, I do."

"Okay, but after we get the answer we both know is coming it's just between you and me until after the fifth month. No buying furniture or tiny clothes. No big announcement in front of friends."

"Roger that."

"So you being pissed for two days wasn't about Hailey?"

"Hailey doused a fire with kerosene."

"And you being ticked today about stopping for coffee?"

"Until you ordered decaf…yeah."

"Why didn't you say anything?"

"I don't know. I guess I didn't want to sound overeager."

"What have you wanted to do?"

"Lay you down. Spread my hand over your belly."

Oh god, his sweetness was tearing her apart and making her feel like a complete witch. "If you want to do those things. Do them. If you want to measure my belly anytime, please do. If you want to test the sensitivity of my breasts, be my guest."

That earned her the flash of a smile. "I sound like a complete dick."

She laughed. "No, you sound like a man who's been struggling with a pregnant wife too scared to let you in, and therefore kept you locked out of the single most important change in our life together. Though believe me, I talked myself into believing it's what was best for you. The baby is yours as much as mine; it was cruel not to tell you."

He took her hand and led her back into the house and into the bedroom. Michal waited, not wanting to ruin this moment for him. Picking her up he placed her on the bed as if she might break and rested on his side next to her.

She bit her lip against the tears as he gently tugged her sweater from her jeans and unbuttoned and unzipped them. Then, with the reverence of a pastor blessing a child, he laid his hand on her belly, spreading his fingers wide.

She swallowed around the emotion in her throat. "I'm afraid there's nothing to feel yet."

"There is for me. There's the place where you're sheltering our child. Feeding him. Protecting him. All the things I can't yet."

He leaned forward and whispered something to the barely formed child within her. Michal pressed the heels of her hands against her eyes and took deep breaths, drowning in her love for the man beside her. She let her hands fall when she felt his face over hers.

"Michal, please hear me and let it sink in your heart. Whatever happens…Whatever. Happens. I love you. I will never be disappointed in you. I will never blame you for any tragedy that comes our way. I will only ever love, protect, comfort, and adore you until I take my last breath. If this is our blessing, it is *ours*. If it is pain, it is *ours*. Do you understand, sweetheart?"

"Yes. We're a family."

He brushed a kiss on her lips and another on her belly. "Exactly. And?"

"I will share both happiness and bouts of terror with you."

"Outstanding."

This time, his kiss was for her alone, and with it, he sealed his promise to her and extracted a promise from her with the kiss she returned. He brushed his lips against hers once more before lifting from her.

"Returning to my original question, are you hungry?"

"Starving."

"Before I shut the fridge, it looked like they left some chili or something for us."

Michal wrinkled her nose. His rough palm smoothed over her belly again as he chuckled, and Michal wondered if he realized he was still touching her.

"No chili. Okay, what sounds good?"

"I could make grilled ham and cheese."

"Okay, you can do that, I'll bring in the rest of the boxes."

"I could help unload after we eat."

"Humor me just tonight, Michal, and let me do the heavy lifting."

"City…"

He brushed a kiss over her lips. "Just tonight then you can pound iron, toss horses, tip cows, pull our pine tree from the ground…"

Laughter bubbled from her and she roped her arms around his neck holding him close. "All right, tonight I will let you coddle me."

"Outstanding."

CHAPTER THIRTY-TWO

MICHAL FLOPPED INTO the truck. "I don't think I've ever shopped so fast for so many in all my life. I should have found a Marine long ago to work up a battle plan for the West End of Billings."

He brushed the back of his fingers over her cheek. "There was a lot of whiteboard work leading up to the exercise, but other than the delayed retreat at Old Navy, it went off without a hitch."

"Now we just have to finish trimming the tree and wrap all of these."

"Sounds fun."

The light in his eyes convinced her he wasn't being sarcastic. He was having a blast plowing through stores crammed with people who'd lost their Christmas spirit after the first store and the twentieth time hearing "Rudolph the Red-Nosed Reindeer". Not her Nick, he was true to his name and reveled in finding gifts for his new family.

"Anywhere else?"

"Nope the candy store was it. We've got everyone covered."

"Long day?"

"A good day."

His mouth curved in a smile. "Getting the official word kicked it off."

She captured his hand and brushed a kiss over his knuckles. "It really was. I didn't think it would be, but it will be hard not to share the news with Mom and Dad."

"Really?"

"This is so different for me, but I'm excited, really excited and hopeful."

"So you won't mind me acting more like an overprotective husband with his pregnant wife?"

She sat back and narrowed her gaze. "How overprotective?"

He shrugged. "Like knowing your job is labor intensive, but telling you a million times as you walk out the door to be careful. Picking up extra chores so you don't overdo it..."

"Rubbing my back and feet?"

"Absolutely."

"No, I won't mind you caring for me, City. I'd like to still keep this news just ours for a few months, though."

"I have no problem with that."

"You don't seem to have a problem with anything today?"

"I don't." He settled back into his seat and shifted the truck into reverse. "I'm Christmas shopping with my off-the-charts wife. I've only been almost run over once by a psycho shopper." He pulled out and into the City Brew a few shops down. "I'm now going to have hot chocolate with my wife..."

"With peppermint."

He nodded. "With peppermint, of course. I'm not a savage."

Michal cupped his face and searched his features. He remained still, letting her see what she needed to and what was missing. Nothing. That's what was missing. He wasn't just making the best of being in Wyoming, he was relaxed, happy, and stupid in love with her. She smiled and caressed his cheeks with her thumbs.

"If you're going to kiss me, Lucky Charms, get to kissing; the line's getting longer inside the joint."

Michal brushed her mouth against his full lips and then ran the tip of her tongue along the seam. His eyelids shuttered, hooding the blue flame burning for her. When she caressed his lips with her tongue, his met hers, and he opened his mouth, deepening the kiss by cupping the back of her head and pulling her close. Michal pressed closer and poured every ounce of love she felt for him into her kiss, receiving his heart back.

When she broke the kiss, he brushed his lips against the corners of her mouth. With a wink he dropped one more kiss on her lips.

She rubbed her cheek against his. "Why don't we get our hot chocolate to go and get home that much sooner."

"You that eager to decorate the tree and wrap packages?"

"I'm that eager to unwrap you."

He pressed his mouth to hers for a quick, hard kiss and shifted the truck in gear and headed for the drive-through. "That's what I like about you Wyomingites, you get right to the point. And I am one hundred percent on board with your point."

"You're a Wyomingite, too, now."

He gave a short laugh. "Yeah, guess I am. I'm one hundred percent on board with that, too."

"AW, SWEET FUCK, Michal!"

Michal smiled at the sound of Nick's surrender to her. Since their quick screw in the truck in the farmyard to the living room and finally bedroom, it had been a power struggle that he'd won. Won, until she finally got him on his back, straddled him and took every last inch of his cock deep inside her sex. She rocked forward, and her smile turned to her biting her lip as his thick, long cock filled and stretched her again.

Leaning back, she rode him hard, his hands around her waist, as he helped her keep a wild pace. His thumb circled her clit, and Michal arched back on a deep grunt. He wasn't touching her breasts, and she figured he was saving that pleasure for when he wanted her to completely fall apart. Bending forward, she captured his mouth in a kiss. Nick cupped the back of her head and deepened the kiss while holding her steady and pounding into her.

She broke the kiss. "Oh god, Nick. Please." So much for her being in charge. Arching back, every muscle in her body tensed, and every nerve sizzled when he fondled her breasts as she continued to ride him and rub her clit.

He brought her back down for a kiss and pushed hard and deep. Michal screamed into his mouth as her body shuddered uncontrollably, and Nick pumped, filling her, his body trembling under her. With a mutual grunt, Michal collapsed on top of him a hot, wet mess. She'd never felt better.

Unable to stop, she ran her tongue over the tempting spot on his chest nearest her mouth. The salt of his sweat mixed with the taste of his flesh almost intoxicated her, and she had to have one more taste. She moaned as he fisted her hair and gave a gentle tug. In answer to his unspoken command, she lifted her gaze to meet his.

His mouth curved in a slow smile. "God I love how drunk you get after I've been inside you."

Michal stretched like a contented cat on top of him twining their legs together. "Mmmm, it's so good, best Christmas ever."

Nick's chuckle rumbled through her. "It's not Christmas yet, Lucky Charms."

"It's felt like Christmas since you first stepped into the barn at the Circle W."

She tried to hide her face after that love-drunk statement, but he wouldn't let her hide. "That was a very feminine thing to say."

She laughed and slid up his body capturing his mouth in a quick kiss. "I know; you've turned me into a real girl."

His laughter joined hers until she went to move and groaned. "I need to feed Bailey and Max, but I don't want to move. Check that, I don't think I can move."

"You want me to do it?"

She shook her head. "I don't want you to move, either."

"If it's going to get done, we have to make the move."

"But my parents arrive in a couple days. That only gives us a couple days to get down and dirty until we're moved to the fold-out couch and…"

"Back up, sweetheart. What?"

Michal forced herself not to laugh at the incredulous look on Nick's face. "Mom and Dad are staying with us. I thought we should give them the bed."

He sat up, and she didn't feel so cocky now; she'd definitely cooled the man off. A dunk in the frozen creek couldn't have done it better.

"Since when? Why wasn't I consulted?"

All teasing left her because his reaction wasn't a put-on. "They always stay with me when they come for Christmas. I didn't even think…are you really angry?"

"Where did they stay before?"

"The Carter Inn."

"And they can't stay there this time because…?"

"Nick, it's Christmas." She moved off him and knelt by his side, but left her hand on his chest. "We can still have sex, we'll just have to be a little bit more quiet." Michal smiled, hoping to restore the good vibes from minutes earlier.

"I don't know why I'm being a dick about this, Michal, I guess it's just…"

"New?"

"Affirmative, and different. And I guess I thought while Esther and John were here we'd have some alone time, too."

"Oh, I'm sorry, I wasn't thinking. I just went with the usual custom. Do you want me to call the Carter Inn?"

"No, we'll go with custom."

"Where did Hailey and Tim have company stay at Christmas?"

"How the hell would I know?"

"I guess I assumed you spent Christmas with them since they had you over for Thanksgiving."

He yanked on sweatpants and a t-shirt. "No, their families gathered for Christmas, or most of the time they went to see Tim's parents."

Michal followed his lead, putting on yoga pants and a sweatshirt. She avoided looking at Nick, certain she'd cry if she did, realizing he'd spent Christmases alone. "We'll have fun, City, I promise. They're good about not getting underfoot."

"Will you be working while they're here?"

She shook her head. "But if you need to, go ahead, we can always head out if you need us to. Even if you just need a break from us, let me know."

Nick pulled her close. "What if I want the folks out of the way so I can do dirty, nasty, wonderful things to their daughter?"

"Well, then that's all you have to say. John could you and Esther head over to Worland or Buffalo, because I need to fuck Michal senseless. Oh, and don't mind the wet spot on your bed."

His nose scrunched. "Nice image, Michal. Also, I'd just soon not have my ass kicked by a seventy-seven-year-old man."

"I am determined this will be an amazing Christmas for you. You are my number one concern."

"Because I'm a poor orphan?"

"No, because you're my husband and I kind of like you just a little bit."

He gripped her hip. "That's not what you said before. You said I was Christmas all the time."

"You're going to bring that up a lot, aren't you?"

"Every damn chance I get."

"You okay with everything now?"

His forehead creased. "I don't know. Guess we'll give it a go this year and see."

CHAPTER THIRTY-THREE

NICK CRINGED AT the sound of Michal tossing her cookies. Jared lifted an eyebrow and shifted his baby girl to his other shoulder. Lucy kept wiping Eli's face from supper, but her gaze shot to the hallway.

Nick cleared his throat and nodded to Anna. "She sure is cute."

"Thanks. You wanna hold her. Sounds like you might need the practice."

"Jared."

Nick shook his head. "Not this, man, no asshole comments about this."

Michal came out of the head her face white until she sat back at the table and pink tinged her cheeks. "So sorry about that."

He took her hand and kissed the back of her fingers. She gave a small smile and hugged his hand with hers.

"Not a problem. Do you need a soda cracker or ginger ale?" Lucy released Eli who beelined to Nick who obliged and lifted him onto his lap. He felt Michal's gaze the whole time. When his gaze met hers, it wasn't hurt in her eyes, but longing and a bit of fear.

She turned her attention to Lucy. "A couple crackers would be great."

"Sure thing."

He watched as Michal's gaze fell on Anna for a few seconds. "It's silly to act like you both don't know."

Nick squeezed her hand, and she smiled at him. "I've dashed to their restroom three times tonight, and I don't want Lucy thinking it was her amazing lasagna." The last word came strangled, and she closed her eyes in the way Nick recognized as her way of controlling another wave of nausea. She opened her eyes after a few breaths, and her smile returned.

He returned her smile before he turned his attention to Jared and Lucy. "Michal's right, you have two of your own. Michal's pregnant. We were trying to wait to announce anything for a few months."

Lucy handed Michal the crackers. "We won't say a thing." She rested a hand on Jared's baby-free shoulder. "We're happy for you both."

"Yeah, Mule, congrats."

"Thanks. We're excited."

To his relief, Michal nodded. "We are. Although I was more excited before the morning sickness kicked in."

"I understand that. With Anna it wasn't so bad, but I swear I spent my first trimester with Eli in one bathroom or another."

"What, mamma?"

Lucy mussed Eli's hair. "Nothing. I was just saying how much I love you."

Jared pushed out of his chair. "Come on, buddy, it's time for you and your sister to go to bed."

"If you'll excuse us for a little bit."

"Sure."

As soon as the family was out of the room, he turned to Michal. "Do you want to leave?"

She shook her head and finished chewing her cracker before answering. "No, I'm much better." Her voice dropped. "You know, we'll have to tell Mom and Dad. It's so obvious."

He brushed the back of his fingers over her cheek. "Yeah, sweetheart, it is. You gonna be okay with telling them?"

"I guess. At first I wanted to keep the baby a secret out of fear, but these last couple days it became more of something I just wanted us to share for this time before everyone knew. But this morning sickness is hitting hard."

He ran the pad of his thumb along her cheekbone. "I know, Lucky Charms, but it's not like we're telling the world, and these are all people who love and support us."

"I know." She leaned into his touch. "I am tired, Nick. Would you mind leaving early?"

"I'll go let them know."

She took his hand. "Let them put their little ones to bed. I can wait."

His hand slid to her belly and he spread out his fingers over her still flat abdomen. He tried to resist doing it often, not wanting Michal to feel pressure, but he couldn't resist in this moment.

She rested a hand on top of his. "If you feel gurgling it's just my insides twisting."

He smiled. "Is morning sickness new for you?"

Pain didn't cloud her gaze, and she didn't flinch. He was seeing something new growing in Michal, and it wasn't his child. It was a confidence, and not just in her work and her abilities, it was in her as a woman.

"Yes. I never had it this bad. I can't even remember having it. To be honest, I feel like crap."

He smoothed his hand under her sweater to rub the soft skin of her belly. The room turned warmer as the scent of pine and Lucy's apple pie clung to the air, and the soft glow of the Christmas tree added a special touch to the atmosphere.

"I'm sorry."

She chuckled. "It's not your fault. Although, as stubborn as you are, it could be your baby is already flexing his will."

"My will? No, he'll have his momma's iron will." He brushed a kiss over her lips.

"You guys up for a game of cards?"

He sat back from his wife, but kept his hand on her belly. "I think we're going to have to decline, brother. We have a big day tomorrow."

Jared's gaze cut from Nick's hand to his eyes. He draped his arm over Lucy's shoulders. "We understand that. So, probably won't see you until New Year's Eve?"

Michal stood and his hand slid from her. "Actually, you'll see me tomorrow. I need to get Mom some of your coconut…" She covered her mouth with her hand, and Nick watched her take deep breaths to fight the nausea.

Nick pushed out of his chair and caressed the back of her neck. "That's how I feel about the coconut truffles, too."

"Fu—

"Jared."

"Fudge you."

Nick laughed until Michal's next words cut his humor short.

"You need to work on your swearing, too, with a baby on the way."

"My language?"

Her smile grew. "Okay, we both need to work on how often we drop the F-bomb. Anyway, I'll see you both tomorrow."

Lucy wrapped Michal in a hug, and Nick smiled when Michal returned the embrace without hesitation. He shook hands with Jared. "I'm stuck working, so I'll say Merry Christmas now."

"You, too, brother. It's good to have you here."

"Good to be here." He glanced at Michal. "Outstanding."

Jared dropped his voice. "You still separating from the reserves?"

"Affirmative. I've already filled out and submitted the paperwork." He cut a glance to Michal. "I made it through four tours, brother, I can't risk number five. Not now."

"Yeah, I got the papers the other day."

Nick lifted a brow. "Really?"

"With Anna now…well, I want to be here." Nick slapped Jared's arm. "I get that. We can get together and drink beer and talk about the good ol' days."

Jared laughed. "Roger. We'll compare beer guts."

They gave each other a nod when they heard the women had stopped talking. Michal wrapped her arms around his. "You ready?"

"Yep."

"Thanks for dinner."

"Our pleasure."

Nick held onto Michal's arm in case they ran into a patch of ice as they walked to the truck. When they were safely in the truck, she winked at him. "A little different than San Diego, huh?"

"What? The six inches of snow, or the twenty degrees turned to ten degrees with the wind?"

"Something like that. Are you going to miss it?"

He shrugged, knowing she wasn't talking about San Diego. "Once a Marine, Always a Marine. In a way, it feels like I'm deserting my fellow Marines. I'll miss the camaraderie and the feeling of making a difference. But it's time." He hooked an arm around her waist and squeezed. "I have a new mission now, and it's a sweet one."

When he stopped the truck in the farmyard, Michal took his hand and rested it under her coat and sweater on the warm flesh of her belly. His fingers instinctively spread. She caught his gaze with hers and smiled. "I meant it when I said you could do this whenever, Nick."

"What are you talking about?"

"I feel your hand there in the night when you think I'm sleeping, and the minute I shift, you move it. I've watched your gaze rest there a million times since the morning sickness started, but tonight was the first time you didn't resist the urge."

"You noticed that, huh?"

"I have. I like your hands on me, City, and I like the connection between the three of us. Our family."

"Our family."

"Hmmm, sounds nice." She rested her head back and closed her eyes.

Nick brushed a kiss to her neck. "You really are whipped?"

Her mouth curved in a small smile. "This race for Christmas has done me in. I must be getting old."

"Not that shit again."

"Whether I'm older than you or not wasn't the question. I'm just saying, traveling from California to race home and do Christmas prep has taken its toll."

"And you're pregnant and now the spawn is revolting."

"Yeah, that, too."

He got out of the truck and walked around, lifting her out. She didn't struggle, but wrapped her arms around his neck and nestled close.

"You really have turned me into a girl."

He laughed. "You're all woman, Michal Walsh, and you were long before I came along."

"Well then, it's nice to be treated like one."

"My pleasure."

"I'm not saying this as an apology, but I am truly sorry I can't make love tonight."

He sat her on the bed and brushed his fingers over her cheek, she rested her face in the palm of his hand. "I won't lie, I'm sorry about that, too. I'll go check on Bailey and Max."

She frowned. "You don't have to do that. I can…"

"Michal."

Her frown disappeared, and she stopped. "Thank you."

Nick made quick work out of checking on the horse and cat, both warm and sleeping and a bit ticked to be disturbed. He headed back into the house, trying to be quiet, sure Michal was passed out. He frowned when she was in the living room on the phone. At least she was in one of his t-shirts ready for bed.

"No, I needed to know despite the source. Thanks, Dan."

She ended the call and turned her attention to him. "Dan said Trevor contacted him about that jerkoff posing as a farrier."

He hooked his coat by the door and toed off his boots. "And?"

"Trevor said he's the other student he was working with when…well you know."

"Wish I didn't."

"Me, too, believe me."

He flopped next to her on the couch. "So, what does it mean?"

She shrugged. "I doubt anything other than he's local and that's why people keep giving him a chance."

"You still don't think it has anything to do with you?"

"I don't." She took his hand and laced their fingers together. "Do you?"

"Don't have a damn clue, sweetheart. I don't know a hell of a lot about horses, but I can't understand someone deliberately hurting them."

Her mouth curved in a smile making him wish he'd said something months ago. "Thank you for saying that. It really pleases me how much you care for horses."

"Well, pleasing you is my top priority."

"And, as with everything, you excel at it."

He frowned. "Why do I feel an op being planned?"

"You said you wanted to be there when I confronted this ass."

He bobbed his head. "I did say that."

"I think we should have someone hire him and confront him there, before he can touch any of the horses of course."

He smiled. "So Worrell and his in-laws are a part of this, too."

"Yes. And the authorities."

"Good call." Nick tugged her hand and Michal responded to the silent order moving to sit on his lap. "Why do you have to talk to this asshole anyway?"

"He's hurting horses in my area. Horses I've had to help or help put down. I know it's out there, but I want to see what kind of crazy does that. I'd also like to beat the crap out of him."

"Huh, huh, huh, sweetcake, no beating the crap out of anyone in your condition."

She dropped kisses over his jawline. "Okay, spoil all my fun."

"If you'd like, I can beat the shit out of him."

"That's sweet, but I don't need you in jail over the holidays. We'll have to settle for him being arrested for animal cruelty and put out of commission."

"Michal, no bullshit, no going into this half-cocked. I'm tempted to kick your friend's ass for calling tonight when you haven't been feeling well. He seems to want to keep this shit stirred up."

She frowned and nodded. "I was thinking the same thing, Nick. I hate to say it, but I don't think it's personal with the farrier. I think it's personal with Dan."

"What the fuck?"

"I wasn't going to say anything tonight, but it was meeting Lydia that really opened my eyes."

"Lydia?"

"Yeah, you dated kind of for the same reason as Dan and me—as friends who needed something from each other at the time. And you two were a couple for a year, Dan and I had two dates. But Lydia was really cheering for us and was happy for you. Even as Dan was encouraging me to go after you, there was just an undertone. Also, with this farrier, it hit me that the first time he mentioned it being personal was when you were at drills and he always seemed a bit pissy that I'd insist he go home to his wife and baby."

His jaw was locked down with such force it actually ached. Michal ran her fingers over the tight muscles.

"Nick, please don't do anything. He wouldn't physically hurt me."

"What the hell does that mean?"

"You know. Like crap like tonight and him constantly bringing Trevor into conversations, like he wants to remind me. But that will end soon. I didn't want to do anything tonight, but after Christmas, I'll tell him we can't work together."

"Won't that hurt your business?"

"No. I just helped Dan because I like helping animals and he didn't have an assistant. He can get an assistant."

"I'm sorry, Michal. That's rough, especially when you thought the man was a friend."

"It's sad, but I can't trust him."

"If you need me to be there..."

"I know. Thank you."

He stood, bringing her up with him. "Now, you need to get some sleep, Lucky Charms."

"If possible you're getting more bossy."

"Yep, get used to it."

"What if I said I wasn't tired?"

He laid her on the bed. "I'm waiting."

"Okay, I'm tired...exhausted, but you're coming to bed, too, right?"

Nick brushed his mouth over hers. "I am. Now, will you get some sleep?"

"I love you, City."

"Love you back, Lucky Charms."

CHAPTER THIRTY-FOUR

"I CAN'T BELIEVE this is going down while your parents are eating breakfast and planning tonight's Christmas Eve feast."

Michal hip checked him. "Don't be grumpy. This will finally be over, and think of all the horses we're helping."

Nick took a deep draw of coffee as they staked out the barn from the Thomas' deck, waiting for Gerald Thomas' signal the so-called farrier was there and set up. "I wonder what Dr. Dan has planned for a new drama to keep you close when this is over?"

She squeezed between him and the rail of the deck so there wasn't a breath between them. "Seems it's you I'm close to."

"Roger that."

"Nick, seriously, thank you for doing this."

"God, Michal, I'd do anything for you. Don't you know that?"

"Yes, I know that." She smiled. "Mainly because you're sleeping with a bar in your back on a fold-out couch."

Nick reached under her coat and sweater and rubbed the center of her back as if she was giving some hint. Michal rested her forehead on his chest.

"All right, sweetheart, Gerry doffed his hat."

Michal nodded and slipped from his warmth. The knot he'd untied with the impromptu back rub doubled. She turned to face Nick right behind her as they reached the bottom of the stairs.

"Just stand back and look menacing."

He put on his aviator sunglasses against the glare of the snow and gave a short nod. Michal frowned.

"I said menacing not sexy as hell."

His mouth quirked in a wicked smile. "Move, Michal. We want to catch him."

Turning, she headed to the barn, but held her hand behind her. Nick's hand closed around hers, and he gave her hand a light squeeze.

Michal's eyes adjusted to the dim light in the barn and the figure in between two stalls. He moved into the stall holding Jared's horse, and her scream exploded.

"STOP!"

The man jumped out of the stall, and Michal lengthened her stride, all nerves gone. "Get away from those horses you sonofabitch."

"If it isn't Mike Fisher."

She refused to flinch at hearing Trevor's last name attached to hers. "It's Michal Walsh, you asshole. And you must have been as cool in college as you are today, because I wouldn't know you in a lineup."

The man hocked and reared back as if he meant to spit on her, and Michal turned her face. An incredibly hostile sound rumbled around her, and she glanced up to find Nick holding the man by his jaw up against the wall.

"Swallow." His voice didn't sound like anything she'd ever heard before. Even at his most pissed off with her, it had never dropped so low and lethal. "Swallow, you goddamn motherfucker, or I will break your jaw and all you'll do is drool." The man wasn't small by any means, but next to Nick's six foot six wall of muscle, he seemed like a Chihuahua up against a Mastiff.

She stood rooted to her spot and silently begged the ass to swallow. She didn't want to explain to her parents that they'd be visiting Nick in the Washakie County Jail. He nodded and she saw his throat work as he swallowed the wad of spit meant for her.

Nick let him drop and stepped back next to her. "All yours."

She slowly bobbed her head. "Thank you."

"Who are you?"

Much more subdued, the man rubbed his jaw. "Bill Kelsey."

Nick glanced at her, or she thought he did; she couldn't be sure with his mirrored sunglasses on, but at the moment, she was a bit scared to see his eyes. Michal shrugged.

"What do you have against me?"

"Not a damn thing. Hell, everyone knew you were fuc—"—Nick took a step forward and Bill slid back—"seeing Trevor on the side." He finally made it to his feet, but kept his distance from Nick and her.

"Holy shit man, I think you cracked my jaw." He glared at Nick.

Nick shrugged. Michal cut a look between the men and continued. "Do you really think you're doing a good job? How could you purposely hurt horses like you do? Do you know how many I've had to help put down, because of your carelessness?"

"I don't give a shit. I'm just trying to make a living like anyone else."

Michal pointed at Bill. "Nick."

His mouth quirked in a half-smile and he started toward the man.

"Holy shit, call him off! I didn't mean to hurt shit! I was going to stop when he paid me to keep going…Call him off!"

She held back her laughter at the high pitched squeal. "Okay, Nick." Even with the sunglasses she knew she was going to pay for ordering him around like her hired thug. But damn, he was good at it.

"Who's he? And why did he pay you?"

"I'm not saying anymore."

Before Nick could advance, Michal walked over and slugged the man right in the gut.

"Damn me, I'm callin' the cops."

"Mr. Thomas already has, I'm sure, since I asked for only five minutes to get some information, and you're going to jail for animal cruelty along with other charges I'm sure from the ranchers you screwed over and the horseflesh you cost them. Now who paid you?"

"Dan Paulson. He tracked me down, and I thought he brought the authorities. I told him I planned to give it up, that I was the fuckup Trevor told me I was in class. He paid me to keep at it and to target a list of ranches he gave me, ranches you'd worked with."

"Why did they go with you?"

"He helped me keep my identity secret. No one really knew who I was. I'm not local, so I gave false names. Hell, he even suggested I dye my hair."

Michal lifted her gaze to Nick, and this time, met his gaze as he took off his sunglasses. His eyes were ice—frozen solid lakes of pure rage. He held her gaze, but addressed Bill. "What was the end game?"

"You'd have to ask him. I always felt set up, like he was going to try to be some big hero."

Nick's gaze followed hers to the man when he started laughing. "Boy, was he dreaming when you already had this big sonofabitch."

Michal couldn't even smile, and Nick looked just as sick. "That's just pathetic."

"It's criminal, Michal. As criminal as this fucker. If you take down one…"

Her stomach twisted. "I know."

"Hello, Mike."

"Back here, Sheriff." She stepped away from Bill Kelsey. "This is the so-called farrier who's been purposely hurting horses in Washakie County and even up in Johnson County."

"Really? Well, looks like it is Christmas."

Bill didn't fight the sheriff as he was handcuffed, or make any accusations against Michal or Nick. Michal sighed. "Sheriff, you'll want to question Dan Paulson about this, as well."

"The vet?"

"Yes, this man claims he was part of it, and sadly, I think he's right."

"Will do. Thanks Michal, and this must be your new husband, Nick Walsh…right?"

Nick nodded. "Nice meeting you, Sheriff."

"You, too, sir. Wish it was under better circumstances."

"Merry Christmas, you two."

"Merry Christmas," they mumbled in unison.

Gerald Thomas entered the barn then and cut a look between the two. "For bringing that ass down, you two don't look happy."

Nick filled him in on the details, and Lucy's father rested a hand on her shoulder. "I'm sorry, Mike. I never would have thought Dan was capable of such a thing."

"Me neither. What I can't understand is how he could condone the pain of all those horses for this. He has a wife and new baby."

Nick rested a hand on each of her shoulders and squeezed. "Michal, this is all on those two assholes; none of it's on you."

She took a deep breath. "What a sadness, though."

Gerald nodded toward the house. "You want to join Patty and me for lunch. You must need some rest, Michal."

She smiled. "Did Lucy tell you?"

The older man chuckled. "No, Patty noticed the signs."

She turned her attention to Nick. "I'd rather go home, but thank you."

He nodded. "Yes, thank you, sir for letting us use your barn and on Christmas Eve."

Gerald laughed. "When are you and Jared going to call me Gerry instead of sir?"

"Give us a few years separated and we might loosen up."

Mr. Thomas laughed and took in Nick's rigid stance. "I won't hold my breath. Anyway, Merry Christmas and tell your folks hi from us. We hope to see them while they're in town."

"Thank you. Merry Christmas," she and Nick mumbled again at the same time and watched Gerald leave.

Nick draped his arm over her shoulders and guided her out. Michal leaned against him. "I need to stop at Jared's and get those truff—"

She slapped a hand over her mouth and stopped walking. Nick rubbed circles on her back and waited while she took deep breaths. Not able to control the nausea, she darted for the house and barely made it to the restroom just inside the house before she lost her breakfast.

Heavy footfalls followed her and she was relieved when he shut the door as he stepped inside.

"You need some crackers?"

"No."

Michal waited for a few seconds before she wiped her mouth with a tissue and accepted a peppermint from Nick with a smile. "Always prepared."

"Marine."

Her smile grew. "Of all things to set off my gag reflex, chocolate."

"I'll go into the store and pick up the truffles just to be on the safe side."

Michal took his hand and he helped her stand. "Good idea." She glanced at the door. "This is a little embarrassing."

"No it's not."

She cupped his face and stared. He smiled. "Looking for something?"

"A sign of the mountain that threatened to break that man's jaw."

His smile dropped. "You'll never see that man, unless someone threatens you again. Scared?"

"Stunned. Turned on. But, no, not scared."

"Turned on?"

"Nick, no one has ever stood between danger and me." She flexed her arms. "Most take a look at these and push me in front of them. You didn't even give it a thought…Yeah, I was and am turned on."

"Michal, you are a strong woman—there is no doubt—but you will never be a shield for me, and I will always fight any battle. Now let's get the hell outta here."

"NICK?"

His arm tightened around her, and he tugged her closer but didn't answer. The lights from the Christmas tree fell on them like tiny blessings, and she didn't even mind the uncomfortable bed. The rest of the afternoon and into that evening Nick had made every effort to erase the sickening start to their Christmas. He'd succeeded except for her feeling of guilt that she'd talked everyone into seeing it done on Christmas Eve instead of waiting until the New Year.

She covered his hand over her belly. "Nick?"

"It's T-Minus three hours until H-hour, Lucky Charms."

She smiled at his impatient tone and snuggled her ass against his groin at the deep rumble of his gravely voice. "How can you sleep on this thing?"

"I'm a Marine; I can sleep anywhere…check that…anywhere my wife isn't staring at me." He moved his hand to her hip to keep her steady. "Or rubbing her ass against my dick. What's wrong?"

"If we're quiet…"

"Then we can sleep."

She chuckled and covered his hand again, this time she smoothed his hand down until it was over her sex. His breath became harsh against her neck, and he dropped a kiss on her shoulder. Opening her legs a sliver she covered two of his fingers with hers and moved them over her clit, turning her head into her pillow to muffle her groans when Nick took over and found her pleasure spots easier than even she did.

He took her earlobe between his teeth and nipped and sucked, and Michal's body jerked against him. "You're so wet, sweetheart. How long have you been thinking of me here?" He slid two fingers inside her and Michal pressed her fist to her mouth.

"Nick, you have to…"

Moving just a bit, he entered her from behind still spooning her. She grabbed a fistful of sheets as his thick cock filled her. He was everywhere in this position. He moved his fingers back to her clit while his other hand molded her breast and pinched her nipples, and she bit her lips against the intense pleasure pain rocketing through her body. She reached back, digging her fingers into his muscled ass, and her head fell forward as he sucked and kissed her neck, leaving his mark on her.

His cock filled her again and again, and with a final thrust, his grunt was low and deep as he groaned with his release. Michal opened her mouth on a silent cry as the intensity of the emotions overwhelmed her only to have him work her body until a second climax shook her as he pressed her lower belly and filled her even more. Michal held onto his ass with one hand and laced their fingers together, gripping his hand with all she had.

He dropped open-mouth kisses on the back of her neck. "Let go of my ass, Michal."

She shook her head. "I don't think I can move anything after that."

His chuckle rumbled through her as he removed her hand from his backside and wrapped her secure in his arms. "That beats reindeer hooves on the roof as a wakeup call on Christmas morning."

"Oh god, Nick, you are so amazing. My body has never been happier."

"How about the rest of you?"

She angled her face over her shoulder and accepted his kiss. "The rest of me...well, the rest of me...happy doesn't even come close.

She gave him a quick kiss and then wiggled from his embrace. She put a finger to his lips when he would have blustered. Tugging her nightshirt over her head, she made her way to the Christmas tree and plucked a small package from one of the branches. She crawled back on the bed.

"I wanted to give this to you when it was just us."

Nick sat up and cut a glance to the dark hall. The bedroom door was shut, and he smiled and opened the gift. She held her breath, hoping he wouldn't think it a cheap thing.

Plucking the ring from the box he lifted and eyebrow. "Did you make this?"

She nodded. "I wanted you to wear my ring, not something we picked up on the fly. It's steel, I hope you like it."

He cupped the back of her head and brought her lips to his for a deep kiss. Reaching over to the bedside table, he handed her a small gift. "You're going to get a kick out of this."

She bit her bottom lip and opened the gift, lifting a small version of the ring she'd forged for him. "How?"

"I'm not as good with metal, but I wanted you to have my ring, too, not some lady in the casino's. I asked your brother to make it. Sorry, I..."

Michal captured his mouth before he could say something really stupid. She straddled his lap and cupped his face, kissing him with all she was feeling at that moment. He smoothed his rough palms up her thighs and rested his hands on her hips for a second before wrapping his big arms around her and holding her close.

"Thank you, Nick. It's beyond perfect."

"As is your gift to me." He smiled. "One Christmas down and we didn't screw up the gifts."

Michal laughed. She covered her mouth hoping she didn't wake up her parents. "I love you, Nick."

"Love you back, Michal."

She took his left hand and slid the ring on his finger. "I take you, Nick Walsh, to be my husband. To love you forever."

He took her hand and slid the ring he'd given her on her finger. "I take you, Michal Walsh, to be my wife. To love you forever and continue even after death."

Michal kissed his lips and rubbed her cheek against his rough whiskers. "Yes, I'm never letting you go."

His arms squeezed her again. "Thank you, Michal."

CHAPTER THIRTY-FIVE

N ICK TUCKED A lock of Michal's hair behind her ear. "No work today?"

She shook her head and finished swallowing her oatmeal. Nick cringed at the thought of eating the stuff, but oatmeal with raisins, butter, and lots of brown sugar was the breakfast of choice for his wife that month.

Looking down at her expanding belly, she cut her gaze to him. "You're funny. I can barely walk, and no horse wants to see this coming at 'em even if I could bend over this big ol' belly." She shifted in her chair. "I'm glad I made arrangements with the farrier over in Worland to take my clients for a few months."

Nick tried to hide his smile, but failed and received a death glare.

"I have a few side projects to work on in the shop, but not sure I'll get to those, either. Full disclosure, I'm fighting a headache and the Motrin isn't getting the job done. You?"

He took her hand and tugged her out of her chair and onto his lap. She cast a glance back.

"I saw that."

"What?"

"The look you gave that oatmeal is the look you used to give me."

She smiled and nuzzled her nose behind his ear, kissing his neck. "You still taste better."

His hand automatically rested on her belly as it had for thirty-seven weeks. He smoothed his palm over the taunt skin and full belly. "I think what hurts is it's oatmeal. A pizza, steak…hell, good Chinese, I can see the competition there, but oatmeal? And in this heat." He shuddered and earned one of her husky laughs.

Her hand rested over his. "What do you have planned on this hot June day?"

"I have a couple of systems to test this morning, then I thought I'd keep you hot and sweaty the rest of the afternoon.

"Mmmm, I like that idea."

"You do?"

"Love it, but it's not happening, City. I'm so miserable right now, I just might kill you if you try to put anything else in me."

Nick choked on a laugh. "Message received and understood. Full disclosure, sweetheart you're looking like you're dragging ass. Are you okay? Doc said to watch those headaches."

She shook her head. "I'm okay…I think."

Nick frowned. "Think or know?"

Michal's cell phone started ringing, and she joined him in a groan. Picking it up, she didn't look at the number just swiped the answer.

"This is Mike."

"Oh." Her hand tightened around his. "I am sorry for you and the baby. Thank you. Best to you, as well. Bye."

Hanging up the phone, she stared at the screen for a few seconds before turning her gaze to his. Where her eyes sparked just a minute ago, pain now dulled the bright green globes.

"That was Lindy Paulson."

He wrapped his arms around her waist and hugged her close. "What'd she have to say?"

"She's taking their son and leaving Wyoming. Going home to Colorado. When Dan gets out, of course, he won't come back to Ten Sleep, and she doesn't care."

"Do you blame her?"

"No."

"I'm glad the sonofabitch pled out instead of making you testify."

She took a deep breath. "Me, too." She turned to playing with the steel wedding ring he wore with pride, a constant reminder of the early morning when they'd repeated their vows on Christmas Eve.

"Michal, no shit, are you feeling okay?"

"Yes, once I got rid of the morning sickness; other than dragging an extra forty pounds around, I've felt great. Today is just one of those days. I actually felt better when I was getting sick."

"Why?"

"It was different from the others, and different was good. There was evidence something was changing, growing."

He continued to rub her belly. "Doc said everything looked good with the baby and you've been keeping your feet up and out of the shop."

"I know." She pushed off his lap and started cleaning off the table. "It's just me. We're so close to holding this little one."

"Michal, you're putting too much pressure on yourself, sweetheart."

Tears formed in her eyes. "That's just it. I haven't put any pressure on myself." She waved her hand around the place. "We have nothing ready for the baby, Nick, and that's on me. I've seen you look at things, but you've been wonderful enough not to push. But now, I'm looking around and feel sick at suppressing your enthusiasm. Then, there's a general panic we have a baby on the way and don't even have a crib."

Nick pushed out of his chair and cupped her sweet face between his hands, catching tears with his thumbs. "Why don't we pull the plug on sweaty, sticky sex this afternoon and go shopping?"

Her shoulders relaxed, and a smile curved her mouth. "I'd like that."

"Then it's done. I'll move things around in the office tomorrow so it can serve as a nursery."

"You just got to move into the office two weeks ago."

"I think our baby takes precedence over a new work space for me. If I'd been thinking, I would have hired the company to build a third room."

"The baby won't need the whole room. You work with Eli in the room all the time."

"Roger, I'll move to one side of the room until we can build on again. Also, if it helps—and she's going to have my balls for this—Lucy is planning surprise baby shower for next week."

"She is?"

"Affirmative. But I'm begging you…act surprised."

"I'll do my bes—" Michal bit her lip and her nose wrinkled.

"You okay, Lucky Charms?"

"Just a hitch of pain. Probably Braxton-Hicks contractions."

"Pain?"

"Yeah. I don—"

"Michal?"

"Maybe I just got too stirred up?"

"Do you think that's what's going on?"

"No." Her eyes were big, and she did nothing to hide the fear. "I'm not scheduled for a C-section for three weeks."

Nick called on every ounce of training to remain calm. "Get in the truck; we're going to Sheridan."

NICK STARED AT the clock on the wall of the waiting room. The hands moved, but time seemed to stop the minute the doctor said Michal needed a C-section stat. She'd said something about a dangerous spike in Michal's blood pressure, preeclampsia they'd called it. At the last visit she'd noticed a slight rise in blood pressure and Michal's ankles were a bit swollen. They were told to watch for severe headaches and Michal was to slow down her pace to a crawl. They'd done everything, but not enough. He wasn't a man used to failure, and he couldn't afford failing Michal. He'd started to follow since they'd planned for him to be present during the C-section, but a stern nurse had informed him plans had changed. It had only been fifteen minutes since they'd taken her into the OR, but by his clock, it was an eternity.

He'd called her parents and Jared and Lucy. All said they were on their way, but he sat alone in the room thinking of all the things he shouldn't be; at the top of the list was life without Michal.

The babies had been delivered. A nurse found him a few minutes ago to tell him he had a baby boy and a baby girl. They were both recovering without any effects from the scare that caused the emergency operation. The doctor got both babies out in four minutes. The way she said it caused Nick's blood pressure to spike as it illustrated just how much danger his wife was in.

It seemed his little girl was already an expert at evasive techniques. The nurse rambled about how women who have children later in life can have twins because ovulation can occur from both sides at the same time. And there was the hidden twins crap, and how on ultrasounds a twin can be missed, and a bunch of information he didn't give a shit about. That Michal was scheduled for her final ultrasound in a few days, which might have had a better chance at revealing a second baby, was just another twist in his already knotted gut.

His babies remained with his wife, and Nick felt like he was a million miles from all three. He rested his elbows on his knees and steepled his fingers under his chin. Despite the situation, his mouth curved in a smile as the image of Michal wrapped in his arms while dancing to the radio on the porch, emerged before him like some sappy movie. As if he hit rewind, the image morphed into their first dance, him pulling her into his arms in the parking lot of the Venetian for an impromptu dance after their wedding, and finally, her dressed to the elevens and making him the envy of every Marine in San Diego at the Marine Corps Birthday Ball. But he shook his head at that image and went back to their first dance. She became the most important thing in the world to him in that moment. She became his world in that moment.

Nick roughly scrubbed a hand over his face ridding it of a few tears that had escaped with the memories. Lifting his gaze to the clock, he groaned.

When the door opened to the waiting room, he snapped to attention. "My wife."

"Is in the recovery room, Mr. Walsh. If you'll follow the nurse she'll introduce you to your babies while mom wakes up."

"Is she? Did she?"

"Fought like a momma bear and everything looks good, Nick." The doctor dropped the formality. "Michal is fine. Your babies will need to spend some time in the NICU, but they're both as healthy and strong as their mother."

"Thanks, doc."

"My pleasure. You and Michal were wise to come right away. It was one of those cases where the symptoms spiked out of control in a short amount of time."

He nodded taking that as a soft blow to the seriousness of the situation. "So, I can see my wife…"

The doctor smiled. "In a little while, Nick. Go see your babies."

Trying to hold back a frown, he realized he'd failed when the doctor patted his arm. "Michal is fine, Nick. Would you rather wait to see the babies together?"

"Affirmative, Doc. If I could see Michal."

"Nurse, take Mr. Walsh to the room." She turned her attention back to him. "Michal will be there in a few minutes."

"Thank you, Doc."

Nick followed the nurse out and to what the nurse called a labor and delivery suite. He'd just folded into a chair when they rolled Michal in on a gurney, and he helped her slide onto the bed flinching with her when her forehead wrinkled in pain as they got her adjusted.

"Lucky Charms?"

Her mouth curved in a small smile, her eyes still bright from the effects of the anesthetics. "Have you seen them, City?"

"No, they're bringing them now. I was waiting for you."

The wrinkles in her forehead deepened. "You okay?"

Nick took her hand and rubbed it against his cheek. "Am now."

Her smile returned. "Nick, we have two babies. *Two.*"

He sank into the chair by her bed. "So I've been told. When you give a man a family, you go all the way."

"Excuse us." Two nurses pushed in separate heated Isolettes. Nick stood and stared at the tiny figures swaddled in striped blankets one blue, one pink. "Who wants the girl and who wants the boy?"

"Uh…"

"The girl. Good choice; a little girl should meet her daddy right away. Hold your arms like this." Nick followed her instructions catching the other nurse handing off his son to Michal. A tiny bundle was placed in his arms. Nick studied the little one who was his daughter.

"Your babies have been examined, and while small at five pounds, they are healthy and should be able to go home in four days when momma leaves."

He nodded, barely hearing anything the woman said. "Okay, we'll leave you all to get acquainted."

THE LAST OF the haze cleared from Michal's brain as she held her baby boy. Despite the nurse's reassurances, she counted all fingers and toes and softly cooed when her son prepared to protest.

Nick folded into the chair next to her, as entranced with the bundle in his arms as she'd ever seen him. He, too, counted fingers and toes then lifted his gaze to hers. "All there."

"Our son, too."

He stretched his neck to peek into the blanket she held. "Fuck me, Michal, two."

"No potty mouth, Nick."

"Sorry." He jostled their daughter. "Sorry."

"Joseph and Beth still good?"

He nodded. "Good thing we prepared for a girl or a boy." He studied Beth. "They're kind of wrinkly."

Michal laughed. "Oh!" She stopped short at the shot of pain from her belly.

"What is it, Michal? You okay? You need a nurse?"

"Sit back down, Nick, I'm fine. I forgot my incision. Yes, they are wrinkly, but they're perfect." She brushed a kiss on Joseph's forehead. "I'll need to feed them soon."

"Do you know how to do that?"

She almost laughed at the horrified look on his face. "We'll call for a nurse soon." Searching his face, she cocked her head to one side. "This is a lot, isn't it?"

"Nothing we can't handle." He continued to hold her gaze. "You've given me more than I ever dreamed, Michal, and you risked your life to do it."

"This is my dream, too, Nick. I look at these babies and it's surreal when I think of where I was a year ago before you came into my life."

"You seemed to be doing just fine, Lucky Charms."

"Then you weren't looking very hard."

"Oh, I was looking and seeing."

"Let's switch."

Nick pushed out of the chair and laid Beth in Michal's arms while taking Joseph. Michal examined Beth as if she hadn't watched Nick doing so, and caught Nick doing the same with Joseph.

"Jared and Lucy will be here soon followed by your parents."

"Why?"

His laughter disturbed the babies and he stifled the humor. "I thought it might be nice to let them know we were having a baby."

"Oh, that was nice of you. I just don't want outsiders."

"Outsiders? Michal they're family."

She wrinkled her nose. "I guess we better call the nurse, and I'll try to feed them before the hordes descend."

He shook his head. "I don't think four people equals a horde. I understand the feeling of wanting it just to be us, but that would be a bit harsh. I'll make sure it's a short visit."

"Nick."

He lifted his gaze from their son to meet her stare. "Yeah?"

"It's kind of funny don't you think?"

"What?"

"A man who's never known a family is the one who taught me the meaning of the word. Have I even told you how much I love you today?"

He lifted Joseph and nodded toward Beth. "Yes."

EPILOGUE

One year later

Nick's large arms circled her waist and tugged Michal close to him. He brushed a kiss on the back of her neck. She chuckled and gave up pounding the red-hot steel, as the iron bands of her husband's arms tightened.

"I'm gross and sweaty, City."

"You're sweaty and hot as hell just like always. For a mother of two, you were amazing last night and this morning, Lucky Charms."

She angled her face over her shoulder. "You were pretty amazing yourself for an old, married man."

He gave her shoulder a small nip and focused his gaze over her. "How can they sleep with you pounding iron?"

Two pairs of eyes from the playpen set up in her workshop shot open, and Joseph and Beth stood reaching for Nick. She laughed as he made a show of groaning, but the grin on his face grew bigger the closer he got to his children.

He sat on his heels in front of the playpen, and Michal joined in his laughter as the babies almost tipped the thing over in their fervor to get to their daddy. "Hey, sweet babies. You learning to be a farrier?"

"Nick, pick them up before they hurt themselves or you."

His deep chuckle filled her heart and soul. "Come on, rugrats." He scooped both up, one in each arm and pushed up to stand.

She shook her head and tried not to drool at the sight. "You're so lucky you can hold them both still. Once they turned into little butterballs, I couldn't do it anymore." She tugged on Joseph's tiny jeans and tickled his tummy, giggling with him. Next, she tugged on Beth's jeans and experienced the same joy at her daughter's giggle.

Once both where sufficiently giggled out, Michal lifted onto the toes of her boots and Nick met her halfway for a kiss. Even holding their babies, he could control the kiss and her, and she smiled against his mouth. Because she trusted him without question, he could command her.

She broke the kiss and started strolling out of the workshop and barn with Nick cradling the children, one against each shoulder. She glanced at Bailey's stall. "I unshod Bailey and turned him out into the field. I swear he had the same look as I do when my boots come off at night."

"I bet. I suppose his sidekick Max has disappeared?"

She smiled. "You know us all too well."

"I love you all too much."

Michal gave in to instinct and sighed like the woman in love she was. She released a sigh again when she turned on the porch to find both Joseph and Beth's heads tucked under his chin. They weren't sleeping, but fighting it like troopers.

"Lucy was right, you are the Pied Piper."

"Just their dad."

She shrugged. "Say what you will, but you've got the touch…with me, too." She winked.

His eyes narrowed in the way they only did for her as desire clouded the indigo slits. "You're asking for it, wife."

"You bet I am."

Opening the door, she let him slide through first, secure in the knowledge he couldn't do anything with his hands full. She should have known better. As he passed by, he brushed his thighs against hers.

Michal cleared her throat. "I thought we'd have the rest of the ham and mashed potatoes tonight. I'll whip up a salad."

"Sounds good to me, you need help?"

"No, you taking care of the kiddos is help enough."

"That I can do."

He folded on the living room floor and sat each twin on their bottoms. They sat staring at him like he was a god. She frowned and wondered if they'd picked up that look from her.

"What's wrong?"

"Nothing." She turned to wash her hands and get supper on the table. He reclined on his side and started playing with their Sing and Play Farm.

He'd chew her out for days if she ever voiced out loud how happy she was she had given him children. It would have been such a loss for Nick not to be a father. In the same breath, she wanted to weep at how amazing it was being a mother. She never minded the lack of sleep or endless feedings and diaper changes, she was determined never to take for granted the blessing she never thought she'd have.

But if she was honest, when they both had croup, she wondered if she'd make it through with all her hair. And this afternoon, when both started howling as if the world was ending and wouldn't settle no matter what she tried, she had to repeat it was a blessing a hundred times over. She smiled, she really was a mother.

"Hey, Lucky Charms, I have to go to San Diego in a couple weeks. You want to strap the young'uns to the top of the truck and come along?"

She tried to give him a look of chastisement, but laughed instead. "Yes, we'd love to go with you. But your children will ride *inside* the truck."

He shrugged. "That works, too. We'll have to take a slight detour to see the Hayes family for final instructions from Hailey."

"Oh, that will be fun. I really enjoyed getting to spend time with them when they came for Thanksgiving."

He started stacking blocks. "Yeah, that was a good time. I don't miss it much, but I do miss drills and getting together with other Marines. At least old Iron Ass lives just down the road."

Michal cut a glance to the babies, hypnotized by their father stacking a wooden block on top of the others. She ignored his language cutting him the same slack she cut herself when she'd released a blue streak while shoeing a spoiled mare earlier.

She sat crossed-leg on the floor and pulled one baby on one leg and one on the other. "Supper can wait a bit."

"Absolutely."

Michal bussed the top of each blond head. "I'm glad their eyes stayed blue."

He smiled. "I was hoping they'd turn green."

She squeezed her babies close, glad they were in a cuddly mood. When Nick sat up though, Beth instantly reached for her daddy. Michal obliged and handed her off, snuggling Joe close and playing Patty Cake with his hands.

"I've got a nice family here."

Michal rolled her eyes. "Yes, you did quite well for a quick summer visit to Wyoming."

"I really did. Outstanding." He tipped his head to one side and stared at her for a minute.

Michal frowned. "What?"

"Just trying to picture that Charlene woman you tried to push on me…"

"You better be joking, City."

His mouth curved in a sexy smile. "You know it, Lucky Charms; you were the only woman I could picture in my life the second I saw you."

"That's much better."

She held Joe to her and rolled to her knees brushing a kiss on his lips. "I love you, Nick Walsh. I'm glad you're a big mule who never gave up on me. I'll never give up on you."

She sat back and joined in his laughter at the look their children were giving them, wide eyes and mouths opened. Joe's forehead scrunched in a frown at being held where he stared at the floor while she made out with dad.

"A thousand men couldn't move me from your side, Michal. We're family."

"Family." She whispered around the emotion blocking her throat and held his gaze as they let all the things they couldn't verbalize flow between them with a look. She had it all and was finally the woman she wanted to be, not because Nick Walsh changed her, but because he didn't want her to change at all.

The big Marine with the bigger heart had taken her iron heart and molded it into something stronger.

AUTHOR'S NOTE

Hello, dear readers! Thank you for picking up a copy of IRON COWGIRL. I hope you enjoyed Michal and Nick's story as much as I truly loved writing it, or I should say, transcribing for these characters. As always, these two stole a piece of my heart, and I'm proud to share them with you.

I certainly enjoyed visiting the town of Ten Sleep and the wonderful people comprising the approximately two hundred residents. The people of Ten Sleep have offered this series a home on the shelves of their stores, and offered information needed to bring the town alive to you as you read the Ten Sleep Dreaming series. I was even provided the name of a local farrier (that's Wyoming local, so that's thirty plus miles down the road outside of Worland) and an opportunity to not only interview him, but to watch him at work. I would like to thank this gentleman for his kindness and assistance; he truly helped me bring Michal to life as she tends to the horses of the area.

My sincerest thank you to each of you who picked up this story and spent some time in Ten Sleep with Michal, Nick, and the rest of the wild Wyomingites there.

Warmest wishes always,

Kirsten Lynn

ABOUT THE AUTHOR

Kirsten Lynn is a Western and Military Historian. She worked six years with a Navy non-profit and continues to contract with the Marine Corps History Division for certain projects. Making her home in Wyoming, where her roots were sewn, Kirsten also works as a local historian. She loves to use the history she has learned and add it to a great love story. She writes stories about men of uncommon valor…women with undaunted courage…love of unwavering devotion…and romance with unending sizzle. When she's not writing, she finds inspiration in day trips through the Bighorn Mountains, binge reading, and watching sappy old movies, or sappy new movies. Housework can always wait.

Connect with me online!

facebook.com/KLynnAuthor

twitter.com/KLynnAuthor

My Website:

www.kirstenlynnwildwest.com

My Newsletter:

www.kirstenlynnwildwest.com/contact_kirstin.php

DON'T MISS CHOCOLATE COWBOY! If you've read IRON COWGIRL and want to know more about Jared and Lucy Worrell, don't miss out on the first story in the Ten Sleep Dreaming series!

Check out CHOCOLATE COWBOY and all my other books at:

www.kirstenlynnwildwest.com/books.html

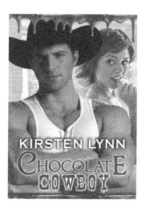

GySgt Jared Worrell wanted one thing—to live and die a Marine. He's made a good start at the first and come close to the second more times than a man should. One call from his mother changes all his plans, and he's headed back to Ten Sleep, Wyoming. The Reserves feed his need to be a Marine, but what does a man do the rest of the year in a town so small it doesn't even have one stoplight? His mom has the perfect solution; Jared should use another talent and become the town chocolatier. He's just recovering from that bomb when she drops another...

Lucy Thomas fell in love with Ten Sleep when her parents fulfilled their dreams of owning their own ranch. Now Lucy is living her dream of photographing Wyoming from its landscape to its people, but she's never really felt a part of the small town where everyone has known everyone else forever. Turning the doorknob to her friend's house brings her face to face with a man whose arms she'd love to call home. He's a Marine, cowboy, and chocolatier...how can a woman resist?

Coming home never tasted so sweet.

Made in the USA
Middletown, DE
22 September 2024

61266362R00156